A SIMPLE VOW

Center Point
Large Print

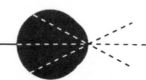

**This Large Print Book carries the
Seal of Approval of N.A.V.H.**

A
SIMPLE
VOW

Charlotte Hubbard

CENTER POINT LARGE PRINT
THORNDIKE, MAINE

This Center Point Large Print edition
is published in the year 2016 by arrangement with
Kensington Publishing Corp.

The text of this Large Print edition is unabridged.
In other aspects, this book may vary
from the original edition.
Printed in the United States of America
on permanent paper.
Set in 16-point Times New Roman type.

ISBN: 978-1-68324-176-8

Library of Congress Cataloging-in-Publication Data

Names: Hubbard, Charlotte, 1953– author.
Title: A simple vow / Charlotte Hubbard.
Description: Center Point Large Print edition. | Thorndike, Maine :
Center Point Large Print, 2016.
Identifiers: LCCN 2016034840 | ISBN 9781683241768
   (hardcover : alk. paper)
Subjects: LCSH: Amish—Fiction. | Twins—Fiction. | Large type books.
Classification: LCC PS3613.A277 S56 2016 | DDC 813/.6—dc23
LC record available at https://lccn.loc.gov/2016034840

A SIMPLE VOW

CHAPTER ONE

E dith Riehl stepped out onto the front porch of her new home, bubbling with anticipation. On this beautiful spring morning everyone in Willow Ridge would be attending the wedding of Ira Hooley and Millie Glick, over at the big house on the hill where Nora and Luke Hooley—mother of the bride and brother of the groom—lived. Horse-drawn buggies were already pulling up the driveway and behind the Hooleys' home as guests arrived, and Edith was excited that she and her two sisters would be among them. Loretta and Rosalyn agreed that helping serve the wedding dinner after the ceremony would be a wonderful way to get better acquainted with folks in their new neighborhood.

As Edith gazed out over the pasture where Bishop Tom Hostetler's dairy cows grazed, beyond the homes and small farms that formed the patchwork of Willow Ridge, her sisters' voices drifted through the windows. They were trying one last time to convince their father to stay for the wedding meal after the service, but weddings hadn't been Dat's cup of tea since Mamm had passed on. He would attend the service only because he was serving as the district's deacon now that his cousin Reuben, the former deacon, had moved back to Roseville to help his widowed mother.

When she heard loud crying, Edith walked to the other end of the porch, wondering where the baby was and why it was fussing. She spotted an enclosed buggy on the side of the road, and behind it two men in Plain clothing and black straw hats were having an agitated conversation.

Don't they realize how they're upsetting that poor wee one? Edith wondered as she hurried down the porch steps. *And where's its mother?*

As she approached the buggy, the men's raised voices became disturbingly clearer.

"What was I supposed to think when I got a phone message from a total stranger, accusing me of—of impregnating his wife?" the taller fellow demanded tersely. He was standing in front of a saddled black horse, gripping its reins.

"And how do you think *I* felt when your name was the last thing Molly uttered before she died?" the other man shot back. " *'Tell Asa I'll always love him.'* Do you know how those words tore my world to shreds?"

Edith's eyes widened. Clearly this conversation was none of her business, yet the crying baby compelled her to walk faster. Perhaps she could suggest that these two men speak with Bishop Tom about their troubling situation—although he was probably already at the Hooley home, preparing for the church service that would precede the wedding.

"I'm telling you I've never so much as *met* your wife, let alone—"

"Shut up! This explains why Molly got so big so fast, and why the twins came two months early!" the man with his back to Edith lashed out. "Not only have I lost my wife to cancer, but I've learned that my marriage of thirteen months was a lie!"

Twins? And their mother's name was Molly— and she died of cancer? Edith's thoughts whirled as she stepped up through the buggy's open door. Two little babies wiggled in towel-lined half-bushel gardening baskets on the backseat as their wails filled the vehicle.

"Oh, look at you," Edith murmured. "Shhh . . . it'll be all right now." She gently scooped the nearest baby, who wore a crocheted yellow cap, into the crook of one arm before lifting its white-capped twin to her other shoulder. It seemed these wee ones had no mother and a very distraught father, and they'd been born into a confusing, distressing situation.

As the men's discussion escalated, Edith stepped carefully down from the buggy. One fellow's voice sounded familiar. She didn't want to believe the scenario he'd been describing, but right now her main concern was for the babies.

"Would you please lower your voices?" she insisted as she came around the rig. "You've upset these little angels so badly that—Will Gingerich? Are these *your* twins?"

"Edith! Thank God I've found you." The handsome young man to whom her sister Loretta had once been engaged removed his hat to rake his sandy brown hair with his fingers. "*Jah*, I believed they were mine until Molly named this—this *other* dog as their father—"

"I'm trying to get to the bottom of that story," the taller man protested, "but—"

"Stop it, both of you!" Edith insisted in a low voice. "These babies are wet and hungry and upset. Your problems will have to wait until we've taken care of more important matters."

Both men stared at Edith as though she were crazy, and maybe she was. What had possessed her to stick her nose into this business, which sounded more dubious by the moment? She had never seen the taller man with the black hair and riveting eyes, and the last she'd heard of Will Gingerich, he'd married another young woman rather quickly after Dat had called off the engagement between him and Loretta. Edith thought her family had left this heartache behind when they'd moved away from Roseville to start fresh in Willow Ridge, but it seemed a brand new batch of problems had popped up like dandelions after they'd left.

"I've come to ask you—your family—a huge favor," Will pleaded. He looked pale, and his eyes had dark circles around them. "I—I have no idea how I'm going to care for these kids, what with

Molly dying. They're only six months old, Edith. I was hoping you and your sisters would take them until I can get my life together and—"

Edith's eyes widened. "Is there no one in Molly's family, or—"

"That's just it," Will continued in a desperate tone. "Molly's *mamm* and grandmother were there at her deathbed when she blurted out *this* guy's name—"

"She was no doubt delirious and unaware of what she was saying," Edith murmured.

"—and then when Molly passed on, her grandmother had a heart attack from all the stress and went to the hospital," Will went on doggedly. "Molly's mother isn't speaking to me now. I've had a lot of stuff thrown at me these past several weeks, what with my wife's being too sick to tend the babies. I trust you Riehl sisters to care for the twins until I get through Molly's funeral and then figure out, well—what to do with them. *Please, Edith?*"

It was indeed a huge favor Will was asking, but how could she refuse? The babies had almost stopped crying. Edith gazed at their precious faces as she swayed from side to side, calming them. By the sound of Will's incredibly sad story, these helpless little souls might not have anyone looking after them—for how long? "Of course we'll take them," she murmured, "but we don't have any diapers or bottles or—"

"I brought all that stuff. I was looking for your house when *this* guy"—Will glowered, pointing at the other man—"caught up to me and claimed I'd accused him falsely."

The stranger looked ready to protest again, but instead he crossed his arms and clenched his jaw. Behind him, his tall black horse nickered impatiently.

"We live in that two-story white house down the road. The one with the dogwoods on either side of the porch," Edith said, nodding in that direction.

"Hop in. I'll give you a ride."

Before Edith could reply, Will jogged around the buggy and stepped up into the rig. As she followed him, she realized just how scattered his thoughts must be, because there was no *hopping in* when she was holding a baby in each arm. Gazing into the backseat, Edith was about to ask for Will's help when a strong arm curled around hers.

"Let me hold them. I'll hand them up after you get in."

Edith looked up into the stranger's face. He had the deepest blue eyes she'd ever seen—as dark as the navy-blue reeds she wove into her baskets. When she realized her arm was tingling as she gawked at him, Edith looked away. "Sorry," she murmured.

"I'm not," he whispered. He released her and stepped back to allow a more proper distance between them.

Edith had known Will Gingerich for most of her life, so she felt a bit traitorous appreciating help from the man who'd supposedly had *relations* with Molly before she'd married Will. The man calmly took one baby and then the other, however, smiling at her as she climbed into the buggy. As Edith situated each of the twins in a basket, she felt his gaze on her—and she felt sorry that the babies had to ride in such ugly, unsuitable carriers.

The rig lurched, and Will drove them down the road without closing the door. "I'm sorry to spring this on you girls," he said with a sigh. "Sorry about—well, I just never saw any of this coming."

"I can't imagine," Edith murmured.

"I hope you'll understand if I'd rather not see Loretta—or your *dat*," he added quickly.

Edith smiled sadly. Her sister and Will had been sweethearts all through school, and their broken engagement was still a sore subject. "It's probably best that way, *jah*."

He halted the horse at the end of their lane. When Edith grabbed the basket handles and started for the porch, Will followed her with a large cardboard box. "You're a godsend, Edith—an angel—and I can't thank you enough," he murmured. "I'll come back as soon as I can, after Molly's funeral."

She nodded mutely, wondering how on earth she would explain to her family about the monumental responsibility she'd just taken on. "So, what are the babies' names? Are they boys or girls or—"

"One of each. Leroy and Louisa." Will kept his eyes on Edith, as though he couldn't bear to look at the children he apparently hadn't fathered. "They were born October tenth, so they'll be six months old tomorrow, and—well, you probably think I'm already a total failure as a father. Give Loretta my best."

As Edith walked to the end of the porch to watch Will's rig roll down the road, she sighed. She'd put on her best purple dress to attend the wedding, and now she'd accepted two babies and a box filled with whatever Will had tossed into it. *What were you thinking? What sort of mess have you gotten yourself into? How long will it be before Will comes back—and what if he doesn't?*

Edith's whirling thoughts were interrupted by the tattoo of boots on the porch steps. She turned to find the raven-haired stranger studying her intently. He removed his straw hat.

"My name's Asa Detweiler, and I live in Clifford—south of Roseville about twelve miles," he said in a low voice. He ducked slightly so that his eyes were level with hers, mere inches away. "I swear to you that I never met Will's wife— never saw *him* before today, when his phone message accused me of fathering these twins, so I tracked him down. Can you believe that, Edith?"

She blinked. Asa Detweiler told a compelling story and had the voice and eyes to back it up. But

14

what did she know about any of the stories she'd heard this morning?

Asa smiled wryly. "I admire a woman who doesn't blurt out the first thing that comes to mind—and who has put the needs of these two babies first," he added. "I promise you I'll get to the bottom of this situation, and I'll be back. Promise *me* that you'll mother these kids—and that you'll hear me out when I return, all right?"

Edith couldn't help gazing into his eyes, as dark blue and mysterious as midnight. Even as she nodded, she sensed that Asa's request, and her unspoken affirmation—such a simple vow— would change her life in ways she couldn't possibly predict.

As Asa mounted his horse and headed down the road, his thoughts whirled like a tornado's funnel cloud. When he'd first heard the phone message accusing him of fathering twins on some young woman named Molly, he'd found the situation outrageous—but now that he'd met Will Gingerich and heard more of the story, he was even more upset. And confused.

He could understand why Will was acting half crazy, because dealing with cancer and grief did that to a man. But how had Will gotten his phone number? If Will's wife had spoken only a first name, what if she'd declared her love for a different man altogether? The whole situation seemed bizarre, and Asa sensed that he could mull it over all the way home and still not have any answers by the time he reached Clifford.

On instinct Asa turned and saw that Edith Riehl was still standing on her porch, watching him. When he waved, she waved back before stooping to pick up the two babies in their baskets. Now *that* young woman was a saint, taking responsibility for twins on the promise that Will Gingerich would return for them. Asa wasn't a betting man, but he figured the odds were about fifty-fifty that Will would come back—and about nil that he'd try to raise the babies on his own. Parenting would be a daunting task for a man alone even under more normal circumstances, and even with help from Molly's family.

Asa shook his head as he imagined the trials and tribulations of tending two helpless babies. *But Edith will handle it. She's a can-do sort of woman whose heart and priorities are in the right place.*

"Let's go, Midnight," he murmured, urging his gelding into an easy canter as they reached the curve where the road left town. His ride home would be much more enjoyable if he thought about Edith Riehl . . . imagined her waiting for him on the porch of a tidy house as his work day came to an end. . . .

Asa heard rapid hoofbeats coming up behind him, but he was awash in his pleasant thoughts—

and he never dreamed a buggy driver would race past him so fast on the narrow road that Midnight would spook and lose his footing in the gravel. Asa cried out as a small rock struck his forehead. He had the sensation of flying through the air—leaving the saddle—

And then he hit the ground and felt nothing at all.

CHAPTER TWO

Nora Hooley couldn't stop smiling as her friends and family members filed out of the house after the wedding. It had given her special joy to see the home she and Luke shared filled with guests—some of whom had come all the way from Lancaster County, Pennsylvania, to celebrate the wedding of her daughter Millie to Luke's younger brother Ira. On this sunny April day with the dogwood and redbud trees in full bloom and cheerful red and yellow tulips brightening the yards in Willow Ridge, her heart swelled with love and fulfillment. God had blessed her beyond her wildest dreams when He'd guided her to this little town and her new life with Luke.

"Pinch me, Mamma! This day's surely a dream," Millie exclaimed as she grabbed Nora in a hug. "I'm so happy, I might just pop!"

Nora chuckled as she wiped away tears of joy. "That's the way it's supposed to be on your wedding day, sweetie—"

"And it's Ira's job to keep that smile on your face for years to come," Luke chimed in as he came to stand beside Nora. He clapped his younger brother on the back. "It's a tall order, but I think you're finally man enough to carry through with it. We wish you both all the best."

With a happy sigh, Nora gazed at her seventeen-year-old daughter. The teal fabric she'd chosen for her wedding dress complemented her ginger hair and sweet, freckled face, and her apron and *kapp* were a pristine white. As Ira stood beside her in his black trousers and vest with a new white shirt, which Millie had made for him, he was the picture of earnest Amish masculinity. Nora had once doubted Ira's intentions—he'd been nearly twenty-nine before he'd joined the Old Order church—but now she believed he was the perfect mate for her Millie. As his wedding gift, Ira had built a new home on the land behind the Hooley brothers' mill. The entire Hooley family had chipped in, so the house was already paid for, but Ira had covered more than half of its expense himself—an investment a younger, less established man couldn't have afforded.

"You'd best head to the Grill N Skillet so you can greet your guests," Nora suggested. "After a long morning of church and your ceremony, everyone's ready to devour the food Josiah and Savilla have cooked up."

"*Denki* for providing our wedding meal—and for your idea to have it in the café," Ira said. "I got so hungry from the aroma of grilled meats coming through the windows, I *almost* couldn't stay through the entire wedding!"

Nora chuckled. "You'd probably have had hot dogs and peanut-butter sandwiches for your meal if *I* had done the cooking," she teased.

Luke laughed and slung his arm around her shoulders. "Everyone knows your talents lie outside the kitchen, Nora-girl—and nobody cares," he insisted as he gazed into her eyes. "We're happy to let Josiah and his sister do the cooking today, and glad the new café's big enough to seat so many people. We'll see you two in a bit."

"Don't go gobblin' down all that roasted pig before I have a chance at some of it," Bishop Tom Hostetler teased as the newlyweds stepped outside. "I *almost* cut the sermon short when the breeze smelled like it came straight from Josiah's smokers."

Nora laughed with him and all the other folks who'd gathered around. "I heard a few stomachs rumbling during the service," she remarked. "Fill your plate as many times as you want and enjoy the rest of our big day, Tom. I—I can't thank you enough for the way you've guided Millie and Ira and the rest of our family."

"Not to mention how you spearheaded the rebuilding of the restaurant and quilt shop," Luke joined in. "Thanks to you, Willow Ridge is moving forward and growing with more young families and flourishing businesses."

The bishop waved them off with a modest smile. "We all pulled together—and you Hooleys are the backbone of our new prosperity here," he insisted.

"Can't help but feelin' a fresh sense of hope and happiness. We've got a lot to be thankful for."

"*Jah*, we do, Bishop," Nora murmured as the people around her nodded in agreement.

"Is it true, what we've heard?" a young woman in the crowd piped up. "Dat's cousin Reuben said the other restaurant exploded on Christmas Eve—and that the fire was set on purpose."

When Nora glanced around to see who'd asked that question, she spotted Loretta and Rosalyn Riehl standing beside their *dat*, peering at her from behind a cluster of other folks. The Riehls had moved into Reuben's house just last month, so they were the newest residents of Willow Ridge. "That's the way it happened—"

"And it's a long story, best told when folks aren't waitin' to partake of Ira and Millie's wedding feast," Bishop Tom interrupted with a purposeful smile. "We're glad you Riehls are here to celebrate with us as we focus on our future—and pleased that you, Cornelius, have taken your cousin's place as our district's deacon, too."

Cornelius, a barrel-chested man who stood head and shoulders above the crowd, pressed his lips together in a tight smile. "You folks have made us feel very welcome," he murmured. "If you'll excuse me, I'm heading home to look into my youngest daughter's latest predicament."

Nora's eyes widened as Cornelius slipped between the other folks and out the door, seemingly set on some grim mission. "May we bring you over a plate?" she called after him.

As the middle-aged deacon put on his hat and strode toward the county highway, his two daughters shook their heads. "Dat doesn't spend much time at weddings since our *mamm* passed on," Rosalyn explained. "And Edith did get herself into quite a pickle this morning."

"*Jah*, we were ready to walk over here for church," Loretta continued, "when we found her with a baby in each arm, telling us a mighty peculiar story about how their *dat* had dropped them off because their *mamm* had died—"

"And meanwhile he was accusing another fellow of being the babies' father," Rosalyn added in an embarrassed whisper. "So it seems we're to look after these two helpless wee ones until their *dat* returns."

"*If* he does—whichever man it is," Loretta added with an exasperated shrug. "It's another one of those long stories best left for another time."

"Oh, my," Nora murmured as the folks around her began to whisper among themselves. "I was wondering why I didn't see Edith sitting with you. She was so excited about helping at the wedding dinner."

"The little twins' dinner—and dirty diapers— were a more immediate concern," Loretta replied wryly. "We can't fault Edith for her soft heart, but we're wondering if she's gotten herself into the middle of a messy situation. I'm sure Dat's going to ask her some hard questions, and maybe insist that she return the babies to Will—the fellow who brought them here."

"It doesn't help that Will was once engaged to Loretta, or that Dat made them break it off," Rosalyn explained, smiling ruefully at her sister.

"Sounds like a matter we need to hold up in prayer, for all of you Riehls and those babies, too," Bishop Tom remarked. "The ladies here in town will help with clothes and supplies, so don't hesitate to let us know what ya need."

Tom and the Riehl sisters made their way outside. The other guests, eager to get to the Grill N Skillet, congratulated Nora and Luke in a steady stream that soon cleared the house. As her husband closed the door and clasped her hand, leading her to the café, Nora chuckled. "Seems there's more to our new neighbors than meets the eye," she said. "The Riehl sisters are such nice girls—and they've mentioned that they make several different craft items, which I'd like to sell in my store. Apparently that Will fellow trusts them to look after his little twins."

"He's probably so overwhelmed by the prospect of caring for them that he doesn't know what else to do," Luke replied. "If you had twins and then passed on, I'd be—well, I'm not sure I'd survive, Nora. You're *everything* to me."

"Oh, Luke." Nora stopped in the middle of the road to caress the brown beard he'd been growing since they'd married five months ago. The hitch in his voice had tugged hard at her heartstrings. "I'm healthy as a horse, and I plan to be pestering you for a long, long time. All right?"

"I sure hope so." A grin lit up his handsome face, and he kissed her quickly. "Although I'm enjoying this extended visit with our family, I'm looking forward to when the relatives head back to Pennsylvania so we have the house to ourselves again. Hear what I'm saying?"

Nora felt heat prickle her cheeks as she smiled up at him. "Loud and clear, Mr. Hooley."

From her upstairs bedroom, Edith heard the front door close, followed by her father's footsteps crossing the hardwood floor and then ascending the stairs. She quickly dropped the two dirty diapers into an old enamelware pot and put the lid on it, knowing Dat would object to the smell . . . just as the babies' fussing would bother him—now, and when he went to bed in the room adjacent to hers. She'd figured Dat would return early from the wedding. He'd had all morning to plan his sermon while Bishop Tom and Preacher Ben Hooley had been delivering theirs during the church service.

"Shhh," Edith whispered. She lifted little Louisa to soothe her, swaying from side to side. "Let's be very quiet, very calm. We'll pray for Dat's patience and compassion and—"

"Edith."

Despite the tightening in her stomach, Edith turned toward the doorway and put on a bright smile. "How was the wedding, Dat? Were there lots of folks from—"

"Tell me again how you came to be responsible for these two babies," he said sternly. "And then tell me how you intend to resolve this *situation* you've gotten us into."

Sighing nervously, Edith sat down on her bed so she could quiet Leroy, who was lying on a towel. Dat hadn't raised his voice, but he habitually spoke in a tone that conveyed his authority—a tone that had always made her squirm, as the startled twins were doing.

"I—I heard a baby crying when I was waiting for you and Loretta and Rosalyn to come down-stairs," Edith began. "When I spotted two fellows having an argument behind the rig the ruckus was coming from, I just had to go and see—"

"And why was their conversation your concern, Daughter?" Dat asked. "Curiosity killed the cat."

"*Jah*, and—like you've told me a dozen times—I used up my nine lives ages ago," Edith replied, hoping to soften her father with humor. "But it was the wee one's welfare I was concerned about, rather than the men's talk. I wondered if the mother was too ill to comfort the crying child—and when I looked into the buggy, I saw *two* babies. They were upset by the men's argumentative talk, no doubt," she added, hoping he would catch the hint.

Her father crossed his arms, filling the doorway with his broad-shouldered form as his disapproval sucked the air from the room. With his thick graying hair and beard, he reminded Edith of an Old Testament prophet about to foretell her doom. He scowled as Leroy began to cry, which inspired Louisa to join in.

"How are we to get any sleep? Or concentrate on our work?" Dat asked above their rising wails. "Edith, you are to return these babies to their mother at once!"

"But I tried to tell you—their *mamm* is dead!" Edith blurted. "Will brought the twins here until he could get through her funeral and—"

"This is Will Gingerich we're talking about, correct?"

"*Jah*, and he'd accused the other fellow of—"

"We *cannot* have Will coming around here on the pretense of seeing his children," Dat stated. "If he's got no wife to raise them now, he'll try to entice Loretta into marriage again. And that matter shall remain a closed book."

Edith scooped Leroy into her arms and stood up so she could rock both crying babies. She was feeling as upset as they were, sensing that no matter what answers she gave her father, they

26

would fall short. "No," she said in a lowered voice. "Will knew it would be better not to see Loretta—"

"He could never carry on an ordinary conversation with me," Dat said, exhaling his disgust. "Tucked his tail between his legs like a whipped dog—and if his wife bore another fellow's kids, then Will obviously wasn't man enough t control her. Maybe not man enough in the marriage bed, either—"

"*Dat*, really!" Edith gasped as her face went hot with embarrassment.

"—so no matter how you look at it, Gingerich has nothing to offer any of you girls," her father continued in a rising voice. "I hope you don't believe that other fellow's promise that he'll get to the bottom of this, any more than you believe that Will figures to claim these babies. It's our Christian duty to return these children to their family. They're not your responsibility, Edith."

Turning quickly to hide her tears, Edith swayed faster as she clasped the twins to her shoulders. Dat made a valid point, but his harshness made her heart shrivel in sympathy for the twins. Her head was starting to pound with their strident cries. She could barely think, much less refute her father's claims.

"I know how you always side with the underdog—how your heart opens wide any time you're around little children," Dat murmured as

27

he approached her. "But I'm watching out for your best interests, Daughter. You entered into this agreement without considering the long-term consequences. What man will marry you if you're saddled with twins who aren't even yours? You'll be stuck at home forever, doomed to be a *maidel*—and a single mother—while all your friends find happy lives with suitable husbands."

Who would marry me anyway? Edith thought sorrowfully. *I'd be a liar if I didn't tell a potential husband that I'm unable to bear his children . . . because Dat didn't take me to the doctor soon enough. If only my appendix hadn't burst. If only the infection hadn't attacked my female organs . . .*

Edith bit her lip against a sob. It wasn't right to dredge up her past resentment—not after she'd forgiven her father years ago, at Mamm's insistence. Dat was standing close enough behind her that she could feel the disapproval radiating from his body as he awaited her compliance. She dared not mention the vow she'd made to that strikingly handsome stranger.

Promise me that you'll mother these kids—and that you'll hear me out when I return, all right? His voice still echoed in her mind, mysterious and compelling.

Asa Detweiler had no idea how desperately Edith longed to be a mother—or that she'd agreed to care for these twins to satisfy her own selfish desires. She'd believed him to be sincere and compassionate, but she dared not mention that to her father, either. Cornelius Riehl had lost a large part of his heart and soul when Mamm passed away, but that didn't mean he'd lowered his expectations for his three daughters. If anything, he held them to higher standards now that Mamm wasn't around to buffer his gruffness, his moods.

"You know how it'll be, Edith," Dat said softly. "Every day you allow these babies to stay will make it that much harder for you to give them up. They belong with their family. Surely Will's wife's mother will wonder where her grandchildren have gone—"

"She's not speaking to him!" Edith blurted, knowing it was the wrong thing to say. "She was there when Molly passed from cancer, breathing another man's name. The shock of it sent Molly's grandmother to the hospital with a heart attack, so the whole family's in an uproar. I can't just—"

"Once again, we see that Will has alienated those who might've helped him in his time of need," her father pointed out. "Any man worth his salt would look after these helpless babies rather than dumping them on someone else. But he knew you'd relieve him of his parental responsibilities, didn't he? Knew you were too kindhearted for your own *gut*."

"Is it really such a sin, being kindhearted?" Edith protested. "Had we three girls been little when Mamm passed, you would've found another wife—"

"That's a lie, and you know it!" he blustered, grasping her shoulders. "Your mother was the only woman in this world for me. Don't you dare presume to understand the depth of my love—and my grief—for her!"

Edith swallowed hard. "I'm sorry. I—"

"I'm leaving this room because I can't stand the racket—or the smell—any longer," he muttered beneath the babies' wailing. "Find a way to quiet them. When your sisters get home, we're packing up these detestable dirty diapers and supplies, and we're returning the whole kit and caboodle to Gingerich. I don't want to hear another word to the contrary."

Edith held her breath until her father's heavy footfalls had gone down the hallway and stairs. As she burst into tears, she held the babies tenderly, still swaying with them, wondering how they would survive without a stand-in mother to care for them. Will was caught up in his own troubles, understandably wounded by his wife's final words—by her betrayal of his trust—not to mention being overwhelmed by the cancer that had claimed her when she should've been experiencing the joy of motherhood.

She had to convince Rosalyn and Loretta to help her with the twins while they sought wisdom and aid from the women of Willow Ridge. If the three of them put their heads together, surely they could find a way to change Dat's attitude. Surely they could keep the twins quiet enough that Dat could work on his clocks undisturbed in his basement workshop during the day and sleep uninterrupted at night.

"That's a tall order," Edith murmured as she gently laid the babies on the towel she'd spread across her bed. She tenderly smoothed their mussed brown hair. "You've got to help me with this, understand? We'll go downstairs for your bottles, but you've *got* to stop crying."

As she stroked their cheeks, Louisa and Leroy gradually got quieter, hiccuping and sucking in short breaths. They seemed small for their age, their expressive faces puckered with concern as they gazed up at her.

Lord, if I've ever needed Your help, it's now, Edith prayed as she gazed at them. *Bring me a sign, a solution. Anything to soften Dat's closed, lonely heart.*

CHAPTER THREE

L uke Hooley gazed around the crowded Grill N Skillet dining room with a sense of great satisfaction. While it was traditional for an Old Order wedding feast to be held at the home of the bride's parents, he and Nora had insisted on hosting the event at Willow Ridge's recently rebuilt and expanded café because it would be a real treat for their friends and family. Josiah Witmer had roasted two hogs, beef briskets, and countless chicken quarters, which he was serving along with the side dishes his sister Savilla had created.

As Luke slipped behind the steam table to chat with Josiah, his stomach rumbled. "You two have outdone yourselves," Luke remarked as the young man set out fresh pans of steaming mashed potatoes and creamed celery. "Everyone's raving about your grilled meats, and the way you've offered the traditional wedding foods along with your specialties."

Josiah flashed a wide smile. "Can't have pulled pork without some baked beans and slaw, ain't so? But Savilla was right—folks are gobbling up the wedding 'roast' she made with chicken and stuffing, too. I suspect we'll run out of the creamed celery before the second sitting of guests makes it through the line."

"We'll have plenty of other food, though," Savilla assured Luke. Her dark eyes sparkled as she set down a bowl of chunky homemade applesauce. "I was astounded when I saw how many different kinds of pies Naomi and the other gals made for us. And Miriam's wedding cake is the prettiest I've ever seen."

Luke glanced toward the *eck*—the raised table in the far corner, where the wedding party sat—and had to agree that the tiered cake his sister-in-law had made was even grander than the one she'd baked for his and Nora's wedding last winter. His brother Ben's wife was out of the restaurant business now, raising their baby daughter Bethlehem, but she still enjoyed sharing her baking skills whenever she had the chance. Miriam's former partner Naomi Brenneman kept the Grill N Skillet's kitchen organized and running smoothly during the daily lunch and supper shifts, which had allowed the Witmers to expand into some catering, as well.

"It's just fabulous, the way you two have grown your business these past months—and attracted so many more folks to Willow Ridge for the rest of our shops, too," Luke remarked. "When Ira and I opened our mill and store last year, we had no idea how busy we'd be, or how many regional farmers we'd need to hire to grow specialty grains for us."

"Not to mention your cage-free chickens and

33

eggs," Savilla said. "We're really glad to have local suppliers for those because we know the eggs haven't been sitting in cold storage somewhere—and the meat's so fresh. Here—" She grabbed a golden-brown chicken quarter with her tongs and put it on a small plate. "This'll tide you over until you and Nora come through the line for your dinner."

Luke laughed, tickled by her sense of humor and hospitality. "You don't have to ask me twice," he teased. "Nora's having such a *gut* time visiting, it might be a while before we sit down."

As he ambled along the outside edge of the dining room, where the tables had been placed end-to-end and covered with long white table-cloths, Luke bit into a perfectly seasoned chicken thigh with a groan of satisfaction. When he spotted his wife, with her auburn hair tucked up under her *kapp* and her freckled face alight with a smile, he let his gaze linger on her. Last spring at this time he'd been footloose and determined to remain uncommitted—a bachelor of thirty determined to live in a state of never-ending *rumspringa*—yet now he craved the company of his unconventional wife, and was contentedly immersed in the Mennonite faith they shared.

As though sensing his attention, Nora turned and smiled at him. Luke's heart fluttered. The crowd ceased to exist for a few moments as her green eyes made him hold his breath. When he saluted her with a chicken leg, they both laughed and went on about their visiting. As he glanced at Millie, so like her mother, and at his younger brother Ira while the newlyweds accepted plates of pie from Naomi Brenneman, Luke sent up a prayer. *Let them find the same happiness You've granted me with Nora, Lord.*

"Quite a party you're puttin' on for the happy couple," a familiar voice behind him said.

Luke turned as his older brother Ben clapped him on the back. "It's the least I can do, considering how you've helped pay for their new home."

"Oh, let's not forget that the aunts kicked in on that, as well as Ira." Ben smiled mischievously. "I felt sorry for you and Nora, what with bein' newlyweds yourselves—maybe lettin' Ira and Millie move into your place rather than expectin' them to bunk in the apartment above the mill."

"Aunt Nazareth and Aunt Jerusalem are so glad to see both of us younger bucks belonging to a church—and married—they said their house money was a thank offering to God," Luke remarked with a chuckle. "Ira and I did keep them on pins and needles for a long time."

Ben, who'd preached the main sermon at the wedding today, shrugged. "I was older than you boys—thirty-five—before I found my Miriam," he said with a nostalgic smile. "Who knew we'd all meet our matches and set up businesses when

35

we came to Willow Ridge? It's a *gut* thing God knew what we needed and got us to the right place at the right time, *jah*?"

"And who could've predicted that I'd give up my English life to join the Old Order and open a clinic here?" Andy Leitner chimed in as he came to stand with them. "Every time I see my kids' smiles—and the rosy glow on my Rhoda's face as she swells with our new baby—I have to pinch myself and give thanks."

"We're blessed to have ya here takin' care of us," Ben said with a nod. Then his smile brightened with curiosity. "Say, Andy, have ya heard anything about that acreage down the road from your corner—directly across from the Riehl place and Bishop Tom's—goin' up for sale?"

"I've heard the English family who owns it is selling because the *dat* and *mamm* can't manage living there by themselves anymore," Bishop Tom said as he joined them. "Guess they're goin' to something called an assisted-living facility."

"Why aren't those kids lookin' after their parents?" Ben asked with a shake of his head. "I can't imagine havin' to move away from the farm you've lived on most of your life, into a place where ya don't know the other residents—or the ones who'll be taking care of ya, either."

Luke considered this information as he looked across the crowded café to see his brother Ira smiling into his new bride's freckled face. "Might be worth my while to check into that land," he mused aloud. "Not sure what I'd do with the house that's on it, but the tillable acres would be a *gut* place for raising more of our specialty grains for the mill, or—"

Behind them, the bell jangled when the door was thrown open. "Where's Andy Leitner?" a woman cried out. "We've found a fellow thrown from his horse alongside the road, out cold!"

Andy rushed toward the door, and Luke felt compelled to go with him. His Aunt Nazareth, now Bishop Tom's wife, had hollered over the happy chatter of the crowd, and she appeared winded from sprinting to the Grill N Skillet. "After we ate, Jerusalem and I were walking over to the barn so she could see our little goats when we spotted a tall black horse, saddled but without its rider," she explained as the three of them hurried out to the road. "Then we noticed a fellow sprawled over in the grass—"

"Stay here and catch your breath, Nazareth," Andy insisted as he smiled at her. "I'll meet up with your sister as soon as I get my horse hitched to the clinic wagon."

"Wonder who it could be?" Luke asked as he and Andy loped down the highway toward the clinic at the next corner. "Most of the locals are still at the wedding dinner or visiting out back of the restaurant."

"Naz didn't seem to know him. Could be an out-of-town guest—or just somebody passing through on a pretty day," Andy said. "*Denki* for coming along, Luke."

Minutes after they reached the Leitner barn, they were rolling down the gravel road that ran past the Riehl place and the bishop's pasture, where cud-chewing Holsteins gazed over the fence at them. Luke had always been in awe of Andy's specialized wagon, which was a small clinic on wheels—allowed by Bishop Tom because it was a horse-drawn vehicle their local nurse could drive to medical emergencies or house calls. Luke's pulse accelerated with the mare's hoofbeats as he gazed up the road. Aunt Jerusalem's white *kapp* caught the sunshine as she waved her arm above her head.

"Wow, that's an impressive horse," he murmured. "Percheron by the looks of it—although he seems to have a limp."

"Might want to have Ben take a look at the horse after we see to its owner," Andy murmured. "The guy's sitting up now. Let's keep him still until I figure out how badly he's hurt."

Andy stopped the wagon a couple of yards from where Luke's Aunt Jerusalem stood, her face etched with concern. "Glad ya got here so quick, Andy," the middle-aged woman remarked. "Now that he's sittin' up, he seems determined to be anywhere but here."

The man had coal-black hair and a grass-stained shirt that stuck out around his suspenders. One side of his face was badly bruised, and he had an open wound in his forehead. He appeared dazed as he looked up at them, and he was placing his hands on the ground as though he intended to push himself up. "Where am I?" he asked hoarsely. "I have no idea how I came to be—"

"Don't stand up!" Andy insisted as he sprang from the wagon seat. "I'll check you over for broken bones and such. I'm a nurse, by the way. Andy Leitner."

The man's dark eyebrows rose. "You look like an Amish man—but you're a *nurse?* I must've really hit my head hard."

Andy smiled as he ran his hands over the fellow's neck and shoulders. "I get that reaction a lot. What can you tell me about your accident?" he asked as he gently grasped the man's upper arms.

The stranger winced. "I'm foggy about that. I think I remember a buggy whizzing past me—must've spooked Midnight awfully bad—"

The gelding nickered in response to hearing its name.

"—and from there, it's a blur," the man finished with a sigh.

"Any idea how long you've been lying here?"

"Nope."

Andy nodded and continued his examination. "Any idea where you are, what town this is?" he

39

quizzed as he assessed the man's eyes and pupils.

"Not really—except I'm on the ground and in a state of pain," the guy added with a short laugh.

"We'll fix that as soon as we can," Andy assured him. "So, what's your name? Where are you from?"

"Ah, my manners are slipping. I'm Asa Detweiler, and I live in—*ouch!*"

"Sorry," Andy murmured. "I'm not finding any broken bones, but you've got some bruised ribs and a bloody forehead. You're going to be sore for a long while."

The guy sighed again as he refocused on Andy's questions. "Clifford."

Andy bit back a grin. "I assume we're talking about a town rather than the big red dog that's in a lot of kids books?"

Asa's expression went blank.

"Sorry. I shouldn't be teasing about stuff like that," Leitner said.

"Clifford's a little town a ways south of here," Luke replied. He was relieved that Asa seemed to be regaining his memory despite his obvious discomfort. "Did you come up to Willow Ridge for the wedding festivities?"

Asa again appeared confused, but then his lean face settled into a scowl. "I wouldn't liken my reason for being here to any sort of festivity," he muttered. "And frankly, I'd rather not discuss it. If you'll just let me get back on my horse—"

"Nope, can't do that," Andy insisted, holding Asa's broad shoulders so he'd remain seated. "Since we don't know how long you were out, I'm taking you to the emergency room for an MRI, in case you've got a concussion—"

"And your horse is in no shape to travel, either," Luke chimed in. He led the tall black gelding a couple of yards and noticed it was favoring a leg. "How about if I take him over to my brother's place? He's our local farrier."

The man seemed torn between concern for his horse and reluctance to stick around much longer, so Luke pointed in the general direction of Ben's shop. "I'll just lead him up the road a few blocks, and we'll take it real slow. I'm Luke Hooley, by the way, and this is my aunt, Jerusalem Gingerich," he added. "We're glad she and Naz found you when they did. We'll look after you and your horse until you're both road ready, all right?"

"Gingerich, eh?" Asa murmured with a hint of suspicion.

"*Jah*, I married Vernon last year," Jerusalem replied. "He's the bishop of Cedar Creek, ya know."

"Ah." Asa smoothed his black hair away from his face as he assessed them all. He winced again as he shifted his position. "Guess I'm not too fired up about riding, now that you mention it— especially if Midnight's lame," he murmured. "I sure have to wonder who raced his rig past us so

41

close—and so fast—that I got thrown to the side of the road."

"And I have to wonder who would've *left* you this way, too," Luke added. "Even Plain boys racing down the back roads for the sport of it would have the decency to stop if they made a horse throw its rider."

"*Jah*, you'd think so," Andy agreed. "Asa, for safety's sake, we're going to put you on a stretcher and carry you to the wagon."

As Luke helped the nurse get their visitor into the clinic wagon, he couldn't help wondering about the real story behind this incident. Had someone from Willow Ridge run this fellow's horse off the road? And why had Asa reacted so sourly to the name Gingerich? Families by that name lived all over this part of Missouri.

Maybe Detweiler was hurt and confused—as any fellow would be after hitting the ground so hard—yet Luke also found himself speculating about the stranger's reasons for being here. The shadow that had passed over Asa's face when he'd refused to answer that question suggested ulterior motives . . . hidden hostility.

Better keep your eye on this guy, Luke thought. *Who knows what secrets he's keeping?*

CHAPTER FOUR

E dith stood beside her bed gazing down at the twins in awe. So small they were, and so sweet—like little angels—now that they'd eaten and fallen asleep. She'd arranged them in large cardboard boxes padded with towels, and finding them beds and more clothing was her first priority. Will's box of supplies had included a very short stack of cloth diapers, half a dozen onesies, a blanket apiece, a half-used canister of powdered formula, and a few baby bottles—not much, considering she had two babies to look after. Molly had probably been too ill to sew for them, and not able to nurse them because of her cancer.

What a heartache that must've been for Molly— and for Will as he watched her weaken and die. Edith sighed. So much about Will's situation and these children was a sorrowful mystery.

I'm watching out for your best interests, Daughter. You entered into this agreement without considering the long-term consequences.

Edith frowned as her father's words taunted her. Dat was right about her tendency to nurture hopeless souls and underdogs, but wasn't that what the Bible urged Christians to do? *What doth the Lord require of thee, but to do justly, and to love mercy, and to walk humbly with thy God?*

The verse from Micah had been one of the earliest Edith had committed to memory—the watchword of her faith. Even as a child she'd rescued little birds that had fallen from their nests and had bottle-fed baby rabbits and deer after their mothers had been hit in the road.

Edith sighed. What future would these poor motherless children face if she didn't care for them? She had to find a way around Dat's refusal to keep them in the house . . . in her life. Already her heart swelled with love as she gazed at Leroy and Louisa.

The clatter of footsteps downstairs alerted her to her sisters' arrival, and she hurried down the hallway. "Shh!" Edith insisted as she leaned over the stairway railing. "I just got the babies to sleep!"

Loretta and Rosalyn's faces were alight with news—and secrets—when they looked up at her. "Where's Dat?" Loretta asked in a loud whisper.

Edith pointed downward, indicating the workshop in the basement.

"*Gut*—you'll never guess what's happened!" her middle sister continued as the two girls removed their shoes.

"*Jah*, Andy from down the road—the nurse fellow who runs the clinic—had to leave the wedding feast to fetch some guy Bishop Tom's wife found on the roadside," Rosalyn went on after she and Loretta had tiptoed up the stairs in their stocking feet. "Nobody knows why he's here—"

"But Jerusalem Gingerich was telling everyone he was thrown from the biggest black horse she's ever seen—"

Edith's breath caught as she followed her sisters into their room.

"—and then we saw him getting out of Andy's clinic wagon on our way home," Rosalyn went on in a low voice. "Luke Hooley was telling the fellow he could stay at their place until he's recovered enough to travel."

"Oh, Asa," Edith whimpered before she could stop herself.

Her sisters' eyebrows rose. "How do *you* know him, Edith?" Loretta demanded playfully. "We just caught enough of a glimpse to see that he was tall, dark, and—"

"Mighty handsome," Rosalyn finished.

Edith's throat had gotten so tight she couldn't get the words out. Her heart was pounding so loudly she could hardly hear herself speak. "That's the man who was arguing with Will about the babies. The one who asked me to take care of them until he came back."

Loretta's playful expression sobered as she crossed her arms. "And you're already head-over-heels for him, ain't so?" she demanded. "Edith, we don't know this man from Adam. What if he recovers enough to go home and he doesn't *intend* to come back?"

"He looks to be somewhat older than we are, so he's surely got a home and a job somewhere else—and maybe a wife," Rosalyn pointed out quietly. "What we don't know about him—"

"What we don't know can't hurt us, because those babies aren't staying here."

The three sisters turned to find their father in the doorway, sternly shaking his head. Edith's face went hot. How had Dat known to come upstairs, to catch them in this whispered conversation? She knew better than to ask, or to protest his ultimatum.

Dat cleared his throat. "If this man was thrown from his horse after a falling-out with Will Gingerich, why do I suspect Will was responsible for the accident?" he asked in a knowing voice. "And if this man is associated with Will and his deceased wife, in a triangle of sin and deceit, nothing *gut* can possibly come of getting further involved in this dubious situation."

Edith knew better, because she'd watched Will leave town ahead of Asa. But she and her sisters remained silent, eyes upon their father.

"This is why we're returning the babies to Will, before you girls get attached to them," Dat went on firmly. "And this is why you're all forbidden to have any further contact with Will or the man he apparently stranded on the road-side. I can see his appearance has already affected the three of you."

46

Edith's cheeks prickled with heat, and she looked down at the floor. She'd never been able to tell even the tiniest fib, and Dat had always been able to anticipate what his three daughters were cooking up before they got away with much. She didn't protest her father's ultimatum—but she didn't agree to it, either.

"Now that you're home from the wedding and those babies have stopped howling, maybe we could have some supper," Dat suggested.

Loretta's hand fluttered to her stomach. "I'm still so stuffed with pulled pork and baked beans—"

"Not to mention those two pieces of pie and the wedding cake you ate," Rosalyn added with a chuckle.

Dat's lips twitched. "Some of us haven't eaten since breakfast."

Edith stifled a sigh. She wasn't hungry, either, but at least Dat was more interested in eating than returning the twins to Will right away. "I'll fix us something—maybe slice and fry those leftover baked potatoes and some bacon."

"I'll gather some fresh eggs to go with those," Loretta chimed in.

"We'll be downstairs as soon as we've changed out of our church clothes," Rosalyn said, gazing intently at their father.

After a moment Dat took the hint and left so the older girls could get dressed. Rosalyn and Loretta carefully hung up their best dresses and grabbed the clothes they'd worn before the wedding, intent on keeping their father pacified.

"Hoo-boy, he's wound up about those babies," Loretta whispered.

"If Dat thinks Will's such a bad apple, why does he insist on taking the twins back to him?" Rosalyn asked with a shake of her head. "I know you've gotten yourself—and the rest of us—into a bit of a bind here, Edith, but I'd have done the same thing as you. It's not the babies' fault that they need care neither one of those men can give them."

Edith flashed her eldest sister a grateful smile and went downstairs to start supper. Neither Loretta nor Rosalyn ate much, and Edith was too lost in her swirling thoughts to do more than pick at her meal. Dat, however, took his time over two platefuls of scrambled eggs, bacon, home fries, and bread with butter. Then, after offering them some, he polished off the two slices of cherry pie and the large slab of wedding cake her sisters had brought home.

"I've been thinking about a suggestion Nora Hooley made," he said as he pushed back from the table. "She wants to display some of my clocks in her store. It's a sure thing that potential buyers would see them better there than in my work-shop."

Loretta snatched at this thread of conversation

like a hen snagging a worm. "Simple Gifts is such a wonderful shop," she replied. "When I was in there last week, Nora was hoping Edith would take in some of her baskets—"

"And your rugs would be just the thing to consign there, too, Loretta!" Rosalyn put in. "Nora sells so many pretty linens and household things. I was thinking to buy a few to use here in the kitchen and—"

"The rugs and curtains your mother made are just fine." Dat focused intently on Rosalyn. "You know how it goes, Daughter. Once you start shopping at Nora's, a lot of money will slip through your fingers before you realize it."

Rosalyn's crestfallen expression tugged at Edith's heartstrings. The cotton curtains were faded from the sun, and the woven rag rugs were patched on the back, so threadbare the girls avoided standing on them when they were washing dishes or cooking at the stove. When they'd moved to Willow Ridge, she and her sisters had hoped Dat might be able to part with some of the items their mother had made, but he seemed determined to keep Mamm's memory alive by clinging to every little thing associated with her—even though those items were falling apart.

The kitchen fell silent, so stuffy Edith longed to open a window—except Dat had always insisted that no one else rise from the table until he did. He didn't like to feel rushed by women clearing away the dishes and removing leftover food.

Finally, he stood up. "After this afternoon's work, I realize how short on replacement parts I am, so I'll be leaving early tomorrow," he remarked. "I like it that the trip to Kansas City is a lot shorter from here than it was from Roseville."

Edith and her sisters nodded mutely.

"Make something substantial for breakfast so I won't have to buy lunch along the way," Dat continued. "I'll let my new driver find his own meal while I'm at the clock-repair store. Every little bit helps when it comes to economizing. Your mother stretched a dollar farther than anyone I've ever known."

When he left the kitchen, Edith and her sisters sprang from their chairs. Rosalyn ran dishwater while Loretta scraped plates and Edith gathered the silverware and glasses. "I need to buy another canister of formula powder," she murmured. "Dat will raise a ruckus if he sees the price sticker on the can Will left, so I'll pay for it out of our stash. *Please* don't tell him I'm buying it, or he'll think we intend to defy him and keep the babies longer. But what else can I do? We don't have enough to feed them through tomorrow."

Rosalyn glanced out the kitchen window. "Folks are still over at the Grill N Skillet for the wedding, so Zook's Market's not open, most likely."

"*Jah*, the stores are all closed for the day," Loretta reminded Edith. "The Witmers have closed the Grill N Skillet for its supper shift so folks can stay at the wedding party as long as they want to. Lydia and Katie Zook plan to help with the cleanup, too."

"Hmm." Edith stood between her sisters, assessing the wedding guests who sat clustered in lawn chairs behind the café. "Maybe if I ask Preacher Henry nicely, he'll let me into his store just long enough to . . . or maybe I'll have to go when they first open in the morning."

"Go now, while Dat's downstairs working," Loretta suggested in a low voice.

"We'll keep the babies quiet for you," Rosalyn chimed in under her breath. "I haven't gotten a *gut* look at them yet."

"Me neither. What're their names?"

Edith gratefully grasped her sisters' shoulders. "*Denki* so much—I won't be long," she promised. "Leroy and Louisa are such sweet little things. You can't help but love them."

Before any more time slipped away, Edith grabbed a couple of twenty-dollar bills from the plastic coffee canister where they kept the money from selling their cage-free eggs to the Hooleys' mill store—a sideline Dat's cousin Reuben had left behind when he'd returned to Roseville. Her pulse pounded as she hurried across the lot behind their house and then strode past the

Brennemans' cabinetmaking shop, toward the back door of the café.

As she'd hoped, Lydia Zook was helping in the kitchen and was sympathetic to Edith's need for formula. As the storekeeper's wife walked her down the road to the white market with the blue metal roof, Edith answered her questions about the babies with what little information she had. It seemed Asa Detweiler was all the talk among the curious wedding guests, but Luke Hooley and his aunts had learned very few details about the man they'd rescued from the roadside.

Once inside the store, Lydia showed Edith to the baby supplies. Plain women didn't use a lot of formula mix, so Edith chose one of the three cans on the shelf and quickly paid for it. "*Denki* so much for helping me out," she said as they left the market.

"Come back tomorrow afternoon," Mrs. Zook suggested. "I'll ask the local gals to bring whatever baby things they can spare to the store for you. You're a saint for taking on a dead mother's twins."

"That would be such a help," Edith murmured. "I can't thank you enough."

As she headed down the road with her sack, Edith felt a surge of gratitude for the folks in this town. Tomorrow was Friday and Dat was going to Kansas City—he'd be gone until evening—so she hoped she'd be caring for the babies at least another day . . . and maybe this outpouring of sentiment and assistance from the neighbors would soften her father's heart. Or maybe, if they heard he was returning the twins to a home where they wouldn't be properly cared for, Lydia and the other women would express their disapproval and change Dat's mind. There had to be a way. . . .

Edith blinked. She'd been so lost in thought that she'd headed the wrong way down the county road—toward Nora and Luke's house on the hill instead of her own home.

Your feet knew where your heart wanted to go. But you can't stay long. Folks will talk—and your sisters are babysitting.

Before she lost her nerve, Edith hurried up the driveway toward the attractive two-story house where she'd heard Asa was staying.

After taking a hot shower to soothe his aching body, Asa put on one of Luke Hooley's plain green shirts and then pulled on a pair of his trousers. He and Luke were nearly the same size, and Asa was grateful that his host had loaned him some clean clothes. Despite a killer headache, he chuckled at the assortment of bold prints hanging in the closet—and at the fact that some of Luke's shirts and Nora's dresses matched. Not every Mennonite husband would be pleased that his woman had sewn such striking garments for him, but Asa suspected Hooley was too enamored of his attractive redheaded wife to fuss about it.

Nice people, these Hooleys. Luke offered me a room, and Nora brought me food from the wedding.

Asa gathered his grass-stained clothes from the bathroom floor. He eased down the wooden stairs in his bare feet, aware of every aching muscle and joint in his body. Andy Leitner had told him he was awfully lucky he'd landed in tall grass rather than on gravel, and that he hadn't hit his head on a nearby tree. Even so, Asa chafed at the local nurse's order to lie low for a few days until they could assess how bad his concussion was—and until his horse was checked out by a vet. He had an entire set of antique bedroom furniture waiting to be restored in his shop—not to mention his mission of finding some Gingerich guy . . . whose first name had escaped him.

Asa shuffled carefully between the tightly arranged pew benches that filled the main level of the house, in awe of how many guests must have attended the wedding this morning. When he got to the kitchen, he lifted the foil from a glass casserole pan sitting on the counter. He inhaled the rich aroma of sauced pulled pork, several pieces of grilled chicken, and a huge mound of mashed potatoes that had been hollowed out to hold enough baked beans for three men. Next to the casserole pan sat a plate with two pieces of peach pie and a big wedge of wedding cake.

These people know how to put on a party. Asa tossed his dirty clothes aside and then opened drawers until he found a fork. He closed his eyes over a mouthful of the pork and let out a blissful sigh. It was an effort not to wolf down the food as a dog would, hungry as he suddenly was. He didn't bother finding a plate or taking his meal to the table. As he bit into a chicken leg, he didn't even care that juice dribbled down his chin—

"Anybody home?"

Asa stiffened, the chicken leg suspended in front of his mouth. Had someone called to him through the screened front door, or was he hearing voices as a symptom of his concussion? Maybe someone had come looking for Nora or—

"Asa? Are you in there?"

He held his breath, desperately trying to match that pleasant feminine voice with a face. He wasn't really in the mood for a visitor, but curiosity got the best of him. "Yeah? Who wants to know?" he called out as he walked toward the front room. He kicked his clothes out of the way so he wouldn't trip over them.

Melodious laughter tickled his ears, and, when he saw a female face, he ached to put a name to it. *She's distorted by the screen,* Asa reassured himself, but he hoped she spoke first so he wouldn't have to admit that he'd forgotten such a lovely young woman's name . . . if indeed he'd ever met her.

"It's Edith—the Edith Riehl who's taking care of the twins."

Twins? "Uh—sure, come on in," Asa hedged, gesturing with the chicken leg. "Pardon my bad manners. Nora brought me some food from the wedding dinner—"

"It smells wonderful," his visitor said as she stepped inside. Her eyes widened as she took in the room filled with benches.

"—and I'm hungrier than a bear coming out of hibernation, it seems."

"*Jah*, I bet you are."

Oh, honey, you don't know the half of it. Asa knew he was staring but he couldn't help himself. This Edith Riehl seemed achingly familiar, just beyond the reach of his recognition as a smile lit her pretty face and her expressive dark brows rose above sparkling brown eyes. When she stopped and nervously pressed her lips together, Asa realized how wolfish he must seem.

"Sorry. That tumble I took is messing with my head. So . . . how *are* the twins?" he asked, grasping at her conversational straws.

"Sleeping like little angels when I left. Lydia Zook opened the market so I could buy some more formula," she explained, holding up her paper sack. "My two sisters are looking after Leroy and Louisa."

Fleeting images of two tiny, wailing babies and the backseat of a rig passed through his mind. Asa smiled, hoping this young lady didn't think he was as lame-brained as he felt. "Guess they're not very old then," he remarked, wishing for a graceful way to get rid of the chicken bone he was holding.

"Born six months ago, Will told me," Edith replied with a shake of her head. "I can't imagine what his family's going through, what with his wife's dying so young from cancer."

Asa sensed he should feel outraged about something, but he couldn't put his finger on it— nor did he want to spoil a nice moment with this lovely young woman. "May I offer you some pie or wedding cake?" he asked hopefully. "Nora brought enough to feed—"

"I really should get home," Edith said as she glanced at the door. "If I'm gone too long— well, I just wanted to check on you. I'm so glad you're up and around, Asa. Are—are those your clothes? How about if I take them home and wash them?"

Before Asa could protest, Edith rushed toward him and grabbed up his shirt and pants. "I promise I won't mix them in with the dirty diapers," she teased.

Asa felt vaguely embarrassed when Edith rolled his pants and shirt together and stuffed them into her grocery sack. "You don't have to do that."

"It's okay, really," she insisted. She gazed up at him from just a few feet away, her smile lighting the whole front room. "We're doing laundry tomorrow anyway."

Before he could beg her to stay, Edith hurried toward the door. When she wiggled her fingers at him, something snapped into place in his mind. "Hey, there's money in my pants pocket. Take whatever you need to cover that baby stuff."

Edith's smile rivaled a sunrise. "That's very generous of you, Asa. Take care, and I'll see you when I can."

When the door banged, the front room suddenly felt very empty. Asa went to the door and watched Edith break into a jog as she headed down the blacktop road. Had he said something offensive? Upset her enough that she was running away from him? Or was his face messed up from landing so hard after Midnight threw him?

Asa wandered into the half bath tucked under the Hooleys' stairway and looked in the mirror. One side of his face sported a huge purple bruise, and he was supposed to put ointment and a Band-Aid on his red forehead wound. He hadn't combed his hair after his shower, and his five-o'clock shadow bristled along his jawline. Luke's apple-green shirt was hanging lopsided at the collar because Asa had buttoned it wrong. And where had that grease spot come from?

Asa sighed. He should probably phone home to say he'd be detained in Willow Ridge for a while, yet he suddenly lacked the energy to make the call. "You're a mess, Detweiler," he muttered as he ambled back to the kitchen.

And that was true before Miss Riehl came calling and made you realize how many pieces are missing from this puzzling situation.

When Edith entered the back kitchen door, voices in the front room told her they had company. She stashed the sack with the formula and Asa's clothes in the pantry, hoping her absence hadn't become too noticeable. Putting on a bright smile, she went to greet their guests.

What a sight it was to see Bishop Tom and Vernon Gingerich, the white-haired bishop from Cedar Creek, standing on either side of Dat near the fireplace while their wives, Nazareth and Jerusalem, sat on the couch holding the babies. Loretta and Rosalyn gazed at Edith as though to ask what had taken her so long, while Dat appeared as edgy as a cat trapped between two curious—but well-intentioned—dogs.

"Bless her, Lydia Zook let me into the market so we'd have enough formula for tomorrow," Edith said as she went to stand behind the sofa. "And she's asking ladies from around town to bring any baby things they can spare for us, as well. What a relief that is!"

"*Jah*, I can imagine it's been a scramble, figuring out how to care for these precious wee ones," Nazareth said as she lifted pink-shirted Louisa to her shoulder.

"And it's an act of true Christian charity, taking them in without a moment's notice, too," Bishop Tom remarked.

When Leroy began to fuss, Jerusalem stood up to walk with him. "What with our little goats living next door, giving such *gut* milk—"

"Why, we could provide all the food you'll need for these little angels!" Nazareth chimed in as she stood up to sway with the baby she held. "At six months, they're old enough to tolerate goat milk, and it's so much better for them than formula."

Vernon's blue eyes twinkled as he considered this. "I can recall several babies in our family who thrived on fresh goat milk when their *mamms* couldn't feed them," he said as he smiled at Dat. "Seems God knew exactly where to bring these little souls who're so dependent upon the charity of strangers. It's a blessed mission you've taken on, Deacon Cornelius. You're an inspiration to us all."

Edith and her sisters bit back grins. With two bishops declaring Dat the epitome of uncon- ditional love, there was no way he could take the babies back to Roseville now—or at least not until they had a stable home to go to.

Dat murmured something about Edith and her sisters being the ones who'd taken charge of the twins. Then he gazed intently at Vernon. "Say, you wouldn't happen to be related to the Will Gingerich who brought us these *angels,* would you?" he asked. "He lives just outside of Roseville—and is apparently caught up in a rather unsavory situation, because as his wife was dying she named another man as the babies' father."

Nazareth and Jerusalem sucked in their breath as Vernon's eyes widened. "Oh my, that complicates things," he murmured. "That branch of the family tree severed itself from the rest of us a couple of generations ago—over some silly feud I can't even recall. But *jah,* Will is my great-nephew. Clearly, I need to venture over that way to visit with him and his troubled family. Sooner rather than later."

"While you're there, I'm sure you'll find a *gut,* stable home these babies can grow up in," Dat said purposefully. "We're happy to help Will in his time of need, but every child should be raised by its own kin."

"That's the best thing for all of us, to be surrounded by a family who loves us," Bishop Tom agreed quietly. "With everyone praying on it, and meanwhile caring for the babies as we're able, I believe God will lead the folks involved to make the right decisions."

"Indeed, we'll look back to this day as a pivotal point when our faith changed lives," Vernon said in a low, eloquent voice. "The babies' lives, of course, but our own, as well. We've been placed in

61

an urgent position of opportunity to be the hands and feet of our Jesus in today's world."

Everyone nodded, considering what the two bishops had said. Edith believed their sentiments possessed the power of sermons, elevating this situation to a higher purpose. She felt even more earnest about carrying out the favor Will had asked of her this morning, giving him—and Asa— the chance to straighten out their knotty dilemma.

Edith found herself thinking about Asa . . . how his dark hair shimmered like ravens' wings, and the way he'd sworn to care for the twins even though he hadn't fathered them. When Leroy began to fuss, Edith stepped over to take him from Jerusalem. "Probably hungry again," she suggested.

"Smells kind of ripe, too," Jerusalem replied with a chuckle. "Better for these wee ones to be with you than with Naz or me. Until we married Tom and Vernon, we'd been *maidel* school teachers all our adult lives, you see."

"*Jah*, we didn't do any baby-raising as young women, and now we're too old," Nazareth continued the story with a chuckle. "I'd probably prick the poor things with the diaper pins—"

"Or put the diaper on the wrong end altogether," Jerusalem teased.

"Puh!" her sister retorted. "Who's the aunt responsible for Bennie's showin' Luke and Ira how to drink the sugar water out of the hummingbird feeders because she didn't realize things had gotten too quiet?"

Jerusalem's graying eyebrows waggled at her younger sister. "And they're the *sweetest* nephews of the bunch, ain't so?" she shot back. "No finer men in Willow Ridge than those three."

Edith laughed at this back-and-forth between the middle-aged sisters, even as Leroy began to wail—which inspired Louisa to do likewise. "If you'll excuse us," Edith said as Loretta relieved Nazareth of the twin she'd been holding.

"We'd best be goin' anyway." Bishop Tom reached for his hat. "My cows'll be wonderin' what happened to me if I don't get to milkin' them soon."

"And we'll be starting back to Cedar Creek," Bishop Vernon said as he gestured for his wife and sister-in-law to precede him toward the door. "I'll get in touch with Will and see how we can help on that end—and meanwhile, we'll keep you all in our thoughts and prayers. It's been a blessing to get better acquainted with you Riehls today."

Edith led the way upstairs, murmuring baby talk to settle the infant she carried, as Loretta and Rosalyn followed her with the other crying baby. Once in Edith's room, they laid the babies on the towels she'd spread upon her bed.

"We'll need to figure out what to use for a crib," Loretta said as she unfastened a diaper. "And we need a changing table, and—"

"Maybe the ladies will bring some of those things to the store for us tomorrow," Edith replied. She deftly removed Leroy's stinky diaper and dropped it into the enameled pail, closing the lid after her sister did the same with Louisa's. "I was amazed that Lydia Zook was willing to organize—"

Rosalyn leaned in close and lowered her voice. "What we really want to know is how your visit with Asa went."

"*Jah*, we saw you heading up the road like a moth to a flame," Loretta whispered. "Is he doing all right?"

"Is he as cute as we're guessing?" Rosalyn quizzed her. "We barely caught a glimpse of him—"

"Are you *happy* now?" Dat demanded behind them.

Edith nearly bumped her sisters' heads as they all straightened at once. Their father's expression told of his frustration—and of how he'd caught them pink-cheeked from scheming again.

"Of *course* everyone left when the babies started bawling," he went on tersely. "But mark my words, Daughters. No matter how *blessed* the bishops claim we are, this is just a temporary fix, until we make Will see the light and take responsibility for these children. I'm going to hold Vernon Gingerich to his promise to move this situation toward its proper conclusion."

"I'm sure he'll do his best on our behalf," Rosalyn murmured.

"He impresses me as a fellow who means what he says and gets right to it," Loretta chimed in.

Edith remained silent. Was that longing she heard in her sisters' voices—the same love she already felt for the babies who wiggled and kicked on her bed? When the sisters began cleaning and diapering Leroy and Louisa, Edith heard their father's footsteps in the hallway and on the stairs. "At least we won't be taking them back to Roseville right away," she murmured.

"I'm glad Bishop Vernon agreed to visit with Will, too," Rosalyn said. "If there's been a mis-understanding amongst members of that family, I'm thinking Vernon will handle the situation a lot better than Dat. With his white hair and beard, he surely must look a lot like God!"

Loretta chuckled at Rosalyn's remark. "The milk from Nazareth and Jerusalem's goats will save us a lot of money, too. All in all, their surprise visit was a big blessing—for us and the babies, too."

Edith smiled, thinking back to her visit with Asa. Had she been a blessing to him? Somehow that idea mattered to her—even if he might not stick around town much longer.

But maybe Leroy, Louisa, and I can convince him to stay . . . even if it's way too soon to be thinking about that.

CHAPTER FIVE

On Friday morning, after Nora had allowed herself to sleep an hour later than usual, she dressed quickly. She and Luke had agreed that because their visitor was supposed to rest, it would be best not to start the noisy job of clearing out the pew benches until midmorning. The cleanup duties were traditionally shared by the newlyweds, so Ira and Millie were also happy they didn't have to get up so early.

Nora smiled at her sleeping husband and padded barefoot down the hall, noting how the morning sunshine glimmered on the hardwood floors of her studio. At the guest-room door she paused, listening for signs that Asa was stirring. Hearing nothing, she opened the door and peeked inside.

Asa was still in bed, and he was looking right at her. His tousled ebony hair and long-lashed deep blue eyes contrasted strikingly with the ivory sheets. His face had returned to its natural tawny color—at least on the side she saw. He appeared alert and rested.

"Sorry—didn't mean to wake you," Nora murmured. "You slept soundly, I hope?"

"Like a rock."

She nodded. "Nurse Andy said rest was the best

thing for you, and that he'd stop by this morning to see how you're doing."

"I feel fine."

Nora found his steady gaze a bit unnerving, maybe because he was such a handsome man . . . probably not wearing much under the sheet and light quilt. "Well," she said quickly, "I'll start breakfast. Ira and Millie are to be here in a couple hours to help with the redding up."

"Count me in," Asa said. "It's the least I can do after the way you and Luke—"

"Nope, you're not lifting anything heavier than a fork. Andy's orders," Nora reminded Asa. "How about if you come over to the Simple Gifts shop with me and write out price tags? Luke, Ira, and Ben can heft those wooden benches back into the pew wagon."

Asa's unusual indigo eyes widened. "Are you ordering me around?"

"*Jah*, I am," Nora replied with a chuckle. "You're not going to make your concussion worse on *my* watch, mister. See you downstairs whenever you're ready for breakfast. Go back to sleep if you want to."

Before Asa could protest any further—or do something provocative like getting out of bed—Nora closed the door and headed downstairs. Their guest seemed much more focused this morning, which was a positive sign of recovery, but Andy had warned her that new symptoms might show up today. They couldn't risk letting Asa ride back home alone, even if his horse had recovered, so keeping him busy at effortless little jobs seemed like her best strategy.

As the three of them ate the breakfast casserole Ben's wife, Miriam, had so thoughtfully prepared for them, Nora stole glances at Asa. Even though Luke's clothing hung loosely on his slim, muscular body, their guest looked much better today. He wasn't much of a man for chitchat, but he thanked them repeatedly for taking him in and feeding him.

"Happy to help," Luke replied as he reached for Nora's hand. "I hope you know you won't be lifting any pew benches this morning, however."

Asa sighed. "So Nora's told me. But it seems she has a plan for keeping me busy in her shop."

Luke chuckled. "Nora's *gut* at keeping guys out of trouble," he replied as he gazed fondly at her. "I can't imagine the havoc I'd be wreaking if she hadn't set me straight and begged me to marry her."

"Hah!" Nora retorted playfully. "You were the one who came begging, Hooley. You and Ira were on the road to ruin when I came back to Willow Ridge last summer."

She rose to pick up their plates, smiling at Asa. "I'll be going over to the shop after I straighten up here—but again, Andy says rest is your best medicine. If you want to go back upstairs and catch a nap, that's fine."

Nora was pleased that when she headed out to the big red barn next door, which housed her Simple Gifts consignment shop, Asa came along. For a moment he stood on the porch, looking out over the panorama of Willow Ridge that spread before them in a patchwork of pastures, farmhouses, freshly tilled gardens, and shops located near the homes of their owners.

"Tell me what I'm seeing here," he said. "Willow Ridge seems more progressive than a lot of Plain towns."

"You've got a *gut* eye," Nora remarked. "Starting on our immediate left is Luke and Ira's grist mill, where they sell specialty grains, along with fresh butter, cage-free eggs, and goat cheese," she began, pointing as she described their view. "Zook's Market with the blue roof is our grocery and dry goods store, and down from that is the Grill N Skillet and the Willow Ridge Quilt Shop, both of them recently rebuilt after a fire at Christmastime. Josiah Witmer and his sister Savilla run the restaurant, with Naomi Brenneman's help. Three Mennonite gals in the Schrock family own the quilt shop."

"And across the road is Ben Hooley's smithy, where my horse is, *jah*?"

Nora nodded, pleased Asa's memory was returning. "You're right! And down at the next intersection is Nurse Andy's clinic. The long metal building behind that is the Brenneman brothers' carpentry shop, and then there's the Riehl place—where our newest resident, Cornelius, makes and repairs clocks. His girls manage the chicken business their cousin Reuben left behind," she went on. "The Holsteins you see are Bishop Tom's, and his wife Nazareth raises goats. That tall white house beside the apple orchard is Micah and Rachel Brenneman's place—Rachel is Miriam Hooley's daughter. Next door to that you see Dan Kanagy's sheep and Leah's beehives and big garden plots where she raises produce to sell at farmers' markets."

Asa was nodding, following Nora's commentary closely. "Sounds like a lot of the women here have businesses. That's unusual."

"We're a hardworking bunch, no doubt about it—but Bishop Tom has the final say about those gals working from their homes," Nora clarified. "Along that road toward Morning Star you'll find an auction barn. Coming around the bend toward this place, we have Matthias Wagler's harness shop, and his brother Adam does home remodeling. And that brings you to my store, Simple Gifts."

As they stepped off the porch, Asa seemed to be thinking about everything she'd told him. "What gets people to come here?" he asked. "Most of the businesses you've named are common enough in Plain towns, but it takes more than locals to support places like your gift shop and a mill store."

Nora smiled as she opened the side door of the barn. Asa had asked a very astute question, which indicated that his mind had cleared since Luke had brought him to the house yesterday. "This is going to sound a little strange, but we have a young woman—Rebecca Oliveri—who's built us all Web sites, and who knows how to make our businesses visible online," Nora replied. "She runs her Web site design business in an upstairs office of the clinic, and she's Andy Leitner's receptionist. As a toddler she washed away in the flood of ninety-three, and then rediscovered her Amish family—her mother Miriam Hooley, along with her twin sisters Rachel and Rhoda. She loves it here so much she's just built a home down the road from Ben's place."

"Wow, that's quite a story—and quite an asset to your community," Asa said as he followed Nora through the back door. His eyes widened as he entered the store. "And *wow* doesn't begin to describe this place, Nora. May I look around before you put me to work?"

The awe in Asa's voice brought a smile to Nora's face. "Please do. We have two levels of furniture, housewares, linens, leather tack, and garden gates—among other things—produced by Plain crafters from all over central Missouri," she told him. "I have to admit that every morning

71

when I walk in here, I'm amazed that we move so much merchandise. I've done better than I ever dreamed possible when I opened last fall."

Nodding, Asa walked slowly between the displays. He stopped to finger a pottery bowl and pitcher set . . . a glorious saddle of tooled leather . . . the star-pattern quilt on a glossy sleigh bed made of walnut. Then he looked toward the upstairs railing, where more quilts and some three-dimensional banners were hanging. "Awesome," he murmured. "Just plain awesome, Nora."

"*Denki*," she replied. "I'm blessed to know so many fine crafters, and pleased that I can provide them with a profitable outlet for their work. And what do *you* do, Asa?"

Several seconds went by. Nora kept watching her tall, muscular guest as he stood in the center of her store. Was he lost in thought, so focused on her wares that he hadn't heard her? Or was he starting to fade mentally, a consequence of his concussion?

Or is he fabricating an answer?

Nora didn't like to think her guest was hiding something, but it wasn't her place to pry, either— or was it? If his story about the young man who'd accused him of fathering those twins was a lie . . . Nora felt entitled to straight answers, if only to watch out for the Riehls.

Asa turned, focusing his cobalt eyes on her. "My brother and I run a furniture business. I do refinishing and repair work, and he does upholstery and caning."

"Ah." Nora smiled, deciding not to challenge his answer. "If you'd like to call to let your family know where you are, my phone's right here," she said, gesturing toward the desk where her computer sat. "I'll get the list of new items we need to tag."

As Nora entered her enclosed office, she observed Asa through the slats of the blinds. He'd seemed very open and sincere until she'd asked about his livelihood. Perhaps she should keep him in sight at all times—because he might exhibit more concussion symptoms, and because he seemed *very* interested in her merchandise. She regretted the worm of suspicion that had crawled into her thoughts after he'd paused for a few moments too long.

He punched some numbers on her phone. "*Jah*, it's me," he said, apparently leaving a message as most Amish folks did. "I'm in Willow Ridge because I got thrown from my horse. I'll be back as soon as we're sure I don't have a serious head injury. Let Hal Gillespie know I'm running late on that antique bedroom set he left with me, okay? Bye."

As Nora carried out a box of labels and her list of new consignment items, she considered what to ask Asa about his business and family. She didn't want to sound nosy—just interested. "I bet your folks will be glad to hear from you," she remarked as she set down her armful of supplies. "It's not every day you get thrown to the roadside and detained in a strange town."

Asa shrugged. "It's just my brother and me living in Clifford—and we tend to go our own ways, picking up or delivering furniture and scouting for pieces to refurbish so we can sell them," he replied. "We sometimes go a few days without seeing each other, so I doubt he's been worried about my being gone."

Nora nodded, although it seemed odd that brothers and partners wouldn't keep closer tabs on each other. "How about the rest of your family? Are your parents close by?"

The rising of Asa's dark eyebrows suggested irritation or impatience—with his family or maybe with her, for asking such a question. "As the youngest sons, we always knew none of the family land would go to us. We moved to Clifford when we found a place to open our business," he replied. "So what's your system for tagging your stuff?"

Although Asa hadn't come out and said so, Nora sensed he and his brother might've had a falling-out with the rest of the Detweiler family . . . wherever they were. She reminded herself that Asa's affairs were none of her business, even though his behavior and words were raising red flags in the back of her mind.

She showed him how she preferred the labels to be written out, following the numbers she'd assigned to each crafter who consigned work to Simple Gifts. Asa set to work, easily fitting his small, tight printing onto the labels. When Andy Leitner entered the shop, however, Asa appeared happy for the distraction.

"Let's look you over, Asa," the nurse said as he opened his medical bag. "Glad to see you focused on a task and behaving yourself for Nora."

Nora chuckled. "He seems a lot more alert after a night's sleep," she remarked. "His bruises are looking better, too."

"He looks to be a sturdy type who heals quickly. His MRI shows that he's got a mild concussion that won't cause any long-term damage to his brain," Andy replied as he studied Asa's eyes. "Comes from being a young fellow who takes *gut* care of himself—or who has a wife looking after him, maybe wondering where he's been."

"Nope, not married," Asa said. "I would like to get home, though. Lots of refinishing work waiting for me."

"Stand up for me." With relaxed efficiency, Andy continued to observe Asa's responses, carefully placing his hands on Asa's shoulders and midsection. When Asa flinched, the nurse nodded. "It'll be a while before your ribs stop hurting. Over-the-counter pain relievers and an ice bag should help, but I want you to stay in

Willow Ridge at least until Monday morning so I can be sure your brain's recovering from that jostling it took. Follow my finger with your eyes while you keep your head still."

Asa's sigh sounded impatient. "That's a long time to be away from my shop. And I promised Edith Riehl I'd get to the bottom of this situation with that Gingerich fellow who says I fathered those babies. I can't do that if I'm stuck here."

"An honorable excuse, but it won't fly," Andy said firmly. "Edith impresses me as a young woman who would want the best for those babies and for you, so work with me, all right? Too many folks who've suffered head trauma get into trouble when they don't rest long enough for their internal injuries to heal."

Asa closed his eyes, quelling the urge to protest further.

"You know, I'm on my way over there to check on those twins," Andy said as he put his tools back in his bag. "How about if you walk along with me, and we can see how your horse is doing at Ben's? The fresh air and exercise will do you *gut*."

"And while I appreciate your help, I'm sure you'd rather be out doing something other than my busywork," Nora chimed in.

Asa's smile confirmed her assumption. As she watched the two men head for the road at a leisurely pace, Nora wondered if her doubts about Asa were off base. Any fellow his age would champ at the bit if he were being detained—and in pain—after an unidentified buggy driver had gotten him into this fix. *She* certainly wouldn't like it if the same sort of accident had happened to her—and she would probably be a lot crankier than Asa.

Nora sat down at her table and wrote out the labels for her new merchandise. Better to be focused on her own business rather than poking her nose into someone else's.

"The vet says Midnight will be feisty and fine again in a day or so," Ben Hooley was saying as Asa stroked his gelding's broad black neck. "He threw a shoe, so I've replaced both of the back ones. Noticed a little tenderness as I worked on him, but that's to be expected. Mighty fine mount you've got here, Asa."

Asa reveled in the presence of his Percheron, in the horse's glossy ebony coat and the bunching of his muscles as he shifted his feet. Midnight was glad to see him, too, and had displayed only a slight limp when Asa had walked the gelding around Ben's corral a couple of times. Innate understanding shone in those intelligent brown eyes as he nuzzled Asa's palm.

"*Jah*, he's got a steady head and disposition—which tells me the buggy that spooked him had to have passed us awfully close and fast," Asa said. He felt worse about his horse's being hurt than he did about his own injuries.

Ben considered this, and asked the obvious question. "Ya didn't hear it comin' up behind ya, then?"

Asa let out an exasperated sigh. "I don't actually recall the accident—"

"And that's normal, right after a bad bump to your head," Andy put in.

"—but I must've been thinking about something else, not paying attention," Asa continued with a shake of his head. "I've wondered about it a lot, but nothing comes back to me. It's not like a horse-drawn buggy sneaks up on anyone."

"For me, the bothersome part is that the driver didn't stop to help ya," Ben said. "We might never know who was responsible."

Asa shrugged, because he'd considered that possibility. "Without anybody to pin the blame on, I'm better off just moving forward. Once Andy says my head's on straight again, I'll go home and get back to work."

As Ben and Andy chuckled, Asa realized he owed the farrier some money . . . and that all his cash had gone home with Edith. He didn't care to let on about how pleased he was to have an excuse to see her this morning—or about how she'd snatched up his clothes when they'd been alone together. As a preacher, Ben might find that detail inappropriate, and Asa didn't want him or anyone else getting the wrong idea. "How much do I owe you for those horseshoes, plus the vet's bill?"

he asked. "I'll bring you the money when I—"

The farrier waved him off. "I'm happy to put those shoes on for ya so you'll get home safely and ya won't have a bad impression of our little town after your accident. We look after folks here."

Asa's jaw dropped. "But a vet charges just for showing up, before he even sees the animal."

"I had the vet here lookin' at one of my mares anyway," Ben insisted. Then he shrugged, a smile lighting his friendly face. "And maybe someday there's a favor you can do for me, *jah*? Or better yet, next time ya see somebody in a tight spot, maybe you'll lend him or her a hand. The Lord loves a cheerful giver."

"These Willow Ridge folks are big on paying it forward," Andy remarked. "Not so long ago I was a divorced English fellow looking to join the Plain faith and this community because I'd found the love of my life here—and she was Amish."

"His Rhoda is my Miriam's daughter, you see," Ben explained. "We had to be very sure this man was sincere in his intentions and his faith."

"I had to prove myself more than most men would," Andy agreed with a fond smile. "Yet this town has made me and my family very welcome. It's a blessing to care for these people, and to see my kids going to school here—growing up in a community that relies upon God and puts Him first."

Asa and Andy took their leave of Preacher Ben, and continued on to the Riehls' place. They walked at a leisurely pace along the county black-top, which allowed Asa time to consider what he'd just learned about the local nurse who'd rescued him along the roadside yesterday.

He knew of communities where English men would've been shut out before a romance had had a chance to develop with a local girl—not to mention church leaders who wouldn't have allowed Andy to practice his medical profession after he'd been baptized into the Amish church. The fact that Willow Ridge had accepted a *divorced* man was the most radical aspect of Andy Leitner's past, however, because the Old Order counted folks who'd left their mates as adulterers—and the church didn't allow anyone to remarry unless their previous spouse had died. The way Willow Ridge had accepted Andy spoke of a deep forgiveness the likes of which Asa hadn't encountered before.

"What do you recall about the guy who brought the twins to Willow Ridge, apparently looking for help from the Riehl girls because he knew them?" Andy asked as the white house with the dogwood trees came into view.

Asa sensed the question was as much a test of his memory as it was curiosity on the nurse's part. "I'd never seen him before—or his wife," Asa added emphatically. "But Edith knew him and didn't bat an eye before agreeing to take in his kids. Except he swears up and down that they're *my* kids."

Andy's eyes widened. "How'd you find out about the babies, then?"

"Got a message on my machine, saying my name was the last thing his wife uttered before she died."

"Wow," Andy murmured. "Any chance he got the wrong phone number?"

"Oh, no, it was my first name he said—and when he mentioned he was bringing the babies to Willow Ridge until he could get things straightened out," Asa continued in a rising voice, "I saddled Midnight and rode up here straightaway to find out what was going on."

Nodding, Andy slowed their pace a bit. "What else can you tell me about this guy? I hate to ask a lot of embarrassing questions once we get to the Riehl place."

Asa gathered his thoughts, hoping to remain objective. "His name's Will Gingerich, and he lives outside of Roseville—the town where the Riehls lived before they moved here," Asa recounted. "He told me he was once engaged to the middle Riehl sister—Loretta, I think her name is—but her *dat* broke it off, and then Will married some gal named Molly. She was apparently pregnant before they tied the knot, but she didn't tell him that part. Somewhere along the line, she got cancer."

"Oh, my." Andy thought about this, stopping at the end of the Riehl lane. "Now that Will is widowed—with two babies who supposedly aren't his—I wonder if he'll try to rekindle his romance with Loretta? You're doing a fine job of recalling these details, by the way," Andy added. "But let's not get into this complicated relationship story while we're here, all right? I just want to be sure the babies are healthy and that the Riehls are handling the situation. It must be a major adjustment to suddenly have two babies in the house."

"Edith was a saint," Asa murmured. "She heard the babies crying and came to see about them while Will and I were arguing. And she informed us that the babies' needs were far more important than our loud, upsetting talk—and then she agreed to take them in until Will could bury his wife and deal with Molly's family. No questions asked. I was amazed."

Andy smiled as he gazed toward the Riehls' tidy white house. "I don't know this family well because they've only lived here a month or so, but I like what you're telling me," he said. "The twins are in *gut* hands—and I've heard that Lydia Zook has organized the women, taking donations of baby clothes and equipment and such."

Asa was once again astonished at the immediate, unconditional generosity the people of Willow Ridge had displayed. When the front door opened and a young woman stepped onto the porch carrying a basket in each hand, his pulse lurched. It was Edith, and behind her came another young woman with baby bottles. "We've arrived in time for lunch," he said with a chuckle.

"A picnic on the porch, by the looks of it," Andy remarked. He returned the other Riehl girl's wave and bright smile. "Shall we make our visit?"

Asa was already walking down the lane, his eyes on Edith as she set the baskets down and settled in the porch swing. Behind the house he saw laundry flapping in the gentle breeze and recognized his own turquoise shirt among a number of gray ones, and dresses in shades of blue, green, and purple. Once again he admired Edith. She'd washed his clothing without any concern that it didn't fit in with the darker shirts and pants—though some neighbor ladies would notice that and wonder what was going on. He felt a puppy-dog eagerness as he got closer to the house.

"*Gut* morning, ladies!" Andy called out as they approached the porch. "At first glance, it appears all is well with you and the twins."

Edith grinned. "It's going a lot better now that Nazareth's brought us fresh goat milk."

"*Jah*, they're slurping it down," her sister chimed in. "They're so much happier; we're guessing the store-bought formula was upsetting their tummies and making them fussy."

"Nazareth's told us to dilute the milk with distilled water, about one part water to two parts milk," Edith said to the nurse. "Are we doing it right?"

Leitner nodded as he observed the babies in their baskets, waving their little arms and legs. "That's the ratio I've heard other Plain ladies speak of. I can check on that when I get back to the clinic and let you know if I find anything different."

Asa had been happy to let Andy initiate the conversation; at this moment he couldn't have talked if he wanted to. What a picture Edith made, sitting in the white wooden swing with a baby cradled in her arm as she held its bottle. She seemed determined not to meet his gaze, yet the pretty roses in her cheeks suggested she was aware of his presence . . . and trying not to let on that she was glad to see him. Or at least he wanted to believe that.

"Asa, you're looking much better than you did when Rosalyn and I caught a glimpse of you in the clinic yesterday. I'm Loretta, by the way," she added. She was holding the other baby, making the feeding process look effortless as she and Edith gently moved the swing forward and back.

"Hi, Loretta," Asa said. "I'm feeling a lot better, too. *Denki* for your concern."

"Oh, lots of folks are concerned," she replied quickly. "The story about you and Will and these babies was all the talk at the wedding dinner yesterday—until Nazareth came to fetch Andy because she'd found you unconscious on the roadside. Then *your* story had everyone chattering."

Asa glanced at Edith, and any sort of reply flew out of his head. Her eyes sparkled, big and brown, as she gazed at him. Soon she set aside the empty bottle, draped a small towel over her shoulder, and stood up to walk as though she'd cared for dozens of babies.

"See how calm and content we are today?" she murmured as she approached him, swaying and patting the baby's back. "Much better than when we first met, *jah*? Louisa, say hi to Asa."

"Louisa?"

"*Jah*, and her brother is Leroy," Loretta said as she, too, stood up and began to burp the baby she held. "I can't for the life of me imagine how anyone could drop these babies off like so much dirty laundry—but we're glad Will dropped them with *us*."

"Sounds like a complicated situation all around," Andy remarked as he walked behind Edith to study the baby on her shoulder. "I thought I should take a look at them to be sure they don't need medical attention—what with their mother passing on and all."

"Such a sad story, that she died of cancer," Edith murmured. "I've prayed that God will guide us all to the right answers and the truth—*for the truth will set us free,*" she added softly.

Asa blinked. What had Edith meant by quoting that particular Bible verse and in such a wistful way? Did she suspect Gingerich had toyed with the facts to convince her and her sisters to care for these kids?

Or does she wonder if you're the one who's not being totally honest?

Before Asa thought about what he was doing, he opened his arms, and after a moment—and the rise of her eyebrows—Edith carefully placed the tiny girl in the crook of his arm. His reaction to the baby's warm, solid weight took him completely by surprise. Asa swallowed hard and couldn't stop gazing into Louisa's little face. When the baby began to squawk, Edith put her towel on Asa's shoulder.

"Hold her upright, like—"

It seemed the natural thing to do, and Asa was rewarded with a belch that made everyone on the porch chuckle. Andy had taken Leroy to look him over, his hips swaying in a rhythm that seemed to come naturally.

"Did I hear correctly that these kids are right at six months?" Andy asked.

"*Jah,* born October tenth, Will said," Edith replied as she tweaked Leroy's nose.

"They're both smaller than I'd like," the nurse remarked as he peered into the boy's ears, "but I believe they'll catch up. I'm glad you've switched them to goat milk. Formula's outrageously expensive, and some newborns don't tolerate it well."

"Nazareth's timing was perfect, too," Edith remarked as she watched Asa and Louisa. "I can return the unopened can of powder to the market—and we won't have Dat asking us how much all this is costing him."

"Where is your *dat*?" Andy asked, glancing through the screen door. "Hi, Rosalyn!"

"*Gut* morning, Andy!" she replied as she appeared with a plate of cookies. "Isn't this a fine scene, with the babies fed and happy, and everyone paying attention to them? The goat milk is a blessing—and our supply's right next door. Life is *gut*. God is *gut*."

Was it his imagination, or had Edith and her sisters ignored Andy's question? Asa had a feeling their father didn't approve of the circumstances surrounding these babies, and he probably didn't relish the crying and the diapers and the change in his family's schedule, either.

Edith helped herself to a warm chocolate-chip cookie and then took another one, smiling up at Asa. "Dat went to Kansas City early this morning to buy replacement parts for the clocks he makes and repairs." Smiling demurely, she held a cookie an inch away from Asa's mouth, silently coaxing him to bite into it. "He won't be back until this evening."

Why did her father's absence make Asa feel like a fox come to visit the henhouse? The aromas of warm sugar and chocolate chips were more than he could resist. As he closed his mouth over the cookie, his eyelids lowered and his lips brushed Edith's fingertips. With everyone looking on, he couldn't give in to the urge to lick the melted chocolate off her fingers, but every nerve in his body was vibrating—every inch of his skin warmed as he met her gaze.

Get a grip. Her sisters are watching—and so is Leitner.

Even so, Edith held his gaze for another long moment before turning the cookie so Asa could take the rest of it into his mouth. He couldn't help noticing how her green dress complemented her complexion and her brown eyes, and how crisp and white her *kapp* appeared against her dark, parted hair.

"*Denki*," he murmured, turning to smile at the sister with the cookie plate. "Fabulous cookies, Rosalyn," he remarked. "In my opinion, home-made cookies are the perfect remedy for what-ever ails you. I feel so much better now!"

Everyone on the porch laughed as they ate their own cookies, but Asa had a feeling they were taking mental notes—honing in on the sparks he and Edith had just created as they stood so close together. Rosalyn sniffed the air and then hurried toward the door. "Better get the next pan of cookies out of the oven! Nothing smells worse than something that's been burnt."

Loretta let out a short laugh. "Well, there's the dis-*stink*-tive aroma of dirty diapers," she countered. "I need to soak several of those before the fumes get too noticeable."

"*Jah*, Dat's not crazy about that part of having babies around," Edith said as the door closed behind her sister. She looked up at Asa again. "Even though I truly love caring for the twins, I hope you and Will figure out who fathered them—but you've got to take care of your own injuries, of course."

For a moment, Asa couldn't remember what those injuries were. "I promised you I'd do that, and it's my top priority when I get home," he murmured. "You seem very comfortable with the twins. They couldn't possibly have a better mother."

"What a lovely thing to say," Edith murmured.

"I agree," Andy said as he handed Leroy to Edith so he could look at Louisa. "But it's the right thing to do, finding out who these wee ones belong to. Or do you think Will Gingerich will eventually raise them as his own?"

Asa bit back a retort, not wanting to sound judgmental. A pickup truck with a magnetic real estate sign on its door was pulling to a stop across the road, so he feigned interest in it as he listened closely to Edith's reply.

"I don't know," she said after a moment's hesitation. "We all loved Will while we were growing up with him, and it seemed the natural order of things for him and Loretta to get engaged—until Dat called off their relationship without much explanation. I suspect Will married Molly too soon after that, and now the big issues of love, marriage, and raising babies have him befuddled."

Asa felt her assessment of Gingerich's situation was more than generous, but he kept his remarks to himself. "That fellow's posting a big For Sale sign," he remarked as the sound of hammering filled the air.

"That place belongs to an English family, and I've heard the parents can't stay in their home any longer." Andy held out Louisa so Asa would take her again. "I've got appointments at the clinic, so I should be going. I recommend you keep the twins on goat milk. Let me know if there's anything I can do."

"*Denki* so much, Andy. Have a *gut* rest of your day!"

How had he and Edith ended up alone on the porch with the twins? Asa had noticed no indication that Andy expected him to return to town with him, so he took this opportunity to get better acquainted with the young woman who'd so effortlessly captured his fancy. It was way too soon to start making romantic assumptions, however. For all he knew, Edith had a steady boyfriend. . . .

He can't be much of a boyfriend if she's gazing at you with such a sparkle in her eyes.

"Our wee ones are nodding off," Edith said softly. "If we put them in their baskets, they'll nap, most likely. Then you and I can visit."

It was the invitation Asa had been waiting for. He watched Edith place Leroy in the basket with a design of deep blue and tan before gently stroking the boy's cheek until his little eyes closed. When she held out her hands to take Louisa, Asa had a sudden flash of a future with this young woman, where all of these pieces fit so neatly into place—her, the babies, a home across the road. . . .

"Those are nice baskets," he remarked, mostly so he wouldn't say something incredibly adolescent or stupid. "A huge improvement over the bushel baskets the babies came in."

"I was glad I had them around," she said as she settled Louisa into the basket with pink and yellow ribbons woven into its upper rim. "I originally made them as market baskets to sell at an auction—"

"You *made* these?" Asa leaned down to study the basket Leroy was snoozing in. "You should consign some to Nora's shop. They'd fly off the shelves, no doubt about it."

Edith's smile made his heart dance. "She's

invited all of us girls to put our crafts in her store—and Dat is already displaying his clocks there. But it seems another project will be taking up my time for a while," she added with a nod toward the twins.

"True enough. But you might not have the babies for long, once we figure out who their father is."

When Edith's face fell, Asa kicked himself for saying that. After watching her care for the twins, he could tell she was totally engrossed in them, as though Leroy and Louisa were her own. She sat down in the swing, patting the cushion as she gazed at the sleeping babies' faces.

"I keep telling myself—just as Dat reminds me—not to get too attached to them," she murmured. "But how can I *not* love them? They've been born into a situation that's not their fault. I believe Will has *gut* intentions, but I can't see him taking these kids back until he's got a wife. And I couldn't blame him for steering clear of marriage altogether, after what he's been through with Molly."

"Maybe she was out of her head with cancer pain, knowing she was about to die," Asa said softly. He sat down on the swing, making the chains creak as he slowly began to rock forward and back. "I have no idea why my name was the last thing she said. Honest. Never met the poor woman."

"I believe you, Asa."

Edith's face appeared so serene, her expression so intense as she gazed at him, that words left him. *You can't lead her on—can't know what will come of further talk with Gingerich, or who else might step forward to admit he fathered these kids.* To relieve the emotion the deep yearning in her eyes aroused in him, Asa focused on what was happening across the road. The truck was pulling away. The wooden sign had lettering large enough that he could read part of it from the Riehls' porch.

"Most For Sale signs simply stick into the ground with metal prongs, so you have to wonder, as substantial as that sign is, if those folks think their farm might be on the market for a while," Asa speculated. "Maybe that's because Willow Ridge is such a small town, a distance from any highways. Might be interesting to know what they're asking for it."

Edith shrugged. "We've not met the owners. All you see is the occasional car going in and out—almost like nobody's living there."

Once again a fantasy flashed through Asa's mind, as though his future was suddenly taking shape—as though God had led him to this place in this moment to give him an unmistakable *sign*. "You know, after talking with Luke and Andy and Nora," Asa mused aloud, "I can see that my furniture refinishing business would be a lot more prosperous in Willow Ridge than it is in Clifford.

My building doesn't even have a display window—and most days we have so few folks come in, I don't think the lack of a window matters."

"Ah. So that's what you do."

"*Jah*, my brother and I work together. I do the refinishing work, and the repairing of the wood, and Drew does upholstery and some caning." Asa pointed to the flat area at the roadside, where the wooden sign now stood. "If we put up a basic metal building with some big windows right there, we'd be close enough to the café and the quilt shop—and the rest of the stores—to attract a lot of walk-in customers. Lots of folks are interested in old pieces that have been restored, rather than buying new furniture that's not made as well. We sell every old dining room table and antique bedroom set we can get our hands on."

"Oh, Asa," Edith said with a sigh. "It would be the most wonderful-*gut* thing if you moved across the road from us. Really it would."

Red warning flags flapped in the back of his mind, and he didn't dare look at her. He'd been thinking the same thing—but Edith's dreamy tone of voice had returned him to reality. "It's not like a snap of my fingers will make that happen," he pointed out. "Purchasing a farm and then moving the furniture business—and getting my brother to go along with such major changes—would be a project every bit as big as the one you've taken on."

"Where there's a will, there's a way."

"What would I do with all that land, though? I'm no farmer," Asa went on with a shake of his head. "And what with the Brennemans having their cabinetry shop on this same road, I might upset the apple cart for their business, too."

"God's will be done," Edith murmured in a voice he could barely hear.

Asa sighed loudly. He'd hurt her feelings. It wasn't what he'd intended, but maybe it was best that he'd burst her rose-colored bubble before she'd made too many wishes he couldn't fulfill. He hadn't come to Willow Ridge looking for a wife—or kids—after all. Taking on a family was a major responsibility he didn't feel ready for, because at twenty-seven he didn't have a business prosperous enough that he could build a home for them. He couldn't ask Edith to live in a sparse apartment above a store, the way he and his brother were doing.

Asa raked his fingers through his hair. As a black van came down the road, creating a dust cloud in its wake, he stood up. "I feel a headache coming on—and Andy's told me I need plenty of rest if I'm to be healthy enough to leave by Monday," he added. "It's been *gut* talking to you, Edith. You're a sweet girl. Better than I deserve."

Before she could respond, Asa took the porch steps two at a time and cut across the back of the Riehls' lot to return to town. The black van turning in at the end of the lane had been parked behind the Simple Gifts shop, so he had a pretty good idea who was driving it. He was suddenly in no mood for Nora Hooley's freckle-faced, forth-right honesty.

CHAPTER SIX

Nora got out of the van and approached the Riehls' porch in time to see Asa's retreat—and Edith's trembling lower lip. She sensed the two situations were connected, so she chose her words carefully. "I sure hope Asa's not running from *me,*" she began as she ascended the wooden steps.

"Said he had a headache."

"Uh-oh. Andy's warned him to pay close attention to possible signs that his concussion's not healing the way it should."

Edith let out a tremulous sigh. "I got the impression it was me he was escaping rather than you. I'll get over it."

Slinging her arm around the young woman's shoulders, Nora decided not to delve into whatever might have gone on before she arrived. She was curious about how Asa and Edith had gotten time alone together on the porch . . . which surely meant Cornelius was working downstairs, unaware of the young man's presence. Cornelius impressed her as a very protective father, with conservative ideas about his daughters spending time with men—especially men nobody knew much about.

"Nora, hello!" someone said from inside the house.

"It's *gut* to see you," the other sister chimed in, and within moments Loretta and Rosalyn were coming out the screen door—then covering their mouths in a hurry.

"Sorry!" Loretta whispered as she looked at the babies. "Didn't realize they were asleep."

"The goat milk Nazareth's brought over has really settled their tummies," Rosalyn remarked with a smile. "It's like the poor little things are finally able to relax and nap."

"They've been through a lot," Nora pointed out. She smiled at the twins, who were sleeping so sweetly in their baskets. "We tend to assume babies don't understand what's going on around them, but they pick up on more than we know. And meanwhile," she continued in an excited murmur, "I've brought over the supplies Lydia Zook's collected for you. I almost couldn't pack it all into my van!"

Edith brightened immediately. "Let's take a look! If we have everything put away before Dat gets home, he can't fuss about us shuffling things around while he's working."

"*Gut* idea," Loretta agreed as the four of them strode toward Nora's van. "If he doesn't see how much stuff folks have donated, he won't preach at us about how we don't need diapers, clothes, and other supplies because the twins won't be staying all that long."

"*Jah*, until Bishop Tom and Vernon Gingerich

backed him into a corner, praising him for taking on these babies," Rosalyn explained as she walked beside Nora, "Dat was going to take them straight back to Will today—except Dat went to Kansas City for clock parts instead."

As Nora pieced together the picture of Cornelius Riehl his daughters were painting, she wasn't surprised; he sounded like most of the Old Order men she'd known while she was growing up. Stern. Autocratic. Domineering. Their father's absence had also provided a chance for Asa to visit with Edith—and probably stay longer than he would have, had the head of the Riehl family been monitoring their conversation and assessing the stranger in their midst.

Rather than dwelling upon Cornelius or Asa, however, Nora smiled as she opened the door on the side of her van. "I think you'll be all set now. You've got stacks of diapers and little clothes, along with bassinets—"

"And look at these bibs!" Loretta said as she grabbed the nearest box.

"We'll be using this baby wash and shampo later today," Rosalyn remarked as she tugged on another box. "And I see ointment and wipes and—"

"Oh . . . *oh,*" Edith murmured as she gazed into the packed van. "A playpen, and a plastic bin full of little toys! This is better than Christmas!"

Touched by Edith's wistful tone of voice,

Nora stopped unloading her van to hug the pretty young woman. "Everybody says you can keep these things as long as you need them," she said gently. "You've been an inspiration to us all, Edith. A reminder of how Jesus told us to love one another and care for those who can't look after them-selves—without question or hesitation."

"*Jah*, when we've fed or clothed the least amongst us, we've done the same for Jesus," Rosalyn said as she started for the house with a box. "You want these things in your room, Edith?"

Edith smiled and followed her elder sister. "You and Loretta are already crowded in your room, so *jah*," she said. "We can shift my bed over to the corner and set up the bassinets first thing. Then we can figure out where to put the playpen so it won't be in the way."

Nora set a couple of other boxes on the ground. She got a good hold on one end of a white wooden bassinet while Loretta grasped the other end. "Edith is so attached to these babies already," Nora murmured. "She's going to be awfully upset if their father steps in to claim them, or if your *dat* insists on taking them back to that guy who dropped them off."

Loretta nodded, lowering her voice. "She has such a soft spot for babies, Edith does. Might be on account of how a burst appendix infected most of her female parts when she was only fourteen," Loretta recounted as they walked. "We almost lost her—had no idea how much pain she was hiding or what was causing it until she passed out and Mamm insisted on getting her to the emergency room."

"Oh, my," Nora said, grimacing in sympathy for what young Edith must've gone through. "Does that mean she can't have children?"

"That's what the surgeon told us."

"What a shame. Edith takes to mothering like a hen to her chicks." As Loretta held the door open, Nora rolled the bassinet into the front room, glancing around. "What a pretty home you have. I was never here when it belonged to Reuben and his wife, but I'm guessing you girls freshened it up."

Loretta laughed. "We spread lots of paint—and elbow grease—but otherwise it's the same furniture we had in Roseville. Dat's not much of one for changing anything that Mamm made or picked out."

Nora nodded, thinking this detail fit with everything else she knew about Cornelius. When she and Loretta went up the stairs with the bassinet, Nora saw that everything on this level was very clean and neat, as well, without any extra embellishment or "doodads." When they entered Edith's room at the end of the hall, however, Nora's eyes widened.

"Which one of you made this rag rug?" she

101

asked, noting how the puffy rows of colors were arranged to form an oval rainbow.

"That would be Loretta," Edith replied with a grin. "This was my nineteenth birthday present, just before we found out we'd be moving here. It's probably the newest piece of handiwork we have."

"My customers would go crazy for rugs like this! Matter of fact, now that Millie's married and has a household to manage, I could use some help at the store, Loretta," Nora said in a burst of inspiration. "You could even bring your materials and work on rugs when we had slow spells. People would *love* to watch you!"

Loretta's cheeks turned pink as she waved off Nora's praise. "That's a toothbrush rug—because I use an old toothbrush with a hole in it, filed to a point, as my needle. Anybody could make one—"

"And you could teach them!" Nora blurted. She knelt to run her fingers over the rows of colorful, puffy stitches, certain that many of her regular customers would flock into Simple Gifts to take a class or two. English ladies were fascinated by Amish women and their crafts, and Loretta had the perfect personality for guiding them through the rug-making process. "What if we put a couple of your rugs on display with a sign-up sheet? We can have Rebecca Oliveri print some posters about classes with you as the teacher, and also advertise them on our Web site,"

Nora went on in a rush. "You'd make some nice money doing something you really enjoy, and you'd be the hit of Willow Ridge!"

Rosalyn playfully elbowed Loretta. "Working in Nora's store would be great fun. You've said so more than once."

Loretta was blushing, her expression vacillating between wistfulness and indecision. "But who would tend the chickens? And gather the eggs every day, and—and help Edith with the twins?"

"We've got the chickens and eggs taken care of before most folks are even out of bed," Edith reminded her. "Rosalyn and I will be fine here at home—"

"You could set your own times to work in the store or to teach your classes," Nora insisted. "Believe me, ladies who like crafting classes are happy to arrange their schedules for a chance to work with someone like you."

Loretta smoothed the bassinet's mattress, shaking her head even as she fought a grin. "It sounds like a lot of fun when you talk about it, Nora, but we all know how Dat would feel about any of us girls working in places where we'd be amongst English."

Nora sighed. She'd anticipated this argument, because she'd heard it while growing up as an Old Order preacher's daughter. "True enough, but you'd be teaching other *women*. I'd be really surprised if any men signed on for this class—and so what if they do? I'll be there the whole time. It'll mostly be one big hen party."

"I'll have to think on it." Loretta gazed at Nora as the two of them headed for the stairs. "I really appreciate your asking me. But I've never worked anywhere, and—well, it would be something we'd have to plan for. Before you make a rug, you have to tear enough long strips of fabric and notch the ends, and that takes some doing. And some time."

Nora sensed she'd gotten her final answer from Loretta—for today, anyway. "You're right; we'll need to plan this out. But I do hope you'll think about working for me, or offering those classes, or whatever you can manage. I'll try to be patient!"

Loretta chuckled. "Patience is a virtue," she quipped. "And sometimes it's one of mine."

They went downstairs and checked on the babies, who were still sleeping soundly in their baskets on the porch. After they all made a couple more trips upstairs with the supplies, Nora enjoyed one of Rosalyn's chocolate-chip cookies and drove back to her store, which she'd closed for her visit to the Riehl place. The sisters had given her plenty of food for thought, and as she entered Simple Gifts through the back door, she realized someone was talking—

Rounding the corner of a display, Nora stopped herself before she loudly demanded who was in her store. Asa was talking on the phone—and she'd given him permission to use it—so she slipped quietly to the front door to remove her note about being gone for a while.

"Think about this," Asa was saying earnestly. "There's property for sale here in Willow Ridge, where our shop would do a whole lot more business than it does in Clifford. Everybody who runs a store here is doing really well—so seriously, let's talk about this when I get back on Monday."

Nora stood still, looking out the door as she considered what Asa was saying. She'd heard Luke and Ira discussing the place across the road from the Riehls, as they were always on the lookout for cropland where their wheat, corn, and specialty grains could be grown.

"It doesn't hurt that there are a lot of unattached women here, either—three of them right across the road from this farm," Asa continued with a chuckle. "That alone would make it worth our while to get out of Clifford. Think about it. See ya."

Doesn't sound like he's got much of a headache. Nora recalled Edith's trembling lower lip, and her idea that Asa had been running away from her—yet now his jovial tone suggested he had plans for more than the land that was for sale.

Nora turned, crossing her arms as he hung up the phone. "Asa, maybe I've got this all wrong," she said tersely, "but if you're playing Edith false, taking advantage of her trusting nature, stop it right now. If you break her heart, I'll see that your business never gets off the ground in Willow Ridge."

Asa's jaw tightened. He stared at her. "What makes you think—"

"I've been around the block a time or two, with men who took what they wanted and then left me to fend for myself," she stated. "So don't start with me, and don't lie to Edith. Maybe you'd better go take something for that *headache,* you think?"

Asa's eyes narrowed, but he had sense enough not to snap back at her. "Yes, ma'am," he muttered under his breath. "I believe I will."

As Edith gently placed Leroy and Louisa in the shaded playpen Saturday morning, she sighed happily. It was a perfect day for planting more of the garden, so she and her sisters had put on their faded work dresses and kerchiefs. "You kids can play with your new toys, and we'll be right here where you can watch us," she said as she put a couple of cloth dolls and balls in with them.

The twins gazed up at her with their dark eyes. After Louisa pushed herself up into a sitting position, so did Leroy. "Bah-bah-bah!" the little girl chattered.

"Bah, bah, black sheep, have you any wool?"

Edith said in a singsong voice, delighted when the twins smiled at her.

"Our lettuce, peas, and onions are off to a *gut* start," Rosalyn remarked as she stuck a stake into the moist, turned earth. From there, she took a second stake and unwound its long string as she walked the length of the garden, making a guideline for planting a straight row. "What say we put the beets and carrots alongside them, and then the potatoes can go at this end?"

Loretta nodded, toting her bin of seed potatoes and a hoe to where Rosalyn had pointed. "The soil's nice and loose there. I've got this job covered!"

With a final smile at the babies, Edith grabbed a hoe and made a shallow trench in the soil. As Edith followed the string, careful not to trample the row of bright yellow-green lettuce beside her, Rosalyn leaned over at the row's beginning to drop beet seeds into the trench. The three of them had worked together in the garden since they were little girls helping their *mamm*, so the planting went quickly. "One row or two for beets?" Edith called out.

"We had way too many beets last year," Loretta said. Beets had never been her favorite vegetable.

"I'd rather have more carrots and turnips," Rosalyn agreed. "This house has a big root cellar, so we won't have to put everything into jars so fast—and beets make such a mess!"

"I'm all for less mess," Edith remarked. "If the babies stay, we'll have a busy summer before we even deal with picking and canning. Do you suppose Dat would agree to getting another deep freeze? Freezing is a lot less effort than canning."

"We can ask him later in the season. Catch him in a *gut* mood and—oh, is that who I think it is, over across the road?" Loretta asked with a rise in her voice.

When Edith reached the end of the row, she turned. She swallowed, hoping her face wasn't turning pink. There was no mistaking Asa's black hair and height as he stood beside Luke Hooley, replacing his straw hat. The two men were gesturing and talking as they looked toward the house that was for sale. A third fellow, English by the looks of him, was nodding as he stood beside them.

You're a sweet girl. Better than I deserve.

How many times had Asa's parting words taunted her since yesterday? And what did they mean? Edith had decided not to mention this to her sisters, who were older and more experienced with men—but they were looking at her, expecting an explanation for Asa's presence. "Asa was sort of interested in how much that place was selling for."

"*Sort* of interested?" Loretta teased.

"As in, he might want to live there?" Rosalyn chimed in. "Now isn't *that* interesting? What did you two talk about yesterday, anyway?"

Edith sighed and started toward the other end of the garden with her hoe. "I'm the wrong one to ask. He was all excited about moving his furniture business here—at least until I said how nice it would be if he lived across the road," she said glumly. "Then he started making excuses. Said he had a headache and took off across the backyard as though I'd caused it."

"A lover's quarrel—or he got cold feet," Loretta remarked.

"It'll blow over," Rosalyn predicted sympathetically. "Asa seems like a really nice guy. And he's *gut* with the twins."

Maybe that won't matter. Maybe the babies won't be staying, and maybe Asa won't be moving here. Edith stuck the corner of her hoe firmly into the soil and dragged it parallel to her previous row, about a foot away. She focused on her work, figuring her sisters were whispering about her as they leaned over the top of the playpen to pay attention to the twins for a moment.

Edith did not figure on hearing her father's voice, however, calling out to the men across the road. "Luke Hooley, is that you?" he said as he strode down their lane. "Got a question about the eggs we're selling at your mill store."

As she and her sisters glanced at Dat and then at each other, they shrugged. Edith hadn't heard Dat expressing any interest in the chickens his cousin Reuben had left behind when he'd traded homes with them—but Dat had been doing some bookkeeping at the kitchen table after breakfast, so perhaps something about the receipts had caught his attention. Loretta went back to planting potatoes while Rosalyn and Edith covered the beet seeds and planted carrots in the next two rows. Their backs were to the road, so Edith jumped when Loretta let out a yelp.

"Asa!" her sister exclaimed. "And what brings you here on this fine spring morning?"

Edith really wished her backside weren't pointing at the sky while she continued along a row with her carrot seeds. Keeping her head down made it easier to follow Asa's conversation without gawking at him, however.

"Luke and I met the real estate fellow and looked at the place across the road," he replied. "Checked out the house and the outbuildings. Luke's looking for more plots to raise his grains, because it'll soon be time to get them planted. He has to find somebody who'll farm for him first, however."

Edith glanced behind her. Dat was still chatting with Luke out by the road—and Asa was walking toward the playpen, but he was looking at *her*. Edith quickly righted herself and felt the blood rushing in her head. She waved self-consciously. Asa tipped his hat before lifting Louisa into his arms.

Feeling compelled to visit with him—*like a*

moth to the flame, she thought—Edith walked into the shade with her hoe. "So what did you think of the house and the property?" she asked, thinking that would be a safe subject.

Asa waggled his eyebrows at the baby, getting a laugh in return. "It's a decent size, overall—but of course I'd have to have the wiring taken out or cover the outlets," he added. He lowered Louisa back into the playpen and picked up her brother. "But I have a lot of hurdles to clear before I cross that bridge—such as convincing my brother that coming to Willow Ridge would be a *gut* move. He's not one for making big changes. And how about you, little man?" Asa asked the boy he'd cradled in his bent elbow. He wrinkled his nose. "Something tells me a change would do you *gut.*"

"I'm headed inside anyway," Rosalyn said as she leaned her hoe against a tree. "I'll take Leroy and then come back to check Louisa."

"I'll get her," Loretta insisted as she, too, set aside her hoe and fetched a baby. "We can't have these wee ones making a bad impression on company, after all."

Edith realized immediately that, once again, her sisters were leaving her and Asa alone together. What could she do except carry on a conversation, trying not to act as though he'd hurt her feelings?

"Would this be a *gut* time to fetch my clothes?"

he asked. "I owe Ben Hooley some money for my horse—"

"They're folded and waiting in the pantry," she replied, wiping her dirt-smudged hands on her old skirt. "I'll go get them."

"If I take them across the back lot, maybe your father won't get after you for washing them," Asa suggested as he followed her toward the rear of the house. "He was quizzing Luke about the price you girls are getting for your eggs, insisting that it costs more to feed the chickens than the Hooleys are paying you."

"Oh, my. Dat watches his dollars pretty closely." Edith's cheeks tingled with embarrassment. "I hope he didn't ask you anything too personal about—"

Asa let out a short laugh. "He shook my hand and turned right to Luke, as though he didn't really see me. Once your *dat* realizes I'm the guy Will blames for fathering the twins, though, he'll have plenty of questions."

"*Jah*, there's that," Edith murmured as she swung open the door to the mudroom. She stepped into the pantry and grabbed the brown grocery sack she'd stashed in the darkest corner. "Turns out we didn't need any baby formula or supplies, so I put your money back in your pants pocket. *Denki* for offering to pay for it."

"You're a peach for doing my laundry." Asa blocked the pantry doorway, casting his tall shadow over her as he smiled. "I'm sorry I left in such a hurry yesterday, Edith. I was hoping to catch my brother in the shop when I called him. But he didn't answer."

"Folks are never waiting by the phone when you want them to be." Edith's cheeks prickled with heat. She hoped Asa would call her after he'd returned to Clifford, even as she realized that if Dat got to the phone shanty before she did, he would assume something was going on between the two of them.

"Before I go home, though, I'm stopping through Roseville to visit with Will," Asa said. "I'm a man of my word, Edith. I hope you'll believe that about me—and trust me to uphold my end of that promise, the way I know you'll care for the twins. Better go."

"*Jah*, bye," she whispered.

Asa's smile looked alluring and mysterious in the unlit pantry, and his bruises and cut forehead were not noticeable in the dim light. He winked at her before he left.

Edith remained in the pantry after she heard the screen door close. She wanted to believe what Asa had said about upholding his end of the vow about the twins . . . even though it might mean those two precious babies would be taken away from her. Once again Edith reminded herself that it wasn't her place to cling to the twins for her own gratification. She was to watch for a sign from God and live the way He was directing her.

The front door banged, and her father settled himself in his chair at the kitchen table. Edith knew better than to dawdle until her sisters came looking for her, so she stepped out into the kitchen and very quietly shut the pantry door.

Dat turned immediately. "I got you girls another fifty cents a dozen for your eggs," he announced smugly. "Told Hooley it was highway robbery, considering how costly his organic chicken feed is—and how hard you girls work at keeping an eye on the birds as they roam around the pasture, and cleaning out their house."

Edith kept a straight face, but inside she wilted. Luke couldn't have been pleased about Dat's challenging his pay rate.

"Hooley impresses me as a *gut* sort, mostly— even though he carried on about that Asa fellow more than I cared to listen to," her father went on. "He says Detweiler's financially solvent enough to consider buying that land across the road, and that he's thinking to pay Asa a nice rental fee for the use of the cropland. Luke also told me how Asa was going to hold Will Gingerich accountable and get to the bottom of this baby dilemma—but I'll believe that when I see it."

Dat studied her, twisting his pencil between his thumb and forefinger. "Cat got your tongue, missy?"

Edith shook her head. "No, I—I'm just listening

to you, Dat, before I go out and plant more garden with Loretta and Rosalyn."

His lips twitched. "I know what you're thinking, Daughter. Asa Detweiler's caught your fancy. He talks a *gut* line—or at least he convinced Luke to partner with him—but you can't help noticing how those twins look just like him. Maybe Will's dead wife was the only one telling the truth."

Edith swallowed hard. She couldn't think of a word to say as she mentally reviewed the babies' faces for signs that Asa had fathered them.

"I predict that if Detweiler actually confronts Will Gingerich, nothing will come of it," Dat went on in a lower voice. "And once he leaves Willow Ridge on Monday, I believe we'll have seen the last of him. Plan accordingly."

Edith did her best not to blink or to let her eyes tear up as she held Dat's gaze.

"It's not my intention to be cruel, understand," her father went on. "I just don't trust Asa—or Will—any farther than I could throw them."

After an intense moment of silence, Dat focused on his ledger again. Edith slipped out the back door, clenching her teeth against a whimper until she was out of his earshot. Her sisters were bent low in the garden, so she took a moment to look past the chicken house to the grassy pasture where the chickens pecked contentedly. When she felt she had her emotions under control again, she went over to the playpen. Leroy clapped his hands and grinned up at her, so Edith picked him up.

Yes, his wispy hair was turning dark—but it was brown rather than black. He was slender, like Asa—but Andy had declared the babies underweight because their mother probably hadn't been able to feed them. It was anyone's guess what Molly Gingerich had looked like, and Edith wasn't about to press Will for details of his deceased wife's appearance. These babies' faces and eyes were still changing—every day, it seemed—so declaring their resemblance to anyone seemed a fool's game.

It's not my intention to be cruel—

"Edith, what's the matter?" Loretta asked as she approached the playpen. "You're looking at Leroy as though he's done something horribly wrong, even though he's just an innocent little baby."

Willing the frown from her face, Edith sighed. "Of course he's innocent, a sweet lamb of God," she murmured. She cleared her throat. "Dat just told me he insisted on Luke's paying us another fifty cents a dozen for our eggs."

Loretta sucked in her breath. "How's Luke to make any profit if he pays us so much more?"

"Is it just me, or has Dat been pinching the pennies harder since we moved here?" Rosalyn wondered aloud as she came to join their conversation. "I thought his clock business was picking up—his workbench is piled with repairs—"

"And he's shipped a lot of new clocks lately,"

116

Loretta put in. "Just Tuesday, the UPS man took five or six of them."

"Folks here have been stopping by to look at his clocks, too," Rosalyn said. "Ira Hooley bought one for his new house, and the Witmers have hung one in the Grill N Skillet with a sign about Dat's business."

When Louisa flapped her arms and let out a little squawk, Loretta leaned down to pluck her from the playpen. "All this talk about clocks and penny-pinching is boring, *jah*?" she murmured as she nuzzled the little girl's cheek.

Edith shifted Leroy to her other arm, thinking she already noticed some weight gain since they'd switched to goat milk. "Maybe you should think about working at Simple Gifts after all, Loretta. Nora wouldn't have carried on about how popular your rugs will be if she didn't believe her customers would buy them, or come to rug-making classes."

"And even if you didn't teach classes, I'm thinking Nora would pay you a decent hourly wage," Rosalyn said. Her forehead puckered as she thought for a moment. "Do you suppose Dat's reacting to the twins' being here? Thinking we'll be out a lot of money, the longer we keep them?"

Edith shrugged. "He knows Nazareth is donating their milk—which she *could* be making into cheese to sell at Luke's store," she pointed out.

"Maybe we should show him all the baby stuff

Nora brought over," Loretta said. "And maybe he just found a mistake in our receipts and it's got him going. He's been a lot more distracted by little things like that since Mamm passed."

"*Jah*, but it's been nearly five years. And he's got us to look after the meals and the laundry and the household chores for him. It's not like he has to fend for himself any more than he did when she was here." Edith steeled herself against tears, knowing they could be contagious. "I still really miss her."

"*Jah*, nothing'll ever be the same," Loretta murmured with a hitch in her voice.

Rosalyn glanced toward the house, squaring her shoulders. "Well, we can't let ourselves get down about it, the way Dat does. Mamm would be disappointed if we went around drooping like rag dolls that've lost their stuffing. Let's brew a pitcher of iced tea and make dinner. We'll feel better after we eat—and so will Dat."

"And maybe we'll figure out what to do about all these concerns," Loretta said as she started for the house with Louisa.

"The best thing would be to turn them over to Jesus," Edith reminded her sisters. She bussed Leroy's downy cheek, feeling better immediately. "But I suppose we'll have to gnaw on them a bit more before we turn loose of them. It seems to be our way."

Before they reached the back door, Leroy

clapped his hands against Edith's cheeks. "Ma-ma-ma-ma *ma!*" he crowed.

Edith's heart stilled. Was he calling her Mama? Or was that wishful thinking and baby babble?

"Woo! Hoo!" Louisa called out as she bounced in Loretta's arms.

"That's the spirit! The twins have it right," Rosalyn said as she smiled at the four of them. "How about if we go for more *woo-hoo* this afternoon, instead of boohoo?"

"I'm all for that," Edith agreed. The twins' bright-eyed smiles were every bit as contagious as her tears would've been, and for that she was grateful.

Chapter Seven

Monday morning, Asa steered Midnight into the lane of the farmstead to which the fellow at the Roseville feedstore had directed him. He sensed a great heaviness about the place—a feeling that everyday life had ground to a halt. Weeds clogged the barnyard fencerow, and the stable door gaped open. The two horses in the pasture trotted up to watch him approach as though hoping for some attention—or were they gawking at Midnight because he stood nineteen hands high and exuded so much more vitality than they did?

Asa frowned. He couldn't see any water in the trough, and the hay feeder was empty. Had Gingerich left the farm and abandoned his horses?

He hitched Midnight to the post nearest the house. It was a modest dwelling even by Amish standards, and the white paint was beginning to peel. On this sunny April day, all the windows were shut tight, and the curtains were drawn. Asa stepped up onto the small porch, opened the screen door—which made the bottom section of screen flap loosely—and knocked loudly on the wooden door. He'd planned his no-nonsense speech all the way from Willow Ridge, his vow to Edith Riehl uppermost in his mind.

Asa placed his ear to the door. Nothing. He knocked again, louder this time. "Will Gingerich?" he called out.

"Go away."

Asa scowled. Will's voice sounded lackluster and weak, but Asa couldn't let that stop him from getting the information he needed about who might have fathered Leroy and Louisa. A father was every child's birthright—and as devoted as Edith was to those babies, she deserved the truth about their *dat* even though she might have to give them up.

"It's Asa Detweiler. Are you going to let me in?" he demanded. Silence stretched long enough that Asa tried the knob.

"I've got nothing to say. Leave me alone."

By then Asa had opened the door enough to see that the front room was dim and unlit. Gingerich sat in the center of the sofa, his elbows on his knees and his head hung low. The place smelled of sickness—stuffy—so Asa left the door open to circulate some fresh air. He almost launched into his prepared speech, but when Will raised his head, Asa held his tongue.

"What do *you* want?" the disheveled younger man asked in a raspy voice. "Can't you see that I'm miserable? I can't stop wondering why my wife had to die—and why she betrayed me. Haven't you done enough damage without coming here to rub my nose in it?"

Asa opened his mouth and then closed it. Will looked horrible—obviously he hadn't bathed or shaved since his trip to Willow Ridge. Dishes were scattered around the front room with half-eaten food on them. Although Asa wasn't the man Gingerich should be angry with, Asa suddenly realized that Will was going by the only information he had—not to mention mourning the loss of a wife whose cancer had eaten her away before she'd wounded him so badly with her deathbed declaration. He saw no sign that Molly's family had brought food or come over to help, either, which ran contrary to their Plain faith.

Will was in a very bad place, emotionally. The last thing he needed to hear was Asa's demand for more information plus an apology for muddying his reputation. As Asa sat down in a worn platform rocker near the sofa, he searched for a way to begin a more positive conversation. The cushion wheezed, and dust flew around him, yet another sign of how long and how deeply the Gingerich household had been immersed in sadness.

Thinking of two perky little faces, Asa smiled. "Leroy and Louisa are doing well with the Riehl girls," he said. "What with the neighbor ladies bringing over beds and baby stuff, and the next-door neighbor donating fresh goat milk, it's like the whole town of Willow Ridge has adopted them. You took them to the right place."

Will looked at him morosely. "You can see why I had to take them *someplace*."

"*Jah*, I can." Asa was determined not to get sucked into Will's downhearted mood, yet everything about this place made him wonder if Gingerich would ever rise above his depression. "I'm sorry you lost your wife. Sorry you learned things about her you didn't want to know."

Will speared his long fingers through his sandy brown hair until it resembled a haystack hit by a storm. "None of this would've happened if Cornelius Riehl hadn't split us up," he murmured with a deep sigh. "Loretta was the girl I truly loved."

Asa didn't really want to hear the history of Will's love life. *But if he talks about his involvement with the Riehls, he might reveal some useful information.* "Loretta seems very nice," Asa hinted. "All three of the sisters impress me as caring and compassionate."

"They are." Will sat taller, as though rousing himself. "It's the old man who's a piece of work. Understatement of the century to call him a control freak. And no man on the face of this earth is *gut* enough for any of his daughters—just in case you're interested."

"I gathered that, *jah*. Met Cornelius on Saturday, when he cornered the owner of the mill store and insisted on jacking up the pay his daughters were getting for their eggs."

Will let out a humorless laugh. "He's all about the money, for sure—which was why he broke off my engagement to Loretta, after he heard my two older brothers were taking over the family farm and I would have to find a place of my own."

"Not what any fellow wants to find out when he's ready to start a family," Asa agreed. "Same sort of thing happened to my brother and me, but we'd been expecting it all along—and neither of us was engaged."

Will nodded. "In some ways, I was just as glad I wouldn't have to deal with Cornelius as his son-in-law," he said in a faraway voice. "Besides being the absolute ruler of the roost, he's got something else going on. . . . Couldn't ever put my finger on it, but he's built a wall around himself, a barrier that keeps folks from knowing much about him. It's gotten a lot more noticeable since his wife died."

Asa had other topics he wanted to touch upon, so he filed these remarks about Riehl away for later.

"But then, who am I to talk?" Gingerich continued with a shake of his head. "I know firsthand about losing a wife now—after months of my constant care did nothing to slow down her cancer. And that's not the end of it. If it weren't for bad luck I'd have no luck at all."

Asa sensed Will was inviting him to join his pity

party, yet he couldn't help saying, "Yeah? How's that?"

Will's lips twitched. "Molly's *dat* informed me at the funeral that I'm to be off this farm come the end of the month. He seemed glad enough for me to be managing it when I married Molly, but now that this paternity question about the twins has come up, he wants me gone. So now I'm a husband without a wife, and a farmer without a farm."

Asa wondered why Molly's family had evicted Will for a situation he seemingly had no control over—or perhaps her *dat* could already see that the place would only go further downhill, given Will's lack of energy. "So what'll you do?"

"I don't have the foggiest notion. Every time I try to think about it, I backslide into this cesspool of a mood, and I can't seem to climb out." Will's eyes widened, and he leaned closer. "What happened to *you,* man?"

Asa blinked, and then recalled the greenish-purple bruise on one side of his face. "I got run off the road and thrown from my horse when I started home from Willow Ridge last Thursday. Had to stay there a few days to be sure my head wasn't messed up."

"Huh." Gingerich considered this for a moment. "You sure it wasn't Cornelius running you out of town for making eyes at Edith? Even if you didn't, he'd make sure you weren't getting any romantic ideas about her."

Too late. I've got more than ideas. Asa kept a straight face as he thought about Will's accusation. It didn't seem very considerate to mention that he intended to buy the farm across the road from the Riehls when Will was losing this place—not that Asa wanted to share his hopes and dreams concerning Edith, either. "I'm pretty sure Cornelius was across town at a wedding by then. He's the deacon for that district."

"Figures," Will said with another abrupt laugh. "He was the deacon in Roseville, too. I was surprised when he left town—guess he traded farms with his cousin, so Reuben could keep a closer eye on his mother. But it seemed awfully sudden, like Cornelius was looking for a feasible reason to leave."

Asa was starting to wonder if Will's resentment about his broken engagement had colored all of his opinions about the head of the Riehl family— and no doubt his current state of mourning was souring his opinion about *everything*. At least Will had come out of his funk somewhat, so Asa decided to venture into the topic he'd come here to discuss. "I—I know this is a touchy subject," he began gently, "but now that some time has gone by, do you have any idea why Molly believed I was the father of those twins?"

"Huh! I'm not sure I know anything about anything anymore—especially when it comes to Molly." Will shifted some food-encrusted dishes on the coffee table and then picked up a rectangular piece of paper. "When I was looking for the white apron she wore on our wedding day, so we could bury her in it, I came across this in one of her dresser drawers."

Asa's heart lurched when he recognized his own business card. DETWEILER FURNITURE WORKS was printed across the top, followed by the services they offered and the phone number, along with his name and Drew's. As Asa looked around at the careworn furnishings in Will's front room, he knew he was grasping at straws. "Maybe she got this card when she stopped by to ask about repairing or reupholstering some furniture," he suggested.

"Get real," Will murmured. "Does it look like we've had any of this stuff redone? It's all been here since Molly's folks lived on the farm years ago—and then rented it out a couple times before Molly and I moved in."

Asa didn't like the way his pulse was pounding. Why was he getting agitated when he had no idea who Molly was or what she'd looked like or—?

There's an angle for you.

Asa cleared his throat. "I don't mean to turn the knife in your back," he said softly, "but do the twins resemble Molly? Or anybody in her family? You're probably tired of hearing me say this, but I really, honestly, never met your wife, Will."

Gingerich exhaled tiredly. "You know how that goes, when people look at babies. Molly's *mamm* went on about how the twins were the spitting image of Molly at that age, while her *dat* insisted they looked like his side of the family. I was just trying to hold everything together here on the farm while Molly was so sick. Fat lot of *gut that* did."

Will looked away, blinking rapidly. "She had a form of cancer with a name so long I can't pronounce it," he explained in a thin voice. "It was so aggressive, and so advanced by the time we found it, her doctor didn't even try chemo. Said it would only make her more miserable."

Asa closed his eyes, wishing he hadn't pursued this heartrending path. "I'm sorry," he murmured. "I'm—well, I don't know what else to say."

Several painfully long moments of silence passed, until Asa couldn't stand to be in the dark, sorrowful room any longer. He stood up, offering his hand to Will. "If I can do anything for you, you've got my number," he murmured despite the irony of that offer. "Take care."

Will didn't respond, and as Asa closed the door behind him he knew how stupid and useless a phrase like *take care* sounded at a time like this. As he walked toward Midnight, the two horses in the barnyard neighed, compelling him to enter the open stable. Asa quickly tossed four bales of hay into the inside feeders and then put two more bales in the feeder outdoors. When he began to pump water into the trough, Will's horses trotted over to drink before the fresh water had a chance to accumulate.

You didn't accomplish what you came to do, but these horses were glad you stopped, Asa thought as he kept pumping water. *And while Will didn't have any answers, he has at least stopped accusing you of messing around with Molly.*

As Asa rode south to Clifford, he pondered what he'd just seen and heard. No two ways about it: Will had taken some nasty hits that made Asa's own accident in Willow Ridge seem minor in comparison. Asa hadn't expected the dismal atmosphere at the Gingerich place, nor had he anticipated feeling sorry for the guy who'd left that inflammatory message on his phone machine last week.

Asa was also aware, as he headed down the single main street of Clifford, that it wasn't much of a town. Spending a few days in Willow Ridge had given him a whole new perspective concerning the future of Detweiler Furniture Works. He wanted not just a change in his liveli-hood but in his life, as well. He envisioned green wheat and cornstalks growing tall around the house across from the Riehl place, as well as a neat metal building housing his much more profitable furniture business.

And he saw Edith standing beside him, smiling up at him with her sparkling brown eyes.

Asa was suddenly willing to raise Leroy and Louisa, no matter whose they were, because he knew how perfectly suited Edith was to be their mother. It was way too soon to be having such thoughts, yet this picture of his future felt so right. Maybe Edith was the reason he'd never taken serious interest in any of the girls he'd grown up with . . . and maybe God had been leading him to Willow Ridge all along, using Will's unfortunate situation to show Asa what his future might hold if he chose to go with it.

Asa swallowed hard. The changes he had in mind had occurred to him so suddenly—literally by accident—that he needed to step back. He needed to analyze what he'd set in motion by discussing the purchase of that farm with Luke Hooley, who'd already begun making plans for the cropland there.

Asa led Midnight into the stable, and tended him. Drew's horse and rig were gone, so Asa went into the shop to assess the work his brother had done and the new jobs that might have come in while he'd been away. The two of them had set up shop in a building that had once been a restaurant, working on the ground floor and living upstairs. They hadn't invested a lot of time or effort in décor; it was very apparent that two bachelors lived and worked here.

Edith—and Nora—would be appalled at this place, Asa thought as he looked around the ground floor. *Why would we want to stay here when we could do a lot more business in Willow Ridge?*

As Asa began sanding Hal Gillespie's antique dresser, he toyed with ideas about moving to a new location—what kind of effort and money it would require. He was so engrossed in his work and thoughts that he didn't hear the back door open.

"So! The lost boy returns."

Asa jumped and turned toward his brother. "*Jah*, and have I got a lot to tell you about my time in Willow Ridge!" he replied excitedly. "Before you think the bump I took on the head has made me crazy, you should know that the nurse there has pronounced me almost as *gut* as new. Says I'm a fast healer."

Drew's eyebrows rose. "You look real *gut*, considering that spill from your horse. But you've gotten friendly with a *nurse?*" he challenged. "I'm already doubting your judgment, chumming up with an English gal who—"

"Nope, Andy Leitner's Amish now, a guy who—like a few other folks there—wouldn't be accepted in some Amish settlements. Yet Willow Ridge welcomes them," Asa said in a rush. "And I've found the ideal place for us to set up shop, too. It's down the road from a busy café and a mill and a fabulous consignment shop where Nora sells Amish—"

"*Whoa.* Hold it." Drew held up his hand, shaking his head at Asa. "What's all this got to do with that Gingerich guy's message about your fathering his wife's babies? The way you tore out of here to confront him, I thought you were going to bite off his head."

His brother's question made Asa realize just how much his worldview had changed since he'd heard Will's original accusation. "Okay, I'll start at the beginning," Asa said with a chuckle. "You might as well pull whatever piece you're working on over here, because this story'll take a while. And I'm sure you'll have questions."

With an expression of mild surprise, Drew took several packages of upholstery tacks from the bag he'd brought in. After he and Asa had carried a fainting couch from the back room and positioned it near the dresser, Drew studied Asa intently. "I can already tell you I'm not wild about yanking up roots to start over someplace else, just on your whim," he said as he laid a new fabric covering over the fainting couch. "But tell me your story. And you'd better make it really, really convincing."

Asa had anticipated his brother's reluctance to move—or to change anything—so as he told of his time in Willow Ridge, he added in all the compelling details he already loved about the town and its residents. "I couldn't believe it when this little gal with a twin in each arm told Gingerich and me to pipe down and stop upsetting the babies," he was saying as he briskly sanded the dresser top. "And then, when she realized she *knew* Will—"

"So you've picked up a girlfriend?" Drew interrupted. He stopped hammering tacks to look Asa in the eye. "You already sound attached to her. What's with that?"

His brother made a good point. Asa had connected with Edith from the first moment he'd seen her, and it had never been his way to rush into relationships. "She's just so caring, and so kind," he said with a shrug. "And so *cute*."

Drew rolled his eyes and began securing the fabric with his upholstery tacks. "And she's okay that Gingerich claims you fathered those twins?"

"She believed me when I said the kids weren't mine. And she's promised to care for them until I figure out whose they are."

His brother eyed him incredulously. "So what happens when you do that? If she's really attached to them, she won't like it if those babies get taken away from her. Probably won't want to see you anymore," he continued with a shake of his head. "And why would you want to live right across the road from her after she blows you off? Might as well rub salt in that gash on your forehead."

Asa flinched. In his excitement, he'd forgotten

about the spot where a piece of flying gravel had hit him. But maybe his brother's tough talk was the reality check he needed.

"Don't let me rain on your parade," Drew went on in a lighter voice. "Tell me some more about Willow Ridge and the property you looked at—except what on earth would we do with a farm?"

"Ah, but see—Luke Hooley wants to rent the crop land to raise grains he sells in his mill store," Asa replied as he resumed his sanding. "So we'd have an income stream even if it took a while for our furniture business to catch on. We wouldn't have to plant or mow that land. Luke's already said he'd advance us the first year's rent on those acres."

"Sounds like you've already settled things, Asa—without bothering to include me in the arrangements. I think this Edith—and all these people—might be leading you around by the nose."

Asa couldn't miss the resentment in Drew's words. "I didn't intentionally leave you out," he insisted. "Things were coming together so fast that, well—you and I really need to go up there so you can see Willow Ridge firsthand. Luke's wanting to get that cropland planted this spring so he can—"

"Luke wants this, and Luke wants that," Drew interrupted tersely. "Why am I feeling like the lone stranger left out in the cold while you've taken up with your new friends in Willow Ridge?"

Asa bit back a retort. It would do him no good to raise his voice to the same level of contention he heard in his brother's questions. "It's not my fault you weren't with me when I got detained in Willow Ridge," he murmured carefully. "You've made some valid points and given me something to think about. Shall we give this subject a rest for now?"

Drew raised his eyebrows, but kept on hammering tacks.

"I'm not letting an opportunity like this pass me by, however," Asa insisted. "I hope you'll visit Willow Ridge with me—soon—so we can make an informed decision about the future I see for us there. Sometimes change is the right thing—the *best* thing, for both of us and our business."

They resumed their work in a silence that made the shop feel too small and stuffy. Asa thought back over his experiences in Willow Ridge even as his brother's questions rang in his mind. He had to convince Drew to at least *see* the place he was talking about and to meet the people who'd taken care of him. . . .

CHAPTER EIGHT

W hen Nora heard the bell above the door jingle midmorning on Thursday, she looked over the loft railing. "It's *gut* to see you girls out and about with the twins," she called to the three Riehl sisters. "Make yourselves at home, and I'll be down in a few."

"Take your time, Nora," Rosalyn answered as she and Loretta set a large box on the desk. "Dat's sent us over with some clocks. We're happy to linger here amongst all your pretty things."

Nora turned to the two English ladies who'd been trying to decide which of her handmade quilts they wanted. "Those girls have taken in two babies whose mother has died," she explained to her customers. "Their father's a clockmaker, and the girls do crafty things, as well."

"Did he make that musical clock by your front door?" the shorter lady asked with a smile. "I was eyeing that one—and the one at the bottom of the stairs—last week when I was here."

"Yes, Cornelius Riehl has consigned several of his clocks recently, each of them different," Nora replied.

The other lady smiled. "Amish folks have such interesting names, don't they?" she remarked. "Go on down and see what they've brought in, if you want to. Annette and I might take a while here. Every one of your quilts is beautiful in its own way!"

Nora sensed that if she gave these two regular customers some time to themselves, they might buy more than they'd originally intended. "Holler if you need me," she said as she started down the stairs.

Seeing two little smiling faces, Nora made a beeline for the babies in their baskets, which Edith had placed on her worktable. "And don't you two look happy today!" she said as she playfully tweaked their noses. "You're traveling in some awfully pretty carriers, too."

"Edith made those for an auction in Roseville—but we moved here a couple weeks before the sale," Loretta said. Her cheeks flushed prettily as she reached into the big box they'd brought. "We wrapped Dat's clocks with a couple of toothbrush rugs I'd made for that same auction, so I thought—well, if you still want to put them in your store—"

Nora's eyes widened as Loretta carefully took a clock from a round rug woven in shades of purple, teal, and cream. "These are wonderful colors! Of *course* I want them," she said as she took the rug and peered into the cardboard box. "And this other one in red, yellow, and blue would be perfect for a child's room."

"Oh, let me see that rug!" one of the ladies

upstairs said excitedly. "Those colors match the flowers in this quilt I keep going back to—"

"Bring both of those rugs up here, Annette," her friend said as the two women peered over the loft railing. "A quilt and a coordinating rug would be just the thing to redecorate my guest room."

Nora chuckled, lowering her voice as Annette came down the wooden stairs. "Quick—decide how much you want for these, Loretta," she said. "And don't even think about asking less than fifty apiece."

"Oh my," Edith murmured.

Loretta's eyes widened. "Oh, I could never charge that much for—"

"Your time and materials are worth more than you know. Don't sell yourself short," Nora murmured. She turned to the customer who was approaching them, holding up the rug done in primary colors. "Isn't this cheerful? And I can think of two or three quilts upstairs it would go with, too."

"I like them both! It's so exciting to be the first person to see them—and to meet the young lady who made them, too!" Annette added as she smiled at Loretta.

"I've got dibs on the purple one!" her friend called down to them. "It'll be perfect alongside my bed, with this quilt that has the four flowers in the center."

"Hold your horses, Tina—I'm coming!" Annette said as she tucked the rugs under her arms.

When she was on her way up the stairs, Nora grabbed Loretta's hands. "Didn't I tell you our customers would love your rugs, girlie?" she murmured. "Those ladies have been fingering the quilts for weeks, so your rugs will seal the deal. I suggest sixty-five dollars apiece—and since I didn't have to tag them, I won't take any consignment fee."

Loretta's mouth dropped open. "I—I was going to ask if you still want me to work—"

"I haven't been this excited since I bought those pottery dishes from you a couple months ago!" Tina called out as she and Annette came downstairs with their quilts and rugs. "My family loves the gifts I find for them here—but this is a present for *me!*"

Nora preceded them to the checkout counter, thrumming with the pleasure she always felt when customers loved the items in her store as much as she did. As she was clipping the tags, the clock on the wall by the stairway played the Westminster chime sequence and then bonged eleven times, filling the shop with its stately tones.

"Can't you just hear that in our front hall?" Annette murmured as she watched the pendulum swing. Moments later, when the clock hanging by the door began to play "Amazing Grace," both ladies stopped talking to listen to its music box.

"Ohhh," Tina murmured, "that's always been my favorite hymn."

Edith smiled at her. "That clock plays several different hymns, along with patriotic songs—and Christmas carols!" she added brightly.

"*Jah*," Loretta chimed in. "You just set the little switch for whichever kind of songs you want, and you can change to a different track anytime."

"I've got to have that for my kitchen," Tina insisted.

"And I want the one with the pendulum," Annette said, clapping her hands together. "Buck will be getting it for his birthday!"

"How about if I pack it for you so it'll travel well?" Loretta offered as she headed for the clock. "And I can show you how the weights and the pendulum hook on, too."

"Oh, this is just perfect! I'm so glad we came here today!" Annette said.

After she'd loaded the ladies' quilts, rugs, and clocks into their car, Nora gazed steadily at the three Riehls. "You see how it works? My customers love my merchandise, but it was the *service* we gave them—and your presence in the store—that made their shopping experience really special today," she explained. "Between the two of them, they spent more than fourteen hundred dollars—"

The sisters gasped, gawking at her.

"—and they'll be back, and they'll tell their

friends about us," Nora continued earnestly. "So thank your *dat* for sending more of his clocks, and—"

"He'll be tickled to see his check," Rosalyn murmured.

"—Loretta, you're a natural at dealing with people," Nora went on as she grasped the young woman's hand. "It was your knowledge of that musical clock, and offering to pack the other one correctly, that finalized those sales. So of course I want you to work here! When can you start?"

Loretta gazed at her with shining hazel eyes, and then looked at Edith and Rosalyn. "Tomorrow?" she replied in a breathy voice. "I—I just don't know what to think about how much those ladies spent."

Nora smiled. She suspected Loretta had done a lot of soul-searching before she'd inquired about working in Simple Gifts, and she admired the girl for overcoming her doubts about dealing with English customers—and probably her fears about what Cornelius would say, as well. "Well, it isn't every day we turn over so many high-ticket items at once," Nora admitted. "But I like it when friends shop together. They give each other ideas—and they tend to fuel each other's, um—*need* for pretty, unusual things."

The sisters laughed, and when little Louisa clapped her hands together, Edith lifted the baby from her market basket. "I think you should do it, Loretta," she encouraged as Rosalyn nodded her agreement.

"And *you* should be making baskets to sell here," Loretta challenged. "You have all sorts of reeds and handles stuck away for baskets you were going to make when we were in Roseville."

"*Jah*, that's true," Edith replied. "Seeing what happened with those two gals makes me think it'll be worth my time. More than I'd imagined."

Nora wrote out two checks and gave them to Loretta, pleased that the Riehl girls had witnessed the way English women loved to shop for hand-crafted articles. "Give your *dat* my best—and whatever you're doing with those twins, keep it up. They look so happy and healthy now! I'll see you at eight tomorrow morning, Loretta."

The shop's calm silence enveloped Nora as she grabbed a rag and a can of furniture polish. Dusty fingerprints suggested that these two mantel clocks had been packed away since Cornelius had moved from his previous home and shop, but cleaning them made the dark wood glimmer. Behind their beveled glass covers, they had ornate faces and graceful brass pendulums. As she polished the back of one clock, the little board that covered the access to the works popped off.

A folded piece of paper was taped to the inside of the board. Across the top it said *Riehl Clocks—Riehl Service, Riehl Timely*, and it was an invoice for four hundred dollars. Nora glanced at the note

Cornelius had tucked into the box the girls had carried in, describing these as musical clocks that he had refurbished—for which he wanted two hundred and fifty dollars apiece. When she fully unfolded the yellowed invoice, she noticed a handwritten note at the bottom: *Shame on you, Mr. Riehl, for insisting that my dear Ervin ordered this clock as a surprise for me the week before he died—and expecting me to pay for it! He did no such thing. Anna Beachey*

"Oh, my," Nora murmured as she read the note again. When she noticed Anna's phone number on the invoice she dialed it, thinking something about this situation sounded familiar. . . . A lady who sounded rather elderly answered.

"*Jah*, Anna?" Nora said. "I'm Nora Hooley, and I just received a clock from Cornelius Riehl to sell in my consignment shop. The invoice with your note was taped inside the—"

"Puh! Never met the man, and I don't want to," Anna clucked. "That clock got delivered to the house addressed to my Ervin, the week after he'd passed away. Had a note sayin' he hoped the little missus would enjoy her surprise, as it played 'I Need Thee Every Hour' and had my name on the face of it. I got all weepy and *almost* fell for it," Anna went on resolutely, "except my cousin Elvina called and said the UPS man had brought her husband George a clock that played 'Jesus Loves Me,' with her name on it. She was so tickled that

143

he'd wanted her to have one last surprise before he'd died, like a gift from the grave to remember him by. Except I reminded her that George had been even more of a tightwad than Ervin."

Nora bit back a laugh at Anna's description of their husbands, but the situation sounded much like the Bible-selling scam from one of her favorite old movies, *Paper Moon*. She'd given up the gadgets and trappings of her English life when she'd returned to Willow Ridge last year to reconcile with her Amish family, but what she'd learned in the outside world had made her wise to its ways. "Did you ladies suspect Mr. Riehl had read your men's obituaries and then personalized those clocks—"

"You got it right, honey," Anna blurted. "When I poked at my name with my fingernail, the fancy sticker came off, and it said *Seth Thomas* underneath. Elvina and I sent those clocks back the next day, as we sure didn't want Cornelius Riehl comin' around to collect his dirty money."

After a few more minutes of chitchat, Nora thanked Anna and hung up. As Nora stared at the two clocks, a worm of suspicion crawled in her stomach. What kind of man took advantage of recently widowed women's vulnerability? It was almost as heinous as watching the funeral announcements and looting the homes of the bereaved when they were at church for the service.

On first impulse, Nora wanted to box up the

clocks and return them so she could give Cornelius a talking-to. If she did that, however, he would surely forbid Loretta to work in Simple Gifts—and might even prevent the girls from crafting their rugs and baskets to sell there.

Keep this under your kapp. *No sense in upsetting the girls by accusing their* dat . . . *and this knowledge might come in handy later. Nothing dishonest about selling the clocks in your shop for what seems like a reasonable price.*

Nora set the clocks at eye-level on opposite ends of the shelf where she'd displayed several Amish dolls and one of Bishop Tom's carved Nativity sets. She wound one of them, smiling at the comforting *tick-tock* produced by its swinging pendulum. After the clock struck noon, the music box played a simple rendition of "Jesus Loves Me" that took Nora back to her childhood, when she'd learned that song at her mother's knee. She set the second clock then, a little bit behind the first one so "I Need Thee Every Hour" didn't play at the same time. The two hymns would remind her of Anna Beachey's story every time she heard them—and remind her to listen for other revelations about the man who'd taken over as the deacon of the local Old Order church district.

If she learned nothing else suspicious about Cornelius, it would signify that he'd given up his dubious habit of scamming little old ladies—wouldn't it?

• • •

That evening at supper, Edith smiled at the twins as they sat between her and Rosalyn in high chairs the neighbors had loaned them. She was grateful that the babies were making happy noises, their tummies full from bottles of goat milk she'd fed them before everyone else sat down to eat. Edith could also feel how Loretta was stewing—working up her courage to talk to Dat.

"When we took your clocks to Nora's shop today," Loretta finally began, "a couple of ladies bought the clocks you'd consigned earlier—"

"So Nora said she'd make out the check at the end of the month, when she pays everyone?" Dat asked as he cut into his chicken-fried steak.

"We brought it home for you," Rosalyn assured him as she beamed at her younger sister. "And the same ladies bought two of Loretta's rugs, along with quilts from the loft. It was quite an exciting visit!"

"When I explained to the ladies about how the one clock's music tracks work—and packed the pendulum clock for them," Loretta said in a rush, "Nora said I was a natural at working with customers, and she asked me if I would work in her store, starting tomorrow. And I—I said yes!"

Dat's knife and fork came to a standstill. "You know it's not our way to allow our young women to work amongst English—"

"But I'm doing it to cover any extra expenses

146

for the twins," Loretta insisted quietly. "When you asked Luke Hooley to pay us so much more for our eggs, I . . . I thought maybe we were running a little short on money and that my wages from the store would help out."

The kitchen went painfully quiet. Dat's expression was like none Edith had ever seen. For a moment his eyes widened as though he'd been trying to keep their financial difficulties a secret. His Adam's apple bobbed above his open collar when he swallowed. Then Dat's face resumed its usual composure, and he found a smile. "Our household expenses are my responsibility," he said in a low voice. "I certainly hope you didn't let on to Nora that we can't make ends meet."

"Oh, no—nothing like that," Rosalyn cut in. "We were caught up in the excitement of watching those ladies buy so much stuff."

"Or—or if you don't want me working out in the store," Loretta continued earnestly, "Nora has also asked if I would teach classes on how to make my toothbrush rugs. Nora will be there, and we could meet in one of her enclosed rooms—"

"Probably of an evening when the store's closed, so there won't be customers," Edith put in. "Nora said you could set your own schedule, Loretta."

She and her sisters watched Dat spoon more mashed potatoes onto his plate and smother them with gravy. When Louisa began to squeal, Edith

147

offered her a pacifier—and Rosalyn did the same for Leroy.

"Your description of the two English women's buying so many items is a prime example of why I don't want you working in Nora's store," Dat explained. He put down his utensils to focus on each one of them in turn. "I'm concerned that your exposure to such extravagant spending will undermine the frugality our faith teaches, or that you will come to confuse your *desire* for something as a *need* for it. Simple Gifts is a wonderful place—filled with tempting items, is it not?"

Edith shared glances with her sisters as they nodded. All of them were enthralled with Nora and her beautiful merchandise.

"Temptation starts so innocently," their father went on in a faraway voice, "that before we're aware of it, we begin to sacrifice time and money we should be spending on necessities in pursuit of worldly pleasure. This is why I'm fine with your making your rugs at home to sell in Nora's store, Loretta, but I don't want you working there. Do you understand my concern?"

Loretta nodded obediently, but Edith sensed her sister was fighting tears. At least Dat's tone of voice was patient, and he seemed intent on looking after their best interests—they had expected him to be angry when Loretta announced that she'd already agreed to work for Nora. The three of them remained quiet, because their father appeared to be considering other things to say. Edith smiled at little Louisa and lifted her from the high chair to cuddle her.

"Another matter that concerns me about Nora—and Luke," Dat continued, "is that they were both raised in the Old Order faith and they left it to become Mennonites. What a disappointment this must have been to their families. And you may not have heard this, but when she was sixteen Nora became pregnant out of wedlock, dropped baby Millie on her brother's doorstep, and then went on to live in the English world married to an English man—whom she divorced before she returned to Willow Ridge."

Edith's eyes widened as she looked at Loretta and Rosalyn. "I—I had no idea," she murmured.

Dat smiled ruefully. "I'm sure Nora doesn't dwell on her past," he remarked, "but we know that Jesus explicitly forbade divorce, and that the Bible condemns those who divorce as adulterers if they remarry. The apostle Paul lists adultery as a mortal sin in his letter to the Galatians, saying those who engage in such activities shall not inherit the kingdom of God."

Edith nodded sadly, rocking Louisa in her arms. Her father had often read passages that pertained to such sinful matters while they were growing up, to prevent them from following the path to perdition. Although their parents had generally avoided the topic of relations between a man and a woman—or how babies were made—Dat had always had plenty to say about the sins of the flesh.

"It puzzles me that Nora's father, Gabe Glick, was a preacher when she was growing up—and Luke's brother Ben is a preacher, as well, yet their families have accepted their unfortunate choices," Dat continued in a pensive voice. "But then, Bishop Tom has also told me that the previous bishop of Willow Ridge, Hiram Knepp, was excommunicated for owning a car, amongst other things—"

Edith blinked. No one had told her *this* story, either, in the short time they'd lived here.

"—and that he eventually became so twisted in his thinking that he set fire to the original café on Christmas Eve and died in the explosion," Dat went on with a shake of his head. "It might be that such permissive behavior amongst the church members began while Knepp was the bishop. Had I known how *progressive* the Willow Ridge district has become—how such serious breaches of the Old Order faith have been allowed here—I might not have left Roseville. Cousin Reuben never mentioned the carryings-on of his neighbors, you see."

Rosalyn playfully rubbed Leroy's nose with her own before lifting the little boy from his high chair. The twins were getting antsy, which in turn made Dat study them as though considering the sinful situation in which they'd been conceived. He picked up his knife and fork to finish his dinner.

"That said, we can't look back," Dat remarked, dragging a bite of meat through the gravy on his plate. "Loretta, I admire your willingness to contribute to our family's income, but I'd be happier if you sold your rugs and budgeted your earnings as you see fit. It's *gut* practice for running your own household someday. A frugal, mindful woman—as your mother was—makes life a joy for the man who marries her."

"*Denki*, Dat," Loretta whispered. "That's what I'll do."

After their father had finished his supper and tucked away a slice of pie, he excused himself to return to his workshop. Edith rose from the table to slip her arm around Loretta, just as Rosalyn did. "I'm sorry, Sister," Edith murmured. "We were all so excited about your working in Simple Gifts."

"We all knew Dat would probably say I couldn't," Loretta responded with a nod. "At least he was in a reasonable mood—"

"And who *knew* about Nora's leaving baby Millie behind, and getting divorced?" Rosalyn whispered with wide eyes. "She's been nothing but nice to us, and to these babies—"

"Dat's calling her a sinner, but aren't we all?" Edith remarked pensively. "Nora's patient and

151

kind—the definition of love given to us by the apostle Paul. Everyone has welcomed her and Luke, so who's to say that Willow Ridge folks are too progressive or permissive? Maybe they simply believe in forgiveness to the same degree Jesus did."

"*Jah*, that's how I see it, too. Sometimes one Bible passage seems to contradict another," Rosalyn remarked as she filled the sink with dishwater. "No matter what Dat says, we're not to judge Nora and Luke—or anyone else. I'm still glad she's our friend."

"Me too," Edith agreed as she situated Louisa in her high chair with a few cloth toys. "Some things are meant to remain a mystery until God sees fit to reveal their meaning. And some day He will."

CHAPTER NINE

Friday morning as Edith put clean, wet clothes through the ringer of the washer, she had time to think about the many topics that had come up during supper yesterday. Dat had left after breakfast for an estate sale in Morning Star, where he'd read that several old clocks were being auctioned off. Loretta had gone to Simple Gifts first thing to tell Nora she wouldn't be working there—but she'd come home with a big bag of fabric remnants she'd bought at the Willow Ridge Quilt store. She was sitting on the porch, keeping an eye on the twins in their playpen as she tore long strips of the fabric to make another rug. Rosalyn was in the basement organizing their jars of pressure-canned fruits and vegetables so they'd have room on the shelves to store this year's crop.

Edith filled the washer with warm water, shirts, and dresses so this load would agitate while she hung the clothes in her laundry basket. When she stepped outside, she gave thanks for the green pasture where red and white chickens pecked, and for the cloudless blue sky, and for the patchwork of farmsteads with white homes, red barns, and tidy shops she could see from their back stoop. She shook out one of Dat's gray shirts and hung it on the clothesline, then did the same with four identical shirts. Edith cranked the handle of the big pulley to bring empty clothesline within her reach while shifting the shirts out over the yard.

How could so much *drama* have occurred in this peaceful little town? How could nice people like Bishop Tom and Lydia Zook and the Naomi Brenneman who managed the Grill N Skillet live and work in such harmony with folks like Andy Leitner and Nora Hooley, who'd divorced their original mates—not to mention Luke and Ira, who'd reportedly led freewheeling lives before they'd married? Some Old Order folks—Dat, for instance—believed that people who'd left the Amish faith had forfeited their salvation by turning their backs on Jesus and His teachings. Yet here in Willow Ridge, Edith sensed no censure or condemnation. The women, for example, knew about the dubious circumstances surrounding Will Gingerich and Asa, yet they'd opened their hearts to see that the twins were cared for.

Lord, I want to avoid the snares and pitfalls of temptation Dat was describing, she prayed as she shook out a purple dress. *But I still want to raise these babies, and I want to befriend Nora, and—*

The *clip-clop clip-clop* of hooves on the road made Edith look up. She sucked in her breath. Could that big black horse pulling the wagon possibly belong to Asa? When Edith stepped off the stoop to watch the gelding, the driver waved his arm above his head and grinned at her.

"Asa!" she murmured as she hurried toward the road. Then, in her excitement, she cried his name out loud. "Asa! You're back! It's so *gut* to see you!"

When he tipped his hat at her sister, Edith realized that anyone in the neighborhood could've heard her calling out Asa's name. But she didn't care. Her heart raced as she jogged behind the wagon, which was loaded with old furniture. Asa halted his horse on the roadside and hopped to the ground. He reached into the vehicle, near the footboard, and brought up a bouquet of fresh lilacs.

"For you, Edith," he murmured as he leaned toward her.

She could hardly breathe. As Asa held her gaze, she fumbled for the flowers and found his strong, warm hand instead. His face was shaded by the broad brim of his straw hat and the raven hair falling over his forehead, yet his smile was so dazzling she might have been staring straight into the sun.

"You look so—your bruise is gone," she murmured when her brain seemed too addled to think of anything else.

"I'm doing well, feeling really *gut*," he murmured. "Seems I had a fine nurse to pull me through after my accident."

Edith's cheeks went hot. Standing here, gazing up at him, it seemed that everything else in the world had disappeared. She was glad the loaded wagon stood between her and Loretta and the neighbors—not that she and Asa were doing anything unseemly. "Are you staying with the Hooleys again, or—"

"This is a very quick trip," he insisted. "I had a load to pick up, and I took the long way home, hoping for a peek at you and the property across the road. Wanted to be sure my first impressions were correct, considering that I took quite a bump to my head last week."

"Come on in," Edith insisted, tugging at his hand. "Leroy and Louisa will be glad to see you—and Loretta and Rosalyn, too. Dat's gone to an estate sale—"

"Temptation, thy name is Edith," he teased, wiggling his eyebrows at her.

She forgot what else she'd intended to say. With his shining black hair brushing his collar and his bottomless indigo eyes drinking her in, and his even white teeth, Edith thought he was the handsomest man she'd ever seen. And his expression told her he thought she was *beautiful*. When had she ever felt so breathless?

"We—we could fix an early lunch," she offered,

"or even just have some coffee and the rest of the apple fritters from breakfast—"

"Edith," he whispered. "I've not been able to get you off my mind. Phooey on fritters. It's you I'm wanting a taste of."

Before she knew what was coming, Asa kissed her. It was the merest brush of his lips, but it sent her into a state of ecstatic euphoria that would keep her floating for the rest of the day. "Oh," she murmured. *"Oh."*

Asa gently ran his finger down her cheek. "I've got to get back on the road, or my brother'll wonder what's waylaid me," he murmured. "But you've given me enough sugar to keep me high all the way home. I'll be back as soon as I can, all right?"

Nodding eagerly, Edith took the flowers he pressed into her hand.

Asa vaulted back into the wagon seat and took up the lines. "Let's go, fella," he said to his horse. As the wagon lurched forward, Asa left her with a parting wink.

For the longest time Edith remained in the middle of the road looking after him. Inhaling the heady scent of the lilacs, she dared to dream of the next time she would see him. He'd only been here for a few minutes, but he'd altered his route to see *her.* He'd changed her whole day.

"Better get yourself out of the road, little sister.

You'll get run down, and you'll never know what hit you."

Edith blinked and looked at Loretta, sitting on the porch swing. Her sister's words finally penetrated the haze of happiness that filled her head, and she strode briskly toward the house. Had Loretta seen Asa kiss her? Edith decided not to say anything, to let it be a sweet little secret. "Asa was hauling furniture back to Clifford," she explained as she ascended the porch steps. "Said he'd be back soon, when he could stay longer. His brother's waiting for him to—"

Loretta's raised eyebrow told Edith she'd been babbling. She stuck her nose into the lilacs again. "Better put these in water before they wilt."

"Might want to douse yourself with cold water while you're at it," her sister teased. "Otherwise you're likely to be drifting like a balloon in a breeze for the rest of the day, silly. He kissed you, didn't he?"

Edith feigned shock and then widened her eyes. "I don't know. *Did* he?"

As she floated into the house, Edith felt confident that her sister wouldn't tattle on her—if indeed she'd seen that kiss—because she'd kept Loretta and Will's romantic activities to herself when they'd been engaged. Nothing improper had happened between Loretta and Will, and while Edith realized it was too soon for Asa to kiss her, she didn't feel any more wayward or sinful than her sister was.

Matter of fact, she'd never felt happier.

As Asa unloaded the wagon at the shop's back door, he noticed clouds rolling in and smelled a hint of coming rain. "Better get this stuff inside, and then we can write up the inventory for it," he remarked to his brother. "That front's moving in pretty fast."

He wondered if Willow Ridge was already getting some moisture—which made him think of the neat green rows of vegetables in the Riehl garden, and clothes flapping on the line, and the way Edith had gazed at him with her sparkling brown eyes.

"Have you thought any more about our buying the farm in Willow Ridge?" Asa asked. "If we don't put our money down soon, someone else is liable to snap it up. The real estate guy said homes in the country are popular for folks who don't make their living farming—hobby farms, he called them."

As he and Drew positioned an antique settee between them, Asa tried to gauge his brother's reaction. Sometimes Drew was a tough nut to crack, yet today Asa detected a glimmer of interest.

"I'd need to know what sort of investment we'd have to make in the property and in a new shop building," Drew said as they eased the settee through the narrow doorway. "And what could we expect to get for *this* place? This building's not in great shape, and when you consider what farmland with a house on it costs, we'll probably need a loan that'll take forever to pay off."

It was a reasonable request—a sign that Drew had at least been considering a change of address. "Luke can probably get me some figures for either frame or metal buildings," Asa replied. "And I'll call the gal who sold us this place, to ask what it'll sell for now."

"I guess our turnover time lately is making me think we might be better off in a bigger town," Drew said. He set his end of the settee down in the back room they'd entered, gesturing at the eclectic collection of pieces they'd bought to refurbish. "Doing custom work for folks who already own the pieces is fine, but some of our stuff sits in the shop a long time before we move it. And hauling pieces around to antique shows takes a lot of effort."

"*Jah*, it does," Asa agreed. "In Willow Ridge we could have a better showroom with windows, plus we could consign some pieces to Nora's store. There's an English gal who designs Web sites for the businesses there, too, and I'm thinking it's time we did that. More exposure means more sales."

Drew chuckled as they returned to the wagon. "Who would've ever thought *we* would be advertising on the Internet? But I'm okay with that as long as I don't have to learn how to use a computer."

"Nora—or that Rebecca gal who does the Web sites—would handle all that," Asa assured his brother. "They could take pictures of our pieces, and update our site when we've sold stuff or when we get new inventory. I'm all for paying her to do that, because print ads don't bring us much business. People don't have many reasons to come to Clifford."

When they'd hefted a drop-leaf table into the back room, Drew got a mischievous look on his face. "Why do I think it's that girl across the road from the farm that's making you so hot to trot to Willow Ridge?" he teased. "What's her name? Enid?"

"Edith," Asa shot back. "And what's wrong with moving where more girls live? It's not like we've got any to choose from here."

"We were stupid not to look into that when we bought this building."

Asa's pulse beat faster. He found Drew's attitude a huge improvement, so Asa decided not to give his brother time to change his mind. "All right, I'll give Luke a call right now and ask him to check on building costs for us. The way I understand it, the Brennemans in town have built a lot of the existing structures—like the café and Ben Hooley's smithy."

"What about a metal building?" Drew suggested. "We'd have less maintenance that way. You know how I hate to paint."

"You're on. Be back in a few."

Asa went to the small room that served as an office to use the phone—a fixture the bishop had allowed them to keep because they had no Plain neighbors with whom to share a phone shanty. As he thumbed through the business cards in the front of the old desk drawer, he couldn't stop grinning. *Edith, this is working out! Keep smiling and praying, and I'll convince Drew to move to Willow Ridge sooner rather than later!*

No one answered at the Mill in Willow Ridge, so Asa left a message with some approximate dimensions for a building, asking Luke's opinion about the most practical options. As rain splattered the window, he pictured Edith sitting on her front porch with the twins in their baskets, enjoying the cool breeze as the rain fell around them.

On impulse, Asa looked up Will's number in the directory and dialed it. He had promised Edith he'd get answers about those babies' father, and it would be good to have an update on Gingerich now that a few days had passed since his visit.

"*Jah*—Will?" he said when someone picked up

after the second ring. "Asa Detweiler. How're you doing?"

"Huh. About the same."

Asa reminded himself to be patient, because he didn't want to put Will off by sounding too cheerful, gushing about his relocation plans. "Not trying to be pushy—and I hope this doesn't sound crass," he said, "but have you heard any new clues about who fathered Leroy and Louisa?"

Will let out a sardonic laugh. "It's not like guys are going to step up and admit to that, you know. But I've got a new wrinkle for you."

"What's that?"

"Molly's *dat* still wants me out of here in a couple of weeks, but her *mamm*—Ruth—stopped by yesterday saying it's time the babies came home," Will replied with a sigh. "She said that we might not know the father, but the twins are Molly's. Says it's only right that family should raise them."

Asa covered his face with his hand. Molly's mother was right—but that didn't mean he liked it. He hated the thought of breaking that news to Edith, too. "How old is Ruth? Twins are a lot of work. Are there other daughters at home to help with them?"

"Nope, Molly was the youngest of eight, and the rest of the girls are married. I'm guessing her parents are pushing fifty."

Asa tried to corral his stampeding thoughts.

He'd known this might happen, but it seemed like the little family of his dreams was being torn apart before he could provide the twins a home. If nothing else, because Molly had called out his name, Asa was willing to accept the blame for a sin he hadn't committed because he believed Edith wanted to raise the babies, too. "So even if Molly's parents didn't feel up to raising twins, they have other daughters who could, right?"

"Yup."

"What if I say I'm their father?" Asa blurted.

"Are you *nuts?*" Will shot back. "After hearing your name as Molly passed on, those folks want nothing to do with you. *Are* you their father?" he demanded. "Because if you're not, you're confusing me—and Molly's family will be even less inclined to let you raise those babies, on account of how one of your stories is a lie."

Open mouth; insert foot, Asa thought glumly. It sounded as though Will had taken his side—believed Asa had never been with Molly—until he'd dropped that last bomb on him. "Bad idea, saying that," Asa admitted. "I'm not their father—"

"After I thought about it—the way Molly never said a last name before she died, and how we've known a few other guys named Asa," Will cut in, "I think I jumped to a conclusion when I saw that card in her drawer and called you. Sorry, man."

Asa's eyes widened. This total turnaround in Will's thinking seemed to suggest he wasn't holding a grudge any longer. "Apology accepted," Asa said softly. "But I can't deny that from the first moment I saw Edith, I've had these rose-colored visions of her and me holding those little kids on our own front porch."

"Got it bad, eh? Edith's a sweet girl."

"The perfect *mamm* for those twins."

"*Jah*, she took to them right away," Will agreed with a sigh. "But that doesn't mean she should raise them, when Ruth wants them back. Unless . . ."

Asa's heart skipped a beat. "Unless what?"

Will let out a short laugh. "Well, I have to get out of this place anyway, so maybe I should move to Willow Ridge—and inform my in-laws that I'm going to continue raising Leroy and Louisa, just like I was doing when I believed they were mine."

Asa's breath caught in his throat. This was *not* part of his picture, Mr. Gloom-and-Doom Gingerich reclaiming the babies he'd dropped off. "Why would you want to do *that?*" Asa demanded. "You've got no source of income, and no place to live—not to mention that raising two babies would leave you no time for a paying job."

"But after the way Molly's folks booted me off this place," Will replied in a rising voice, "why should I turn the twins over to them? It's not like

I could've cured Molly's cancer—and it's not like I knew about her pregnancy before I married her. They haven't exactly had any faith in me or done me any favors, have they?"

Asa was still unclear about what Gingerich had in mind for those little kids, but the energy in his voice was a distinct improvement. Maybe Will was ready to turn the corner, to climb out of his emotional pit and get on with his life. Although resentment wasn't a very positive emotion, maybe it would give Gingerich the incentive to move on. Maybe a change of scenery would prove beneficial, and if Will lived near the twins—

"Wait a minute," Asa said tersely. "Don't you dare tell me you're thinking to marry Edith so you can—"

"Not to worry, Detweiler. It's Loretta I'd intended to spend my life with, remember?" Will pointed out. "Not that I'm exactly in a position to court her again."

Asa gripped the receiver, composing his thoughts. This conversation had taken a totally unexpected turn—for both of them, he suspected—and he needed to keep Will's ideas from spinning out of control. It occurred to Asa that if he did Gingerich a huge favor, he could expect one in return.

"What if—what if I know somebody who's looking for a fellow to farm some ground for him?" Asa asked before his better judgment could get in the way. "And what if I could find you a place to stay?"

"I will *not* stay in Cornelius Riehl's house," Will blurted. "I'm not *that* desperate. But what've you got in mind? I'm all ears."

Will sounded excited now, as though he'd discovered a new purpose for his life. Asa knew he'd have to tread carefully, because until he made a call or two he didn't know if he could deliver these carrots he was dangling. "Promise me you'll leave the twins with Edith."

"Huh. You've already pointed out the reasons I can't raise them right now," Will said. "Why would I remove them from a home where three sweet, caring young women are willing to look after them? But if I got a job, I could pay for their food and clothes and—"

"And you can prevent Molly's parents from claiming them. Right?"

Will cleared his throat. "I haven't told them where Leroy and Louisa are," he said softly. "So if I vacate this decrepit old place without leaving a forwarding address—without saying anything until after I get settled—that'll give us some wiggle room until Ruth writes to her kin in this area and puts them on the lookout for her grandchildren."

Will had gotten a raw deal, so Asa didn't feel so bad about getting swept up in his scheme.

After all, Asa was offering Gingerich a whole new life while he was piecing together a future for himself with Edith. He had everyone's best interests in mind. "So, if I find you a job and a place, the babies stay with Edith? We're in this together?"

"For better or for worse," Will replied with a chuckle. "Man, if you really can get me out of this house and back to work—"

"I'll call you tomorrow."

"—I'll owe you, big time."

Asa sighed with relief. He'd made some tall promises, and that meant that he, too, would have to get his act together. Very quickly. "Well, I'll be talking to you—"

"Oh—before you go—"

Asa held the receiver tighter against his ear.

"—one of my long-lost relatives—Vernon Gingerich—stopped by to check on me," Will went on. "Said he'd lost contact with my family due to a feud a few generations ago. He knows about the situation with the twins and offered me a place to stay and a job in Cedar Creek. But I turned him down."

That name rang a bell, but Asa wasn't sure why. "How come?"

"Why would I want to live in Cedar Creek? I don't know anybody there," Will countered quickly. "He was a nice old guy, but I wasn't wild about being beholden to a total stranger who seems intent on reconnecting with this branch of his family tree. You know?"

Asa considered this for a moment. Families sometimes separated over differences of faith and opinion, but most folks he knew worked toward reconciliation rather than remaining isolated by such issues. "Matter of fact, I *don't* know," he replied. "Is there another feud brewing in your family? You haven't mentioned their reactions to this baby situation—only that your two brothers squeezed you out of the family farm."

There was a pause. Asa heard Will breathing, thinking.

"Let's just say Mamm and I aren't on the best of terms because she chose Homer and Harvey to stay on the home place after Dat died—which happened a year ago last January." Will cleared his throat. "What with Molly's getting so sick and taking care of the twins as best I could, I, um, haven't ever taken Leroy and Louisa to see her. Not that she came here, either."

Asa glanced at the wall calendar. He thought back over what little he knew about Gingerich and did some quick mental math. "So you lost your *dat* early last year. And when you lost any claim to your home place, Cornelius broke up your engagement to Loretta—"

"And then along came Molly, with parents who set us up on their smallest farm." Will sighed.

"The twins arrived, um, two months early, and we found out about Molly's cancer. She passed on just a few days short of our first anniversary."

Asa's mind reeled as he considered this unfortunate series of events. "No wonder you're messed up—I mean—I didn't intend to—"

"No, go ahead and say it," Will cut in with a sad laugh. "It's been one thing after another after *another* for more than a year. I'm ready for some peace and quiet. I just want to mind my own business without any more upsets, you know?"

Suddenly, Asa liked this guy more than he'd ever figured on—especially considering the reason he and Will had met. "Say your prayers and start packing, Gingerich," he said with a sense of renewed purpose. "We're going to make *gut* things happen, for both of us."

CHAPTER TEN

L ate that afternoon, Luke sat down with a pen and paper and punched the Play button on his phone's message machine. He and Ira had spent most of the day driving around to inspect the plots of ground where their corn and popcorn would soon be planted, as well as to look at the oats and wheat their farmers were raising for the mill. They'd collected several cases of fresh eggs, as well. Now that a heavy, steady rain was falling, Nora had closed Simple Gifts a little early and had come over to the mill's store to keep him company.

As she often did, his wife tidied the containers of goat cheese, butter, and other packages in the refrigerator case. Luke played his messages, jotting a few call-back numbers as he watched Nora work. He smiled to himself as she leaned over, her backside in the air as she restacked cartons of eggs to allow space for fresh ones. A familiar male voice pulled him out of his distracted state, however.

"Luke, it's Asa, and my brother's warming up to the idea of moving to Willow Ridge." Detweiler's baritone voice filled the mill store with an undercurrent of excitement. "What do you suppose a shop building's going to cost us on that farm we looked at? I'd like an idea both for a frame building and metal. I don't want somebody else buying this place, so I'll be coming up there tomorrow. *Denki* for all your help."

Luke smiled, pleased at this news. This afternoon he and Ira had again discussed the farm across the road from the Riehls—the tillable acres were level for the most part, and if he and his brother could get this deal moving, they'd still have time to plant popcorn and oats. His eyebrows rose as the next message began to play, because it was Asa again. He sounded urgent.

"Luke, call me real soon, will you? I've got a farmer for that place we're looking at, and he wants to start right in!" Detweiler said in a rush. "When I get there tomorrow morning, let's be ready to talk money with the real estate guy and put down a deposit." *Click.*

With a short laugh, Luke checked the times on Asa's two messages. "Now what happened in the twenty minutes between his first call and the second one, that he was able to find a fellow to farm for us?" he wondered aloud as he dialed Asa's number.

Nora straightened to her full height and looked over at Luke. "This is moving along mighty fast—"

"*Jah*, Asa doesn't let any grass grow under his feet."

"—so don't forget that until Asa chased down

that fellow with the twins, he hadn't set foot in Willow Ridge," she reminded him. "*I* think his main reason for coming is Edith Riehl—and that relationship hasn't had time to gel, either."

Luke nodded at his wife as someone picked up the phone on the other end. "Detweiler Furniture Works. Asa here—and how can I help you?"

"Asa, Luke Hooley. Sounds like things are hopping like popcorn on your end," he said with a chuckle.

"Luke! *Jah*, the heat's on and things are popping, all right," Asa said. "My brother's convinced our furniture business will be more profitable in Willow Ridge. And you'll never guess who else has come around—and he wants to farm that place we've been looking at. It's Will Gingerich!"

Luke's jaw dropped. "Will Gingerich? The fellow who dropped off his twins with the Riehl girls and accused you of being their *dat*?" He met Nora's wary gaze as she crossed the store to sit on the edge of his desk.

"*Jah*, due to a lot of circumstances beyond his control, Will's been booted off the place he was farming for his wife's folks," Asa explained excitedly. "He wants to see that Louisa and Leroy are taken care of, so coming to Willow Ridge will be the fresh start he needs to move beyond all the tragedy that's hit him lately. I think it's the right thing to do, bringing him into the mix."

Luke considered this information, in light of the

various hoops they had to jump through to get the farm under contract. "How about if I ask the Realtor to meet us here at one o'clock tomorrow? We can put down enough earnest money to keep somebody else from buying it before we make our final decision—"

"I'm ready. Let's *do* it, Luke."

Exhaling in surprise, Luke met Nora's curious gaze. "That's a big decision—a big move for you and your brother—considering you've seen this place only once," he pointed out. "A deposit will buy us time to consider all the angles—"

"I'm in. There's only one potential fly in the ointment."

"What's that?" Luke asked. "Is your brother hanging back because he's not been here to look at the place?"

"Oh, Drew'll come around," Asa assured him, "but our building won't sell for nearly enough to cover that farm—and we think it might take a while to find a buyer. Folks aren't exactly pounding down the doors to acquire property in Clifford, and—well, let's just say the upstairs apartment looks like a couple of bachelors live there, and the shop area doesn't exactly sparkle, either. But we'll make it work," he insisted.

Luke had to smile. "Brings back memories of when Ira and I moved to Willow Ridge, just on Ben's recommendation, and then we bunked above the mill—until a couple of redheads made us change our ways," he added as he smiled at his wife. He paused to see if Asa would offer any more information about his other motivations for moving to Willow Ridge.

"Women have that way about them, ain't so?" Detweiler said with a chuckle. "I can't deny that the sight of Edith with those little twins is working on me. But we've got no time for romance until Drew and I are relocated and you and Ira get Will situated. He'll be needing a place to live, too, by the way."

"You don't ask for much!" Luke teased. He winked at Nora, just because he loved to watch her freckled cheeks turn pink. "The apartment above the mill is vacant. And if that doesn't suit him, I'm thinking some of the older folks around here—like Nora's parents, maybe—would rent him a room in exchange for some help around their place. Ira and I have to talk to Will before we hire him, though," he added matter-of-factly.

"Of course you do. As many changes as Will's gone through this past year, I suspect he has times when he doesn't really know *what* he wants," Asa stated. "Seems to me plenty of other folks have found fresh starts in Willow Ridge, though. I like the idea of giving him a chance at work he's *gut* at, near the twins."

"Can't fault you for that," Luke replied. "We'll work this out, Asa. I'll call the Realtor right now and talk to Ira. See you tomorrow."

As Luke hung up, he was slightly amazed at what had just transpired. "Sounds like we're in business," he remarked when Nora's insistent gaze prompted him. "The Detweilers are coming to Willow Ridge, and Will Gingerich is, too. I've got to get ahold of—"

"Wait just a cotton-pickin' minute!" his wife blurted. "You can't tell me you're going forward with this deal on Asa's say-so during a phone call. What if his brother backs out? What if their place in Clifford doesn't sell? What if Will changes his mind—or what if someone in his family takes those twins to live with them?"

Luke smiled patiently as he dug around in the desk drawer for the real estate agent's business card. "Those are all *gut* questions that any prudent businessman would ask, pretty lady," he replied. "But truth be told, Ira and I haven't gotten this far by always being rock-solid on the details. We tend to do things on the prayer-and-a-promise system—like when we left Lancaster County to come here," he added. "We prayed for steady work and *gut*-looking girls, and we promised to stick together no matter what. Worked out pretty well, don't you think?"

Nora sighed in exasperation. "All right, fine! But whatever you and Ira scheme up is on your money. My store's not going to subsidize whatever you invest in—"

"You're exactly right. This is mill business—

and not so much your business, if you get my meaning," Luke teased as he dialed the phone. "For your concern and your caring ways, I'm taking you to supper at the Grill N Skillet, all right?"

Nora's lips lifted. "I know when I'm being shooed off and shut up," she replied with a shake of her head. "But I reserve the right to say 'I told you so' if this deal blows up in your face."

Luke chuckled as he watched her head back into the storeroom. "*Jah*, Chuck? It's Luke Hooley. How about if we meet you at the farm we've been talking about tomorrow? We'll have some earnest money for you—and you might as well bring the paperwork to start processing the purchase."

"Well, now!" Chuck replied. "Sounds like things have fallen together fast. Any idea how long it'll take for a loan to get approved, or—"

"It'll be a cash transaction. Soon as we get signatures all around, we'll be *gut* to go."

After arranging a few more details, Luke hung up the phone with a sense of great satisfaction. Nora, who'd been restocking the fridge with fresh eggs, gazed at him meaningfully from across the store. He understood her concern, because she was an astute business owner in her own right. She'd created her own success despite a previous husband who'd ditched her and a father who had initially refused to accept her back into her Amish family.

But going through with this farm deal just felt *right,* for a lot of compelling reasons.

Luke stood up and stretched as he peered out the window. "See there? The rain's stopped, and I bet there's a rainbow in the sky somewhere—a sign from God that all's right with His world," he said. "We'll go to supper as soon as I tell Ira what's up. I love you, Nora-girl."

"It's a *gut* thing you do, Luke," she teased. Her smile told him she wouldn't pester him about this matter any further. "Where would I be without you in my life?"

Luke was glad he didn't need to worry about that. He blew Nora a kiss and headed out the back door toward the new house on the hill, jubilant about this day and the many gifts God had given him.

CHAPTER ELEVEN

As Asa rode around the bend and got his first glimpse of Willow Ridge on Saturday, he perked up and paid attention. "Whoa, Midnight," he murmured to his Percheron. "A lot's riding on what we do today."

Rather than heading straight up the road toward the Riehl house, he took the curve that went past the farms and homes on the side of town he hadn't yet seen. He passed a couple of mailboxes with *Brenneman* on them, where a newer home sat slightly behind one that had been built years ago. Sheep grazed in a pasture behind the place with *Kanagy* on the mailbox, and Asa saw white bee-hives tucked among the apple trees in a small orchard. Farther along, the road curved up a hill and he passed the Wagler Harness Shop. A large wagon with *Wagler Remodeling* painted on its side was parked at a house that sat back from the road.

Asa smiled, inhaling the sense of peace and prosperity that enveloped this picturesque little town. The red barn that housed Simple Gifts glowed in the morning sunlight, and alongside the river behind the Hooleys' large white house he saw the big wooden mill wheel turning—and the new home behind it, which belonged to Ira.

"What do you think, Midnight?" Asa murmured

as he rode along toward the county highway. "Is this place calling to you the way it is to me?"

Midnight shook his black head, easily topping the next hill to head toward Zook's Market with its blue metal roof. Asa caught sight of the Riehls' backyard in the distance, but forced himself to focus on the other places around town rather than rushing over to see Edith. He had so much to tell her!

A lot depended upon his meeting with Luke and the Realtor. He believed the Hooley men were on board, but he couldn't stake his future on his wishes and impressions. There were dotted lines to sign and large checks to write out— after Asa took another look at the house and the land and the price tag attached to them.

He hitched his horse to the rail alongside the Grill N Skillet and went inside for an early lunch. The café appeared sleek and new inside, with sturdy wooden booths along the walls and several tables and chairs filling the center of the dining room. The home-cooked aromas that filled the place told him these folks knew how to cook— and from the look of the buffet tables, they were ready for a crowd.

An attractive young woman with black hair tucked under her *kapp* filled his water glass and nodded toward the steam table. "Help yourself to the lunch buffet," she said. "We just opened, so more food will be showing up soon."

Asa was amazed at the assortment of grilled and smoked pork, beef, and chicken—not to mention several salads and the best-looking mac and cheese he'd ever seen. A guy with dark wavy hair and a matching beard walked behind him with two big baskets of rolls and biscuits.

"Finding enough?" he teased as he set the breads on the serving table. "Don't believe I've seen you here before. I'm Josiah Witmer, and you've already met my sister, Savilla."

"Asa Detweiler. This is my first visit—but it won't be my last," he replied as he spooned food onto his warm plate. He already felt so comfortable with these people that he dared to reveal why he was here. "I'm thinking to buy the farm across from the Riehl place, and I'd be relocating my furniture refurbishing business here, as well. If you don't mind my asking, how's your business? Your place doesn't look like it's been open all that long."

Josiah studied him. "Detweiler, eh?" he murmured. "You wouldn't be the fellow they found out cold on the roadside the day of Ira and Millie's wedding, would you? We were so busy serving the wedding dinner I didn't get much chance to hear how that story played out."

"That would be me," Asa replied with a laugh. "The fall from my horse knocked some things into place for me, you might say. But it's a big risk I'm taking, moving here with my business and my brother."

Nodding, Josiah plucked a warm roll from the basket and balanced it on the edge of Asa's heaped plate. "My fiancée and I took a wrong turn in a snowstorm last winter and got stuck here. Best thing that ever happened to us," he added with a warm smile. "We've got a baby now, and my sister has joined us—after we sold our place in Iowa. Even though the previous café, um, *exploded* on Christmas Eve, the *gut* folks here were rebuilding the place—expanding it for us— within a week. I'm a grateful man. I owe this town and the people here more than I could possibly repay."

"Wow," Asa murmured as goose bumps prickled along his arms. "That's quite a testimony."

"Your lunch is on us, Asa. It's our way of saying welcome to Willow Ridge."

As he savored his food, Asa observed the folks who came in—several of them English, with Mennonites and Amish, as well. From his table he could see cars and buggies pulling in along-side the Willow Ridge Quilt Shop, housed in the other half of the building, and the smiles on the women's faces told him they loved shopping there. He glanced at the wall clock, tossed down money for a tip, and waved at Josiah in the kitchen on his way out. Clearly the Grill N Skillet attracted all manner of tourists and families— and across the road, a handful of Plain fellows waited to have their horses shod at Ben Hooley's smithy, as well. He saw a car and a couple of buggies parked at Andy Leitner's clinic, too.

Asa noticed a pickup parked near the For Sale sign at the farm, so he clucked to Midnight to move him along. A glance toward the Riehl place told him the girls were busy inside, and that was just as well. He had to concentrate on business now. He couldn't allow romantic fantasies about Edith, Leroy, and Louisa to distract him—not when he was securing a future for himself and his brother, along with Will Gingerich.

"Hope I haven't kept you waiting," Asa said to Luke and Chuck as he dismounted. "Just ate a fabulous meal at the café while I talked to the owner about Willow Ridge. I'm ready to buy this farm and *be* here!"

Luke crossed his arms with a sly smile. "You're about half an hour too late, Asa. Somebody's already bought the place."

Asa felt as though Midnight had kicked him in the chest. All the breath left him as he stared first at the real estate agent and then at Hooley. "But—but I thought we agreed yesterday that—how did *that* happen?"

Luke didn't reply for a moment that seemed to last forever. Then he clapped Asa on the back, laughing. "Not to worry, man," he said as Chuck chortled along with him. "Ira and I bought the place, and we're going to have the acreage with the house and the road frontage surveyed so you can buy that part from us. You and your brother didn't intend to farm it for yourselves anyway, right?"

Asa's gut tightened as he took in this startling change of plans. "No, but I thought—"

"This way, you won't be up to your ears in debt for half your life," Luke explained. "When your place in Clifford sells, that money'll probably cover the cost of the house, the buildings, and the land they sit on. You can move in any time, and you can pay me whenever you're ready."

Turning on his heel, Asa exhaled hard to keep from saying something he might regret. He looked at the house, a modest structure set back from the road and shaded by mature maple trees and a few evergreens. A barn and a couple of outbuildings sat farther back. He gazed out over the untilled acres awaiting a fresh crop, searching for words. He'd come to Willow Ridge believing this little slice of paradise would be his and Drew's. . . .

"You okay?" Luke asked after a moment.

Asa repositioned his straw hat and faced Hooley, who stood as tall as he did. "I figured we were partners in this deal. If you'd had plans to buy the place outright, maybe you could've told me that," he said tersely. "I was counting on the rental income you were going to pay me for the crop land to keep us afloat until my brother and I got our furniture business established. This changes everything."

Luke cleared his throat. "I can understand why you'd feel I double-crossed you," he began in a calm voice, "but Ira and I have our reasons for wanting ownership rather than a rental agreement. We like you a lot, Asa. But we could see the deal falling through if your brother decided he didn't want to move here—because he's not even visited Willow Ridge, after all. And we've not met him."

"I asked Drew to come along today, but he trusts my judgment about whether this move's right for us," Asa stated stiffly. "He stayed in Clifford to spruce up our apartment and shop before the real estate lady looks at it, so the building will bring a better price. Do you have a problem with that?"

"Nope, I understand where he's coming from. Ira's letting me handle this real estate business, and he's minding the mill store right now," Luke replied. "And while I admire the way you want to provide Will Gingerich a job and a home, I haven't talked to *him* yet, either."

Hooley studied Asa for a moment. Detweiler's gaze was confident without being cocky, and he showed no sign of backing away from the decisions he'd made. "There's a lot of money riding on this deal, Asa, and several pieces of the puzzle are still loose on the table yet," he pointed out. "I want to be sure the crops will be planted soon and properly tended—which might fall through if Will changes his mind. And if somebody from Will's family takes the twins from the Riehls, I can see this whole arrangement tumbling like a house of cards."

Asa pressed his lips together. He still didn't like the way Luke had taken the entire real estate transaction into his own hands—had taken total control—yet he could understand the reasoning behind Luke's decision. "*Jah*, it's amazing how much is riding on two little babies," he said with a sigh. "My brother and I still want to do business in Willow Ridge. And Will is coming partly so he can raise the twins as his own—"

"So where does that leave you and Edith? And how's Will going to raise those babies while he's farming full-time?" Luke blurted incredulously. "Are we talking about a—a three-way relationship here? Your best intentions—and who will be doing what, with whom—still seem a little iffy, if you'll pardon my saying so."

Asa laughed, at himself mostly. "It's complicated," he agreed. "I can see why you have your doubts, and why you and Ira might not want to take the same leap of faith I did. But I'm trusting God to guide us to the outcome He intends. I believe the details will all work out."

"I believe that, as well," Luke said. "And I believe I've removed a lot of the risk involved by purchasing the farm. I'll sell the house acreage to you when you're ready. You'll still have your home and shop, while Ira and I have the tillable land."

"Seems to me both families are getting what they want," Chuck remarked as he looked at Asa. "And this way, the Hooleys will be footing the bill for the seed, fertilizer, and other farming expenses—part of which would otherwise be coming out of your pockets, before you and your brother can get relocated. It leaves you more money to build a new shop and fix up the house a bit, too. That might not be high on *your* list, Asa, but I bet it'll make the lady in question happy."

Edith. Asa glanced across the road, but none of the Riehls were outside. The Realtor's remarks made sense, because when all of the *T*'s were crossed and the *I*'s were dotted, what mattered most to him was Edith's happiness and the twins' security within a family who loved them. "I see what you're both saying. I'll get adjusted to it," he murmured. "So what happens now?"

Chuck's weathered face creased with a smile. "The Hooleys can close on the deal this week. The house is already cleared out, so you and your brother can move in any time after the papers are signed."

"Ira and I hope to meet with Will as soon as possible," Luke said earnestly. "He can live above the mill and start planting oats and popcorn as soon as he gets here."

"I suspect he'll be here in a day or so. He's traveling light." Asa extended his hand to the Realtor and then to Luke. "My brother and I will move in as soon as we get ends tied up in Clifford and we have a new shop building in place."

"Go talk to the Brenneman brothers," Luke said, pointing to their long white cabinetry shop down the road. "Aaron's putting together some numbers for you, so you can decide between frame and metal construction. Once they've got the materials together, he's thinking they could have the building in place by the middle of May."

Asa's eyes widened. Today was the eighteenth of April. "That seems mighty fast."

Luke smiled. "The three Brennemans make a *gut* team—and they'll have help from a lot of other men in town, come time to raise the building—as they did when they built the new café and quilt shop," he explained. "We consider it an investment in your success."

"Many hands make light work," Chuck said with a nod. "You Amish fellows know how to do it right, too."

Asa felt his insides relax. As he let go of his initial resentment, he realized that he and Drew hadn't really lost anything . . . except the financial crunch they would've felt if they'd taken on the whole farm. "Sorry I got so touchy," he murmured. "This arrangement isn't what I'd figured on—but you're right. It's better."

Hooley's smile lit up his face as he reached into his shirt pocket. He pulled out a key on a key ring with the Realtor's company logo on it.

"I was hoping you'd see it that way, Asa. I thought you'd like to look around the house again as you plan your move."

"We'll let you know when it's all signed, sealed, and delivered so you can move in," Chuck added.

As Asa closed his hand around the key, a sensation of lightness filled him. Another chunk of his future had just fallen into place—before he'd even arrived in Willow Ridge this morning. Surely this was Providence at work.

Go tell Edith what you've done!

As Edith ran dishwater, she glanced out the kitchen window. "Dat seems pleased to have a couple of clock-repair calls today," she remarked as his rig rolled down the lane. "Do you think our money's tight? Or was he pestering Luke for more egg money because Dat always goes for the highest dollar he can get?"

Rosalyn shrugged as she carried their dinner plates to the sink. "Could be a carry-over from when Mamm used to tell him he should charge more for his repair work."

"*Jah*, she thought he should've been asking more for house visits, especially," Loretta reminded them. "When he works on grandfather clocks, or for folks who can't bring their clocks in, it takes time away from his shop repairs."

Leroy let out a funny-sounding squawk and started laughing, which prompted Louisa to make noises of her own. Edith chuckled, scrubbing the dishes quickly so she could play with the babies sooner. "Maybe everybody's in a better mood today," she remarked. "When I stood on the bathroom scale and picked up each of the twins, I was pretty sure they'd both gained a pound since they've started on the goat milk."

"Not a bad catching-up for a week and a half," Rosalyn said. She made a funny face at Leroy to make him laugh again. "We should get a baby scale—"

"Knock, knock! Anybody home?"

A male voice coming through the front screen door made the three sisters look at each other. Edith's heart began to pound, for it sounded like Asa—but rather than appear too eager, she kept washing the dishes while Loretta went to the door. Only yesterday Asa had stopped with his wagonload of furniture, so she hadn't figured on seeing him again for a while.

"Look who's here," Loretta said with a teasing edge to her voice.

Composing her face, Edith turned her head while she kept swishing dishes. Asa looked so good, it was all she could do to remain at the sink. His hair fell shiny and soft over his forehead and ears as his dark-eyed gaze met hers. "I—it's so *gut* to see you again!" she blurted. "Let us fix you a plate or—"

"I ate at the Grill N Skillet before my meeting

with the Realtor and Luke," he replied. His grin held secrets as he lifted Louisa from her high chair and rumpled Leroy's hair.

"So you're looking at the farm across the road?" Rosalyn inquired. "We've seen a few cars going in there this week."

"Luke and Ira Hooley bought it this morning, for the cropland. They're selling the acreage with the house and buildings to me—and my brother," Asa added quickly. "Meanwhile the Brennemans are working up plans for the new shop building we'll need."

"*That* all fell together fast," Loretta blurted.

Edith's hands went still in the dishwater. She was too giddy to speak.

"So you're moving to Willow Ridge?" Rosalyn asked as she tidied the kitchen table. "Here—we've got some crumb cake left from dinner, Asa. Help yourself!"

Asa's grin made Edith's heart turn a cartwheel. He eased into the seat nearest Leroy's high chair and playfully patted the boy's hands on the tray. "You kids are looking fat and sassy," he said in a sing-song. "And we're making sure you can stay here, too, Will and I."

"Will Gingerich?" Loretta smoothed her *kapp* nervously. "Last I knew, you two fellows didn't have much *gut* to say to each other."

"We've made our peace. It's a long story, but Will's coming to farm for the Hooleys—before the weekend's out, most likely," Asa added. He bussed Louisa's cheek and gently put her back in her high chair so he could hold Leroy.

"Oh, my," Edith whispered.

"Oh, *my*," Rosalyn echoed. "If he's going to live in that house across the road, Dat'll have a cow."

"Nope, the Hooleys are renting him the apartment above the mill." Asa gazed at Edith over the top of Leroy's downy head. "I was hoping for some female guidance, far as what might need to be done to that house before we move in. Any way you girls can come and look it over with me?"

Edith's imagination ran wild. She dared to dream that Asa's plans for that house included her and the twins, even as she reminded herself that she'd first seen this handsome man only nine days ago. "But—so—well, how does Will fit in, far as the twins are concerned?" she asked. "Surely he doesn't figure to raise them in that apartment!"

Asa made a silly face at the boy on his lap, laughing along with him. "Will still doesn't know who fathered these kids—says it must've been one of the other Asas he and his wife knew—but that doesn't matter so much now. He wants to pay their bills and treat them as though they were his. He knows they'll do better here with you girls caring for them while he works, though."

"Hmm," Rosalyn murmured. "Dat might be

having twin cows before this is all said and done."

"Sounds kind of confusing," Loretta ventured as she dried the plates.

Edith saw nothing confusing about it at all. Asa was making faces and talking to the twins as though he'd been around babies all his life. If he had plans for that house and for her, it seemed only natural that the twins would be there with them. She *so* wanted this dream to come true, but she reminded herself to behave rationally. "I say we look at the house now," she suggested, "while Dat's making his house calls."

"Let's finish these dishes and get over there," Rosalyn agreed.

By the time Asa had polished off a wedge of crumb cake, Edith and her sisters were pulling the sink plug and hanging up the dish towels. They quickly put the babies in their baskets and started across the road. Rosalyn and Loretta chatted excitedly about Asa's plans to move to Willow Ridge, while he dropped back to walk beside Edith. He shifted Leroy's basket to his other side so he could stroll closer to her.

"Hope I'm not making you nervous," he murmured as he gazed down at her. "Things have fallen together pretty fast."

Edith had to pull her gaze away from Asa's so she could think straight. "What's your brother saying about this? He's not even come to see our little town."

"He's getting our building ready to sell this weekend. I'll bring him here soon, though," Asa replied. "Drew agrees that our business would be a lot more profitable if we lived almost anywhere other than Clifford."

As Asa put a key into the front door, Edith gazed out over the front lawn, gripping the handle of Louisa's basket. The English couple who'd lived here had planted several rose bushes around a bird bath in front, and she thought the vine climbing the trellis at the side of the porch was a clematis. A swing was hung from the porch ceiling, out of the weather and covered with a sheet. As her sisters entered the house, commenting about what they saw, Edith hung back a bit to take everything in more slowly.

Had Asa really wanted all of their opinions about what this house needed, or was this his way to bring her here while they could be properly chaperoned? And why would any man ask a woman's opinions of a place unless he really cared about what *she* wanted?

Maybe you're reading way too much into this. You'd better hold your horses—

"What do you think, Edith?" Asa's voice cut through her thoughts. "I have so much I want to talk to you about, but I'm trying to slow myself down. Ask me questions, or—or say what you really think about the place."

Edith looked for something to make a rational

comment about. "Well, first off, all the electrical outlets will have to disappear," she remarked.

"I'll be asking Bishop Tom how he wants me to do that," Asa said. "Sometimes Amish folks remove all the wiring and the breaker box, and sometimes it's enough to remove the outlets and switches and cover the openings."

"Ask him about installing solar panels, too." She looked inside a couple of the kitchen cabinets and then gauged how a table would fit in the center of the room. "Lots of folks are using solar energy in their shops and for charging their buggy batteries and such."

"*Jah*, that's a sign of how progressive Willow Ridge is, compared to a lot of Plain places—another reason I really like this town," Asa added. As they heard Loretta and Rosalyn walking in the upstairs rooms above them, he came to stand beside Edith. "The main attraction is you, though, Edith. Please tell me to back off if I'm taking this all too fast, all right?"

Edith held her breath, gazing at his handsome face. Now that his bruises had all but disappeared and the wound on his forehead blended in with the creases there, he looked healed. Rested. Comfortable with Will Gingerich—and with her.

Is he going to kiss me again?

Asa raised his eyebrows as though he'd read her thoughts. "We'd best behave ourselves," he murmured, gesturing toward the ceiling as her sisters' footsteps made the floor creak.

"You're right," Edith said as she moved a couple of steps away from him. "It's important that we talk about—well, a lot of things."

Was it too soon to discuss the fact that she couldn't give him children? They hadn't even been on a date—

"May I take you for a ride this evening, Edith? Let's go for an early supper so you can show me around this area before it gets dark."

"Or we could take our ride first, to be sure you see everyplace you want to," she suggested. "I'll ask my sisters to look after the twins."

"Just this once, I'd like that," he agreed. He made a point of looking around them then, walking to the doorway of what had probably been a dining room. "If we knocked down this wall, we'd have room for a bigger table, don't you think? I always thought it was odd for families to have a separate room to eat in when the kitchen is where the food's prepared."

Edith's heart swelled. He was already looking toward the times when their families would join them for meals on Sundays and holidays. "I was just thinking the kitchen would be awfully cramped with a table opened all the way out," she said. "Seems you've already thought of the solution to that."

When they heard footsteps on the stairway, Asa

grinned at her. "Tonight then? Say, four o'clock?"

Edith nodded eagerly. She spent the rest of her time in a euphoric state, aware of looking around in four bedrooms and commenting about the pretty woodwork on the main level and so many built-in shelves in the basement . . . but she barely saw these details for stealing glances at Asa. His smile was so confident, and he was so easy to be with that Edith could easily envision herself spending the rest of her life with such a wonderful man. Even the smiles on her sisters' faces suggested that they, too, admired Asa for making such important decisions so quickly—and for being able to afford them. When he'd walked them all home, he tipped his hat and said he'd be discussing the new building for Detweiler Furniture Works with the Brennemans this afternoon.

Edith stood on the porch watching him ride Midnight down the gravel road toward the cabinetry shop. "What do you think, Louisa?" she murmured to the baby in the basket she held. "Is Asa too *gut* to be true?"

"Well, if *you* don't want him, I'd sure keep him company," Rosalyn remarked as she went inside. "He's closer to my age anyway—"

"And he seems a lot more outgoing than the other single fellows we've met since we moved here," Loretta chimed in. "You have to admire him for talking things through with Will, concerning the twins. A lot of guys would steer clear of a girl who's agreed to raise two babies for however long it takes to figure out where they should live."

Oh, but they should live with me—and Asa, Edith thought longingly. She looked at her middle sister as they all went in the house. "And how do you feel about Will's being here? What if he's coming mostly to be with *you* again, Loretta?"

Loretta sighed. "I'm not sure that arrangement will work out anymore," she said hesitantly. "After all Will's been through, he's not the same man I was once engaged to. And Dat's already warned us of *his* suspicions concerning Will."

Edith nodded. At nineteen she felt a lot less experienced than her sisters about dealing with men, because she hadn't dated much in Roseville. Yet she felt ready for a serious relationship. For a home and a husband.

You've brought me to this time and place for a reason, Lord. Show me Your way.

Chapter Twelve

As Asa pulled up to the Riehls' house a few moments before four, he was pleased to see Edith waiting for him in the porch swing. She looked fresh and pretty in a dress of deep cinnamon that suited her complexion. Her apron and *kapp* were snowy white, and he was again struck by her simple beauty, a radiance that came from within her.

"Asa! Ready to see all the sights?" she asked as she sprang from the swing.

"I am. But if your *dat*'s home, I'd like to meet him," he replied as he removed his hat. "I hope to start off on the right foot so he doesn't think I'm sneaking around or stealing you out from under his nose."

When her dark eyes widened, Asa saw himself reflected there—and he liked it. If the eyes were the windows to the soul, he longed to consider himself connected to Edith on such a deep level.

"He's still out on some clock-repair calls," she replied. "And if he met up with Bishop Tom or Preacher Ben, they're probably discussing church business. They do that every now and again."

Asa couldn't help noticing a sense of mischief and relief on her face. "I suspect your father's very protective of you three girls—especially now that you're in a town where he hasn't known the eligible men for very long," he commented. "I'll meet him when we get back. Shall we go?"

Rather than putting down the buggy's metal step, Asa lifted Edith into the rig before springing up beside her. As he clucked to Midnight, it felt so right to have her sitting to his left, as she would do on all their rides . . . and at their kitchen table after they married.

"What a pretty courting buggy," she remarked as she turned in the seat to look at it more closely. "I really like this burgundy upholstery. Did your brother do it?"

Asa smiled. "This is Ira Hooley's rig. I came on horseback to make better time riding up here this morning," he explained. "When I told him I'd be with you, Ira was pleased to loan it to me. Everyone I've met thinks you're a fine new neighbor, Edith—an asset to the community. Not that I'm surprised by that."

The flutter of her long lashes against her pink cheeks enchanted him. "The Hooley family deserves credit for being a mainstay of Willow Ridge," she said. "They've provided a lot of jobs and services with their mill, and with the crops and chickens they hire folks to raise—and at the smithy, too. Before Ben arrived and married Miriam—who ran the café before the Witmers took it over—I'm thinking this town was a lot like other Plain settlements."

"Small and a bit sleepy," Asa said with a nod. He steered Midnight toward the county blacktop that would take them out of town. "But enough about the Hooleys! I want to hear more about *you,* Edith—about what you like to do when you're not gardening and making baskets and tending babies."

Edith turned away as though a bothersome thought was troubling her. When her brow furrowed, Asa sensed something was seriously amiss. "Edith?" he whispered as he reached for her hand. "If I said something that upset you—"

"No, I . . . before this goes any further between us, there's something you should know, Asa."

His eyes widened. He squeezed her hand, so small and delicate in his grasp, wondering what could possibly weigh so heavily on her mind.

"Maybe our first date is the wrong time to bring it up," Edith murmured, "but when I watch the way you play with the twins, I can tell you love babies—and what a *gut* father you'll be . . . but I can't give you any children, Asa."

He stopped breathing. Steering Midnight to the side of the road, Asa searched for words. Anything to bring a smile to Edith's dear face again. "You're awfully young to be thinking—I can't see how you have any way of knowing—"

She faced him again, summoning her courage. "My appendix burst when I was fourteen," she whispered. "I had no idea why I was feeling so

201

bad. Dat kept saying it was a nasty case of the flu—until I passed out from the pain, and Mamm made him take me to the emergency room. You know how it is with Plain men, not wanting to set foot in a doctor's office."

"*Jah*, my *dat*'s the same way," Asa replied as he took both of her hands. "So what happened?"

Edith shrugged. "I guess I nearly died during the surgery. I don't recall much from when I was in the hospital," she replied in a faraway voice. "The surgeon said the infection had gotten so bad inside me that some of my, um, female parts had to come out along with my appendix. He said I'd never have babies—"

When Edith turned again, shuddering with the effort of holding back tears, Asa wrapped his arms around her. "I am so sorry," he murmured. "That has to be hard for you to accept, seeing's how *you* love little ones, too."

"I—I just thought you should know before we committed to anything. I'll understand if you don't want to see me anymore."

Asa felt so bad for Edith that his chest ached as he rocked her in his arms. "All the more reason I want *you* to raise Leroy and Louisa," he said as he rested his head against hers. "Truth be told, Will and I have made a pact to keep Molly's family from taking the babies home with them. It's a bit underhanded, I suppose, but he has the kids' best interests at heart. Just as I do—and you do."

Edith ran a finger beneath her eyes and wiped the moisture on her apron. "I've always known that Will or Molly's family might insist on raising them," she said, sniffling loudly. "But they're such precious little souls, and they're doing so well now."

"I believe—and so does Will—that a younger set of parents should be raising them," Asa insisted in a whisper. "It was no accident that he brought them to you instead of to his or Molly's parents. His heart's in the right place."

"*Jah*, I've always believed that about Will," Edith admitted. "His family gave him the short end of the stick—and then so did Dat."

Asa smiled against her *kapp*. Edith was so kind, so willing to think the best of people. "But enough about Gingerich," he murmured. "I admire you for telling me such a difficult secret, Edith. It's still you I want to spend my time with—long beyond today, if we can make that work out."

When she turned in his embrace to smile at him, Asa felt dazzled. Her lashes were still damp with unshed tears, making her brown eyes appear huge and accentuating her innocence. He'd dated a number of girls when he'd been younger, but none of them held a candle to Edith.

Asa slowly lowered his lips to hers, consecrating this moment—the intimate information they'd shared—by sealing it with a kiss.

She closed her eyes and sighed . . . allowed

him to move his lips over hers before she responded with a sweetness that seared his soul. Asa suspected no one else had ever kissed her—not that he would ask. What Edith had shared with him seemed even more special now, and he vowed to love and honor her always.

When he clucked to Midnight again, he chuckled. "Guess I didn't exactly pick a private spot, did I? Anybody could've driven by—"

"But they didn't!" Edith cut in. She was blushing prettily, looking happy again. "If you continue in this direction, we'll soon pass the new house Rebecca Oliveri lives in, and beyond that is the farmstead the Witmers own."

Asa nodded, looking down the blacktop as the horse reached road speed. "Rebecca's the gal who designs Web sites, right? I need to talk to her about setting one up for our furniture repair business."

"*Jah*, she works fast—and she's so reasonable, even Dat says she's worth every penny," Edith replied. "Never thought I'd see the day when he advertised online. He thinks computers are the root of all evil."

Asa chuckled. "As with any tool, computers can be used for *gut* or for wicked purposes," he remarked. "Seems to me the businesses in Willow Ridge are prospering largely because of Rebecca's expertise—yet another sign of how progressive your town is."

"Soon to be *your* town," Edith said happily.

Asa felt immensely pleased at how easily they conversed. Soon they were driving into New Haven, the next sizable town. They enjoyed supper at the pizza place, and, by the time they were leaving, it was all he could do not to ask Edith if she'd marry him. His heart knew no other woman would ever suit him, but he wanted to do this right. Asa wanted Cornelius Riehl to see that he was capable of supporting Edith and their family, and—although it wasn't traditional to ask for it—he hoped to receive her father's blessing before he proposed.

They were pulling out of the parking lot when Edith gasped. "Oh! There's someone behind those evergreens. I hope Dat's not been following us on the sly."

Asa turned quickly in the seat, but he saw no sign of anyone. "Do you want me to go back and look?"

She waved him on. "No, no! It might've been my imagination," she admitted sheepishly. "Loretta caught Dat spying on her and Will once, when they were engaged, but I don't see how Dat could have known where we were headed. You must think I'm pretty silly."

"I think you're *pretty*," Asa countered, hoping to make her feel more at ease. "But I want to assure your father I've got the best of intentions, so there'll be no running from him or hiding. At twenty-seven, I'm not a kid in his *rumspringa*, after all. You deserve a man who honors his promises—and honors you, too."

Edith sucked in her breath. "Oh, Asa. What a lovely thing to say. Maybe if I quit ducking Dat's sternness—face him square-on about my feelings for you—he won't seem so intimidating anymore. You deserve a grown woman who states her convictions and stands by them, no matter who questions our relationship."

Asa's heart stilled. The *clip-clop* of Midnight's hooves punctuated the pause that begged a very important question. "May I court you, Edith?" he whispered.

She tucked her arm under his, leaning into him. "I thought you'd never ask," she said with a giggle. "I'm so happy I could just pop!"

When Asa entered the house to speak to her father, Edith remained outside to give them some privacy. As she gazed at the colors of the sunset, she prayed that Dat would listen to Asa . . . would believe that he was a decent, hardworking man who truly loved her.

The sound of the screen door closing made her look up. "How did it go?" she whispered as she joined Asa on the porch. "What did he say?"

Asa's smile appeared subdued, but he sounded hopeful. "It'll all work out," he murmured as he held her gaze.

Edith nodded, sensing she shouldn't ask him to elaborate. She said good night to Asa on the porch, knowing better than to kiss him. She watched him roll down the road in the buggy, however, briefly reliving the wonderful time she'd had talking and eating pizza . . . and agreeing to court him with the idea that they'd marry. *Soon! Let it be soon,* her thoughts sang.

"We need to talk, Daughter."

Edith closed the front door against the chill of evening, reminding herself of how she'd decided to face up to Dat rather than cowering beneath his stern gaze. Loretta and Rosalyn, who'd put the babies to bed, sent her sympathetic glances from the couch. Loretta's toothbrush "needle" moved swiftly in and out of the oval rug she was making, while Rosalyn sat alongside her keeping the long strips of fabric from tangling.

Dat gazed intently at Edith from his recliner. The oil lamp beside him flickered, making his crow's-feet and facial creases more pronounced. "I'm only going to say this once, Edith," he stated. "It's too soon for you to be thinking of marriage to Asa Detweiler. What you perceive as love and devotion are merely the romantic fantasies of a young, inexperienced girl."

Edith steeled herself against his criticism, knowing she had to tread carefully. "How old were you and Mamm when you courted?" she asked, although her mother had told her that story long ago.

"I was twenty-six and she was—but that was different!" he insisted. "We'd known each other all our lives."

"Asa's twenty-seven, and established in a business," Edith ventured hesitantly. It felt so foreign, standing up to her father. "He's buying the acreage and house across the road, and he and his brother are building their shop there."

"But his whole scheme—this do-gooder inclination to raise those twins—is a ticket to disappointment!" Dat declared. "And he's told me he's gotten Will Gingerich involved, as well. I predict that someone in Will's family will come to claim those babies any time now, and you and your sisters will be left heartbroken."

Edith glanced at her sisters, who appeared very focused on Loretta's rug. She didn't expect them to speak up—they'd spent their lives obeying whatever Dat said, after all—but she felt very lonely and vulnerable. If only Mamm were here to buffer her father's verbal blows . . .

Edith took a deep breath. "Asa came to speak to you because he—he doesn't want you to think we're sneaking around, or—"

"Puh! For generations, Amish couples have made their plans first and announced them to their parents later," Dat interrupted. "Now that I know Detweiler's intentions, I can disagree with them and thwart him every chance I get. You're too young to marry him, Edith. End of discussion."

Resentment swelled within her, a defiance she'd been taught to subdue all her life. Rather than hang her head and slip away in defeat, however, Edith let out the breath she'd been holding. With a last look at Dat's inscrutable expression, she went resolutely to her room to check on the twins.

Leroy and Louisa slept sweetly in their bassinets. Edith felt such a fierce love for them, such a determination to see them through their trials and tribulations, that she had no inclination to cry over the cross words her father had just flung at her.

And that was a start, wasn't it? For once she hadn't cowered before him. She'd spoken her mind, quietly, though she'd gotten no valid answers in return—for her mother had been seven years younger than her father, only nineteen when they'd married. Just as Edith was.

Help me through this, Mamm, Edith prayed as she gazed out into the darkness. *This will all work out for those who love the Lord—and for these precious little twins.*

CHAPTER THIRTEEN

A s church let out over at the Wagler place,
Luke watched out the window while kids
rushed from the house with whoops and whistles
to release their pent-up energy. He recalled those
three-hour Old Order services that had seemed
endless when he'd been young. He greatly
preferred the more concise sermons and services
at the Mennonite fellowship he and Nora now
attended. He turned toward her, smiling at the
way she sat in the recliner with her shoes kicked
off, reading a craft magazine.

"Ready to head next door?" he asked. "I'm
hoping Will Gingerich has arrived—and it'll be
interesting to see how Cornelius is reacting to
Asa's being here for the weekend. Never a dull
moment in that family, it seems."

Nora dropped her magazine to the floor. "And
I'm looking forward to a lot of *gut* food I didn't
have to prepare myself—and to visiting with
everybody. It was such a busy week, I've hardly
seen my parents or the newlyweds."

"We can guess where Ira and Millie have been
hiding themselves," Luke teased. "I'll grab the
lemon cake you made."

"Hope it's fit to eat. If it weren't for box mixes,
I wouldn't bake." Nora smoothed her apron over

her colorful floral dress, chuckling. "The beauty of the common meal is that you don't know who brought what unless they mention it. If folks make faces when they taste my cake, I'll keep my mouth shut."

As they walked down the hill to the Wagler place, Luke reveled in the brisk April morning. The lush green grass, cream-colored dogwood blooms, and the deep pink redbud trees made spring his favorite season. In a few more weeks the mid-Missouri heat would set in, and they'd be praying for rain. When they stepped inside the crowded Wagler house, Nora joined the ladies in the kitchen while Luke headed into the main room, which had been greatly expanded for church by taking down most of the interior walls.

The men were rearranging the wooden pew benches and setting up tables for the meal. Luke spotted Asa and made his way through the crowd, greeting everyone along the way. He noticed a shorter, compactly built fellow with sandy hair and observed the ease with which he maneuvered a long wooden bench. Was this Will? Even camouflaged by his white shirt sleeves, the muscles bunching in his shoulders suggested that this young man was well acquainted with physical labor.

"Hey there, Asa!" Luke spoke above the other men's conversations. "Quick now! What were the sermons about this morning?"

Asa straightened to his full height, chuckling. "Bishop Tom preached on the parable of the prodigal son—about how God welcomes us all home when we see the error of our ways and ask His forgiveness," he replied. "Your brother spoke on the virtues of being a *gut* Samaritan, helping folks who're down on their luck.

"And this, by the way, is Will Gingerich," Asa added as he gestured toward the sandy-haired fellow. "Will, this is your new boss and landlord, Luke Hooley."

Luke stuck out his hand, sensing that Will hadn't smiled so brightly in quite a while. He was a nice-looking fellow with a sad reserve about him—and a handshake that left no doubt about his physical strength. "Glad you made it for church, Will," he said. "This is a tight-knit district of *gut*-hearted souls. You know they're tolerant and forgiving if they allow a fellow who signed on with the Mennonites to come eat with them after church."

Will chuckled before his expression waxed more serious. "I appreciate your taking a chance on me, Luke," he said earnestly. "Lately I've felt like that fellow in Ben's sermon who got beaten and left for dead, so it means a lot that you've offered me a job and a place to stay just on Asa's recommendation."

Luke returned Will's steady gaze. The words of warning he'd planned—the rules he expected his new, untested farmer to follow—went unsaid. "Let's chalk it up to God's providence that some cropland came up for sale, and that you're available to work it," he remarked. "Maybe later today we can walk the farm, and figure out what crop will grow best in each field. I'll show you your apartment, too."

"Looking forward to it." Will's lips twitched. "I think I'll sleep better now, without all the ghosts that haunted my other place—and where I can keep an eye on the twins. They already look so much healthier and happier than when I brought them here."

Luke nodded. "They have a lot of guardian angels in Willow Ridge. Hard for folks to resist those bright eyes and cute faces."

"You've got that right." Will brightened. "Will you eat with Asa and me? We could compare a lot of notes and be readier for me to start work tomorrow if we talk now, *jah*?"

"I like the way you think, Will."

As they devoured sliced ham, macaroni salad, and other cold dishes the women had set out, Luke enjoyed getting acquainted with Will. It amazed him that Gingerich and Asa seemed like close friends despite the accusation that had nearly brought them to blows last week. After they'd enjoyed some coconut cream pie and lemon cake, the three of them rose from the table. Luke wasn't surprised that Asa made a beeline for Edith.

"Detweiler's got it bad," Luke remarked as he watched Asa pick up the twins' baskets to follow Edith out the back way. Even as he joked about Asa's devotion to his new girlfriend, Luke felt a twinge of envy because they already looked like a close family. Maybe someday he and Nora would make a baby. . . .

"You're right." Will's response cut into his thoughts. "And Cornelius is taking *bad* to a whole new level."

When Luke followed Will's gesture, Deacon Riehl's expression made his jaw drop. "*Jah*, Asa told me he'd stated his intentions after he brought Edith home from a date last night. He suspected she'd catch some flack after he left."

"I think they're both going to catch some now," Will murmured, shaking his head. "It was the same for Loretta and me when Cornelius decided we shouldn't be engaged anymore. I lost all claim to our farm when my brothers took it over, you see."

Luke watched Cornelius follow Edith and Asa outside, wondering why the head of the Riehl family always seemed so unhappy. From outward appearances, he had a nice home, three caring daughters, and a clock business that was off to a prosperous start here in Willow Ridge—not to mention a steady income from the eggs they supplied to the mill store.

"Let's head over to the farm," Luke suggested as

he stood up. "You'll have time to get acquainted with folks after we finish our walk-around."

Will smiled at the folks Luke introduced him to as they made their way between the tables. Once they were outside, they strolled quickly along the county blacktop. "I'm not much *gut* with names, but it seemed like most of the folks I just met are Hooleys," he said lightly. "You and your brothers seem to be the pillars of Willow Ridge."

Luke considered this as they passed the café. "We can't forget about the women," he said. "Without Miriam, my brother Ben wouldn't have become nearly so successful—and I credit my Nora with the shaking up I needed to make the mill profitable. The gals here run their households, of course, but most of them are also engaged in some sort of business activity."

"Really? That's different," Will murmured. "Most bishops wouldn't allow that."

"Bishop Tom finally convinced Miriam she should be staying home with their baby, Bethlehem, but before that she started baking around three every morning and didn't go home from the café until about twelve hours later," Luke explained. "Her sister, Leah Kanagy, takes a lot of homegrown produce to the farmers' markets—and keeps bees. Seth Brenneman's Mary makes Amish dolls for Nora's shop."

"And I suppose Loretta Riehl is still making rugs. And I bet Edith's weaving her baskets when the twins aren't keeping her busy," Will said as he gazed wistfully toward the tall white house where they lived.

"*Jah*, and Nora's selling those in her shop, as well. And meanwhile, here we are," Luke said as he gestured toward his new farm. "I take possession of the place next week, but the previous owner's fine with our getting into the fields while the weather's right for planting. What do you think?"

Will stood at the roadside, taking a long look at the lay of the land . . . the stubble and dried stalks from last year's crops. "Nice and flat," he murmured. "Doesn't look to have many low spots where water collects after a heavy rain, either. I hope it's not a problem that I don't have any draft horses or equipment. You probably wonder about the state of my affairs, considering how I packed all my earthly belongings into one buggy and wagon, which my two horses pulled."

"Ira and I didn't come to Missouri with much more than some bags of seeds and the clothes on our backs," Luke said with a shrug. "Earlier this year we bought a team of mules from a fellow in Bloomingdale—east of Cedar Creek—and we latched onto some bigger planters at an auction, too. We finished planting our places east of town this week, so the mules and equipment are coming here next."

"You've got some of Jerome Lambright's mules?

Hot dog!" Will said with a grin. "I watched his teams perform at a farm show last year. Fine-looking animals—and they have a lot of endurance bred into them."

"Jerome trained this team especially for farming. Picked them for their temperaments when they were first foaled, and kept the six of them together while he worked with them." Luke liked the way this conversation was going. It was a point in Gingerich's favor that he didn't insist on working with Belgians, as some farmers did. "We'll get the oats in first. By the time they're planted, the weather'll be warm enough to plant the corn and popcorn."

Will studied Luke for a moment and then gazed out over the fields again. "You and Ira must be doing really well, considering how you came here with practically nothing," he murmured. "It's my dream to own my own farm someday, but my wife's doctor bills and my family situation have set me back."

Touched by Will's pensive admission, Luke quickly gripped his shoulder. "Ira and I've been blessed by a lot of favorable circumstances we didn't foresee when we came here. Let's start believing that the same blessings will come your way now that you've moved beyond your troubles."

"*Denki* for that thought, Luke," Will murmured. "I'll do my best to believe it—and I'll do my best work for you and Ira, too."

As they walked across the front field to assess the land beyond the house and the outbuildings, Luke sensed that Will Gingerich would be yet another blessing—another asset to his and Ira's expanding mill business.

But you'll have to keep Cornelius Riehl's nose out of your business—and Will's, he thought. If Riehl started in on Will about the circumstances of the twins' birth—or what an inconvenience they were—Luke suspected his new farmer might lose his focus or want to leave town.

He kept this thought to himself as he and Will ambled back toward the Waglers', where clusters of men sat in lawn chairs and kids played tag and hide-and-seek. When Will headed toward the girls who were playing volleyball—which included Loretta and Rosalyn Riehl, Savilla Witmer, Hannah Brenneman, Katie Zook, and Nellie Knepp—Luke had to smile at his instincts. All of those girls were single and would probably welcome Will's attention, or his help on their side of the net.

Luke waved at Nora, who was helping Miriam and Lydia carry the leftover desserts to a table beneath the trees. He continued toward the back pasture to see how the Waglers' alfalfa was looking, as he'd put in an order for several bales of it to feed his horses and mules. When he passed the stable, he heard familiar voices—but he sensed his brother Ben and Bishop Tom were discussing church business, so he left them to it. Luke paused at the wire fence, immersed in the sight of the rich green alfalfa crop. The river formed a natural boundary to the north, widening as it approached his mill.

". . . went to the Riehls' yesterday to pick up a clock he'd cleaned for me," Ben was saying. "Cornelius was out on a call, so Rosalyn took me downstairs to the shop. Did you realize that his workbench blocks the vault door?"

Luke stood absolutely still. Why would Ben care about where the clockmaker's workbench was?

"Now why would he do that?" Bishop Tom asked in a concerned tone. "Come time that somebody needs a cash advance from our Aid fund . . ."

"I didn't quiz Rosalyn about it, of course," Ben continued. "I don't think Cornelius would be careless enough to tell the girls the district's vault is behind that wooden door—or how much money we've accumulated in it."

Luke swallowed hard. It wasn't any of his business, what the bishop and a preacher were saying about their district's "bank," because only the leaders of the church knew where it was kept. Every Amish community stashed an aid fund in a secret place, adding to it when members contributed their offerings twice a year—and dipping into it to cover disasters, such as when the Sweet

Seasons Bakery Café and the Shrocks' quilt shop had burned down last Christmas. Because he was now a Mennonite, he *really* shouldn't be privy to such information—but Luke couldn't help over-hearing the two intense voices that carried over to him on the breeze.

"Maybe it's just his way of makin' sure the girls don't discover the money when they're cleanin'," Tom said. "He was the deacon in his Roseville district, too, so he knows the location of the fund shouldn't get out to anybody else."

"I just thought it was odd," Ben replied. "The door's padlocked, remember—"

"*Jah*, you're right. So the girls wouldn't stumble onto that money anyway."

"—and only the three of us have keys. But now *two* of us can't get into the vault if Cornelius isn't home," Ben continued urgently. "It's not like you or I are going to clear off the clocks he might be working on, and maybe drop the cogs and pieces lying loose on his workbench."

"It's a puzzlement. I'll have to think of a way to ask him about this without seemin' suspicious," Tom said. "It was just so convenient that he was already a deacon when he traded houses with Reuben. . . ."

Maybe too convenient? Luke walked toward the mill, away from any further information he didn't really want to know. He didn't like to assume that Cornelius Riehl had barricaded the vault door for nefarious reasons—just as he didn't want to believe Loretta's father had broken up her engagement to Will simply because the other Gingerich brothers had displaced him. He shook his head over Cornelius's demand for higher egg pay—claiming it was a way to cover the extra costs of keeping the twins.

Let it go—but keep it in your mental file, Luke thought as he circled back to the Wagler place by way of the road. He had a lot of more pleasant things to think about on this sunny afternoon, and his redheaded wife—looking pretty in her flowery dress as she smiled at him from her lawn chair—was definitely one of them.

As Asa rode into Clifford that evening, he was filled with so much urgent news about the farm and Edith and Will—and Edith!—to share with his brother that he felt like a kernel of popcorn dancing in a hot skillet.

The For Sale sign on the shop building caught him up short.

Asa sat astride Midnight for several moments, staring. Not only had Drew gotten the place listed with Kristin, the real estate agent, but the windows were so clean they glimmered. In what little daylight remained, he could see that the whole place appeared freshly renovated. Had the facade been painted?

After he tended his horse, Asa went inside and

turned on the gas shop lights. The large main room had been painted pale sage, and although their in-progress furniture pieces were all pushed to the center, he could tell the wood floors had been cleaned. Even the back storage rooms and the office looked tidier.

"Drew?" he called out as he took the apartment steps two at a time. "Hey, what-all did you do while I was in—"

Asa stopped short in the apartment doorway. The rooms had that hushed feeling that told him his brother wasn't home. Here, too, the walls were now pale gray-green, and the sparse furniture huddled in the center of the main room. It was a shame their home and shop looked better now than they had while they'd lived here the past few years. And it was a miracle that the transformation had taken place in the day and a half he'd been gone.

The stove had been cleaned, and so had the kitchen floor. On their tiny table, Asa found Kristin's business card and the invoice from a cleaning and painting service for thirteen hundred dollars.

Money well spent, Asa thought as he glanced into the bedroom. Now the building was ready for prospective buyers to view, and it stood a better chance of selling for more money.

At the sound of Drew's boots on the stairs, Asa went out to greet him. "Wow!" he said as his brother entered the apartment. "Fine idea, getting the place spruced up."

Drew smiled as he set a pizza box on the coffee table. "Kristin's the one to thank for that suggestion—and for knowing who could do the work so fast. How're things on the Willow Ridge end?"

Asa grinned as he plopped down on the couch. "You won't believe how fast the pieces are falling into place," he began. As he explained about the Hooleys' purchasing the farm, planning to sell them the acreage when they were ready, Drew nodded.

"That makes a lot of sense—saves us from having to invest so much, too." He took the chair nearest the coffee table and helped himself to a slice of the steaming pizza. "And what did you do about a building for the shop?"

"The Brenneman brothers across the road had already prepped some sketches and crunched some numbers for us," Asa replied eagerly. As he showed his brother the paperwork Aaron had given him, summarizing their construction choices, Drew seemed a lot readier to relocate.

"I vote for the metal building," Drew said after he'd glanced at the figures. "It costs more, but it'll require less maintenance. It'll make us look prosperous from the get-go, too—because if Willow Ridge is like most Plain towns, the shops are frame construction or even outbuildings that have been repurposed."

223

Asa's eyebrows rose as he helped himself to the pizza. His brother was making some astute observations. "*Jah*, Nora's Simple Gifts shop was once a high-dollar horse barn, and the other places look pretty typical. Wooden buildings painted white, mostly. We really need to get you up there to meet—"

"I'm ready to move," Drew cut in. "The prospect of getting this place ready to sell was holding me back, but my time was well spent this weekend. Watching those guys paint with their sprayers and then clean the windows and these old floors was *amazing*." He eyed Asa with a cryptic smile. "But not as amazing as Edith, if the shiny-bright smile on your face is any indication of how you spent your time with her."

Asa laughed out loud. "Edith! How can I describe her with mere words?" he said, aware he was being a little melodramatic. "Long story short, we're courting!"

Drew's eyes widened. "*That* was fast."

"It's meant to be. Just looking into her big brown eyes, watching her tend the twins—who're growing like weeds thanks to goat milk from the bishop's wife—tells me she's the woman God chose to be my wife." Asa ate for a moment, wondering how much personal stuff to share. He didn't want to betray Edith's trust; the two of them had talked of some very personal matters.

"If it weren't for her *dat*'s objections, I could see us getting hitched very soon—"

"Why does it matter what he thinks?" Drew challenged. "You're both of age, right? And both already members of the Old Order church. Right?"

Asa sighed. He suspected Edith had been subjected to more of her father's lectures after he'd left this afternoon. It bothered him that Cornelius Riehl was so quick to find fault with him, and with Will—and with everything else, it seemed. "We wanted to do this on the up-and-up, because two little babies are involved," he explained. "But when I asked Edith's *dat* for his blessing, he laughed in my face. He thinks this whole situation is even more dubious now that Will Gingerich has moved to Willow Ridge to farm for Luke Hooley."

Drew considered this as he went to the fridge for two cans of soda. "How's Edith handling all this? Most girls would obey their *dats* and call off the courting on their fathers' say-so."

Asa smiled. "Not Edith! She says my commitment to her has inspired her to stand up to her father, and to live life the way she sees fit. She's one of a kind, Drew."

Pausing, Asa dared to make a sudden leap of faith. "I'm going to get a letter from our bishop and present it to Bishop Tom in Willow Ridge, to prove I'm in *gut* standing with the church here.

225

Once he publishes our intention to marry, there's nothing Cornelius can say! Then we can set our date for whenever we're ready!"

"That should make your intentions perfectly clear to everyone who matters," Drew said with a decisive nod. "And it establishes the two of you as a family where those twins will grow up the way they're supposed to."

Asa smiled warmly at his brother. "*Denki* for your vote of confidence, Drew. It means a lot that you're willing to change your whole life on this whim I've had about moving to Willow Ridge."

Drew shrugged. "What's left for us here in Clifford? We've always been loners—outsiders— here in a town of mostly English. Our parents might not like it that we're moving farther away, but they'll be happy about your finding a girl to hitch up with. Now they'll start prodding me to do the same."

"*Jah*, that's how it works," Asa murmured. "Will was getting acquainted with the single girls on Sunday. He had several of them to choose from."

"That's all I need to hear!"

As they polished off their pizza, Asa felt grateful for his brother's change of heart. He'd always suspected that Drew stopped to visit a girlfriend or two while Asa was on furniture-finding trips or making deliveries, but he hadn't pressed for the details because his brother tended to keep his love life to himself—probably so their parents wouldn't hound him about settling down.

Asa smiled. Someday soon he'd go tell their parents his good news—but he had other priorities, too. "I'm going to deliver that bedroom set to Hal Gillespie tomorrow. My goal now is to finish the other projects I've taken on for customers around here so we don't have to haul those pieces to Willow Ridge," he reasoned aloud. "And I'll call Aaron Brenneman tomorrow, to get him going on our new building."

"Cool! I'll upholster and sell the pieces we've already got, rather than going to any more sales." Drew looked around at the walls of their main room. "If it's all the same to you, I'd like to finish off the upper level of the new shop as an apartment, so I won't be horning in on you newlyweds."

Asa was surprised his brother felt that way, but he reminded himself that Drew hadn't yet seen the house they were buying. "Plenty of rooms where we're going—four bedrooms and an attic that could be remodeled, if you feel the need for more privacy," Asa insisted. "That way you wouldn't have to scrounge up your own meals, or—"

"Maybe I like the idea of coming and going without interrupting your um, *schedules*," Drew put in with a knowing smile. "And maybe sharing a house with two babies will be more of an adjustment than I'm ready for. Although . . . if I think sharing your place will work out, we could rent out the apartment. It would be another source of income."

Asa considered this idea. He might feel the same way if he were going to be the bachelor rather than the new husband in this situation. "Might as well have the Brennemans finish the upstairs while the place is under construction, then. They'll do it faster and a lot better than we would."

"Can't argue with that."

Asa smiled. It felt good to reach this level of understanding with his brother. The whole shift to Willow Ridge would go much more smoothly now that Drew seemed ready to make the move.

I want to move there tomorrow—load up the stuff and be there when Luke signs the final papers, he thought eagerly. *Having patience is the hardest part.*

CHAPTER FOURTEEN

Nora looked up from tagging new merchandise Thursday morning, returning Edith's bright smile as she came inside. "*Gut* morning, girlie. I just opened the shop, and you're my first visitor."

"Dat went to Kansas City for clock parts, so we got an early start to our day," Edith replied. "I have these three bigger baskets for you, and a few smaller ones in the buggy yet. I'll be right back!"

As Edith jogged outside, Nora picked up the largest basket and admired the intricate tricolor pattern at its upper rim. She was always excited when her crafters brought in items unlike anything else in her store, because fresh merchandise kept her regular customers coming back.

"These are fabulous, Edith!" she said when the girl returned with another basket that held several smaller ones of various interesting shapes. "They all look so tightly woven and sturdy. And every one of them is different!"

"Here's my inventory list," Edith said, handing over a piece of notebook paper that listed her eight baskets and her prices. "This was a *gut* way to use up some of the dribs and drabs of supplies I had—"

"Every crafter accumulates those," Nora put in.

"—and it kept me busy after Asa went back

home on Sunday," the girl continued in a rush. "I—I won't have time to make more baskets for a while, though. I'll be sewing my wedding dress and apron, and I told Rosalyn and Loretta I'd make their new side-sitter dresses, too."

Nora nearly choked in surprise. "You're already planning your wedding? But you've only known Asa—"

"Two weeks today," Edith said with a giddy grin. "He asked if he could court me this past weekend!"

Nora bit back a lecture. She didn't have the heart to spoil this young woman's dreams. "Well, congratulations," she murmured as she searched for appropriate words. "Have you set a date?"

"We'll do that soon," Edith replied with a confident nod. "My sisters and I saw a bulldozer across the road today where the new Detweiler furniture shop will be, so if the Brennemans are getting the foundation ready, it won't be long before the building goes up. I'm thinking Asa will be here to look it over this weekend."

Nora couldn't help but be happy for this dear, compassionate girl, yet she still had reservations about the whole situation. "Asa's a very nice guy," she said. "And Luke's glad he recommended Will Gingerich to do the farming, but—"

"You think it's too soon, don't you?" Edith asked with a hint of disappointment. "Believe me, Dat's already read me the riot act. I'm either too young to marry, or this is all moving too fast, or he's determined that Will or his family will claim the babies and things won't be the same between Asa and me."

Nora cleared her throat. "Those reasons have occurred to me, too," she murmured. "The voice of my own experience is crying out to warn you of the pitfalls you're too ecstatic to see, Edith. What's your hurry? Once Asa and his brother move here, you'll have all the time you need to get better acquainted. To be sure you're suited to each other."

Edith looked away, feigning interest in the pottery pieces Nora had been tagging. "I—I love him, Nora," she whispered. "He's all I can think about."

Nora grasped Edith's hand. "I know all about what you're feeling," she said gently. "When I married Tanner I was barely eighteen. I thought he was the handsomest, most industrious, most loving man I could possibly find. That was after I'd had Millie out of wedlock and left her for my brother and his wife to raise. I was getting by on what I earned cleaning a couple of motels that Tanner's family owned."

Edith's brown eyes widened at this information. "You married an English fellow?"

"Yup. I didn't think my family here would ever accept me again. When wealthy, up-and-coming Tanner proposed to me, I thought he'd be my ticket out of perpetual poverty," Nora recounted quietly. "I believed him when he vowed to love, honor, and cherish me. But he was older and more worldly, and after about ten years I discovered he was seeing another woman."

Edith sucked in her breath. "What did you do?"

"What *could* I do?" she asked, squeezing Edith's hand. "Tanner divorced me, without warning. Said I was boring and unsophisticated. I had to get smart fast, because he thought I was too naïve to press him for more money. I hired a lawyer and went after a *much* larger settlement than Tanner was going to give me.

"As I was licking my wounds, figuring out what to do with my life, I realized I hadn't had the vaguest idea about what real love was all about," Nora went on. "I'd been so enamored of Tanner's looks and wealth and sweet-talk—thrilled that he wanted to be with somebody like little *me*—I totally missed the signs that he was only playing games."

"That was really cruel of him."

"*Jah*, but it was really stupid of me, as well," Nora said earnestly. "I rushed in with my heart all aflutter instead of having my head on straight."

"But then you found Luke," Edith said, her smile returning.

"And from the first, I knew him for a flirt and a flatterer. He thought it'd be a feather in his cap to land an English woman who drove a fancy car and could afford the biggest house in Willow Ridge." Nora's eyebrows rose as a catlike smile overtook her face. "I didn't believe a word Luke Hooley said—and I told him that to his face. Made him prove himself every step of the way."

Edith considered this, but the lovestruck glow remained on her face. "It'll be that way with Asa, I just know it. He's such a fine, sincere man—willing to take on somebody else's kids, too."

"But once you're hitched, it's forever," Nora insisted. "For Amish couples, divorce is never an option."

Edith sighed. "I'm so ready to have a family, Nora," she whispered. "And ready to be out from under Dat's roof, too. Asa's nothing at all like him, you know."

Nora's heart went out to the young girl standing before her. She had her doubts about some of Cornelius Riehl's business practices, but it wasn't her place to pry. "*Jah*, I wanted to live anywhere except with my *dat*, too. He was a preacher—and when he found out I was pregnant, he wouldn't have believed that a bishop from another district had taken advantage of me, so I didn't tell him that part at first," she explained. "I lived with an aunt until Millie was born, and then I left. I know all about having a *dat* who makes you follow all the Old Order rules and then casts you aside when you don't measure up."

Edith's expression wavered. She appeared

caught between Nora's hard-luck story and her own rose-colored images of love and romance.

"Just think about what I've said, okay?" Nora asked. "If Asa's the right man for you now—the husband God wants you to have—he'll be all the more loving and wonderful, say, six months from now. And by then, he'll have established his new shop so he can focus more on you and the twins."

"You might be right," Edith mused. When one of her father's clocks chimed and its music box played a short melody, she waited for the song to finish. "But like that clock, my life's ticking away, and I don't want to miss a minute of living with Asa. I've got plans for freshening up the house, making it ours, and—well, I need to be going," she added quickly. "My sisters are minding the twins, and I told them I'd be back as soon as I picked out our dress fabric at the quilt shop."

Nora kept her sigh to herself. *You can lead the horse to water . . .*

"*Denki* for speaking your mind, and for looking after me, Nora," Edith murmured. "Your words and friendship are such a gift to us girls now that our *mamm* is gone."

"Any time I can help, let me know," Nora insisted as her young friend headed for the door. Her warnings and advice had gone in one of Edith's ears and out the other, but Nora had spoken her mind. She'd expressed similar doubts to her daughter Millie about marrying Ira, yet hadn't that relationship turned out to be mature and mutually beneficial for her seventeen-year-old daughter and Luke's brother?

I hope I'm just an old mother hen who's clucking too much, Lord, Nora thought as she wrote out tags for Edith's beautiful baskets. *After all, I don't know everything, the way You do.*

Asa bounded up the steps to Bishop Tom's porch and knocked exuberantly on the door. On this beautiful Friday morning he felt like a man on his way to a finer life than he'd ever imagined. As he heard footsteps inside, he couldn't keep a wide smile off his face.

"Bishop Tom, *gut* morning!" he said when the door opened. "If you've got a minute, I'd like a word."

"Sure I do, for a fella like you," the bishop said as he swung the door open. "I was mighty excited yesterday, seein' a dozer doin' the dirt work for your new shop."

"They're to pour the foundation today, so I wanted to be here," Asa said. He stepped into the large front room, removing his straw hat and jacket. "Aaron says he's got his crew constructing the metal sides already, too, so once the concrete's set, the main walls can go up pretty fast."

"Those Brenneman boys are a fine team," Tom

remarked, gesturing for Asa to follow him. "If we talk in the kitchen, we can probably sample some of the goodies Nazareth's takin' from the oven. Ya timed this visit just right, Asa."

"*Gut* morning, young man!" Nazareth said as she deftly flipped a pan of sticky buns onto an oblong tray. "I'd figured to take fresh milk over for Leroy and Louisa, so maybe you'd like to do the carrying. Bet you're headed that direction anyway."

"I am, and I'd be happy to take it," Asa replied. His eyes widened as the bishop's wife plated two large, pecan-crusted rolls and carried them to the table. "It's the least I can do if you're going to feed me this way—and *denki* so much for providing the milk that's making those babies grow so well. How much do I owe you for that?"

Nazareth waved him off. "My little goats are tickled to help out. Truth be told, they give more milk than I have time to make into cheese for the mill store anyway," she admitted. "Think of it as labor you're saving me."

Asa was speechless for a moment. Where else had he ever experienced such generosity? Although he got along fine with the folks in Clifford and the neighbors near his parents' farm, he couldn't imagine them donating milk on a regular basis for babies who weren't even local. "Well, again, *denki* from Edith and Will and me," he said as he loosened the outer layer of his sticky bun with his fork. "You're a lifesaver, Nazareth—literally."

"*Jah,* she's a keeper," Tom remarked. When he smiled at his wife, his face glowed, and his crow's-feet deepened. "And it was a fine sight, as well, watchin' Will work the field nearest the road with a team of Percheron mules. We had him over for dinner yesterday. Nice young fella."

"He's pleased to be farming for Luke and Ira. Ready for a fresh start—and oh my word," Asa blurted. "This sticky bun is the *best,* Nazareth."

She beamed at him from the kitchen counter. "I enjoy watching you young men tuck away so much food. Tom and I are of an age we have to cut back some, if we're to squeeze through the doorways."

The bishop laughed along with Asa, and then looked at him intently. "But ya didn't come here to discuss us gettin' old and tubby," he remarked as he cut into his roll. "Ya looked like a man on a mission when I answered the door."

Asa pulled an envelope from his jacket pocket and handed it to the bishop. "It's a letter from my bishop back home, telling you I'm a member in *gut* standing—because I want you to publish my plans to marry Edith at your next church service."

Bishop Tom's mouth fell open. "I'm all for young folks gettin' hitched," he finally managed to say. "But this is feelin' rather *sudden,* son—"

"Why, it was the day of the Hooley wedding—

just a couple weeks ago—when Jerusalem and I found you on the side of the road," Nazareth recalled. "Are you sure you and Edith are ready for this? Some folks'll wonder if you're not healed from that hit you took on the head."

Asa chuckled. He'd figured his announcement would cause a stir. "I *am* back in town partly for a follow-up visit with Andy Leitner about my concussion," he replied. "But otherwise, it's just a case of two hearts beating as one from the moment they met."

Bishop Tom read the brief letter and set it away from his plate. As he cleared his throat, he focused intently on Asa. "I hope you're not gonna tell me ya got carried away, so now you're savin' Edith from any embarrassment nine months down the road."

Asa's fork clattered to his plate. He had *not* expected the bishop to hint about *that*. "Absolutely not," he insisted. "Edith's not that kind of girl, and I wouldn't turn her into one."

Tom let out a relieved sigh. "All the same, it's feelin' a bit rushed."

"We haven't set a date yet," Asa pointed out. "I just want everyone here—especially her *dat*—to know my intentions are honorable. Long-term."

"*Jah*, it's forever," the bishop insisted as he glanced at Nazareth. "I'd not wish my previous humiliation on anybody, after my first wife left me for an English fella. When the marriage vow's broken, it stirs up turmoil God never intended His children to suffer." Tom looked away, as though recalling this event still caused him pain. "Lettie's leavin' shattered our family, even though our kids were grown and married," he murmured. "Had Nazareth not come along, I'd still be a desolate man today."

Asa's eyes widened. He thought carefully about how to word the question that came to mind. "You . . . you remarried, Bishop? I didn't think the Old Order allowed—"

"We got word that Lettie was killed in a car accident with her English husband," Nazareth explained as she came to stand beside Tom. "Even so, folks looked askance on our relationship for a while. We're just saying, Asa, that you'd better search your soul long and hard before you take Edith as your wife. It's a noble idea, raising those babies together, but it'll bring challenges you can't foresee. I'll go milk the goats now and let you fellows talk."

As his wife left the kitchen, Tom's gaze followed her with a gratefulness that touched Asa's heart. "I haven't heard that you're any closer to knowin' who their father is," the bishop continued. "That revelation alone could upset your apple cart in a major way."

"Will and I have talked about that," Asa murmured. "We figure his wife took that secret to her grave—especially if she never told the man responsible that she was in the family way."

"Will's a case in point. The way Vernon Gingerich understands it, he and Molly married pretty quick," Tom continued. "And ya can see how *that* disaster might've been avoided had they taken more time to court. Sad to say, but Will's folks suspect Molly and her parents knew of her condition and were understandably eager to get her married off."

Asa's eyes widened. He'd talked at length with Will, but Gingerich had never hinted that he'd suspected Molly's condition when they'd married. Maybe that's why her parents had provided the couple with a home and a farm, such as it was . . .

"Well," Asa finally replied, "we're not worried about that being the case with Edith and me. When I saw the way she put the twins' welfare ahead of everything else, I had to stand by her. It was the sort of commitment that made me love and respect Edith completely."

The bishop nodded. He went over to the calendar on the kitchen wall. "All right then, I'll announce your engagement on our next church Sunday—which'll be May third," he said. "But that doesn't mean ya have to set your date right away."

Asa nodded, sensing it was best to leave the subject as it stood. He and Tom visited about Asa's furniture business until Nazareth came in through the back door with two large pails. She opened the freezer and stuck two bottles of frozen water into each bucket. "We cool this fresh milk down immediately, so it doesn't smell so *goatsy*," she explained. "If you'll take this on over to Riehls', the girls will know to refrigerate it right away."

Seeing that as his cue, Asa put on his hat and took his leave. He walked carefully along the gravel road so he wouldn't slosh the milk, gazing at the tall white house where Edith and the twins lived. He'd accomplished the first of his missions—the one he'd anticipated as the biggest challenge—so he could relax and look forward to seeing Edith . . . hopefully take her along when he went to deliver the two large checks he'd brought with him.

When Edith opened the door, her smile was further proof that his plans with her were right on track. "Milkman, making a home delivery," he quipped. "Tom and Nazareth send along their best."

"They *are* the best," Edith replied as she escorted him to the kitchen. "We keep this milk in the extra fridge in the mudroom. I'll return those bottles and pails later. Right now I'm tickled to see *you,* Asa!"

"Hi there!" Rosalyn piped up as Loretta grinned at him. They were stirring something together on the stove, probably for the noon meal.

"Happy to be here. It's a big day," he said as he leaned over the side of the playpen. "And you kids make every day seem like a big day. Come here and see me."

He gently lifted the twins into his arms. When both Louisa and Leroy began laughing, smacking their hands on the sides of his face as though they recognized him, Asa felt ten feet tall. He reveled in their downy cheeks, bright eyes, and cheerful dispositions, anticipating the day when he could live with the twins . . . as their father.

He looked at Edith. "How about we take these two on a stroll? I'll be stopping to talk with Aaron, Andy, and Luke this morning, and I'd like you to come along."

"We can put them in the double stroller Annie Mae Wagler loaned me," she said as she went back into the mudroom to fetch it. "It dates back to when her brothers Josh and Joey were wee ones. She'll want it back when her own twins are born this summer, but meanwhile, we enjoy having it."

"*Jah*, they already love it," Loretta remarked as she chopped an onion into the pot on the stove. "We took them for a ride yesterday to watch the big dozers dig the hole for your shop foundation."

"While I'm here, I want to check on the concrete the crew's to be pouring today." Asa held the twins lower so Edith could position each of them in a stroller seat. "Aaron said his Mennonite buddies would be helping with some of the heavy equipment, so the shop will get built a lot faster." When he heard footsteps on the basement staircase, Asa turned. "*Gut* morning, Cornelius! Anything you need us to do for you while we're running our errands around town?"

Asa liked it that Edith's *dat* appeared surprised at his offer. At least for a moment, he'd caught the dour man off guard.

"It's the last Friday of the month. You can see if Nora's got any checks for us," Cornelius replied.

"Will do. See you all later." Asa walked ahead of Edith to open the door for her, and once he'd lowered the front end of the stroller down the porch steps to the ground, they headed toward the road.

"Oh, but this is fun! It's so *gut* to see you, Asa," Edith exclaimed. "What with all the activity across the road, you and your brother will be able to move in pretty soon."

Asa gazed down at her. Once they reached the gravel road, he took over pushing the stroller, keeping it to the side where the grass was mowed shorter. If this was how it felt to be a family, he couldn't wait to be doing it full-time. Forever.

"I gave Tom a letter from my bishop, saying I'm in *gut* standing with the Old Order church. He's going to announce our intention to marry on your next church Sunday," Asa blurted. Then he wanted to kick himself. "I—I guess I got so excited I forgot the obvious, and now I'm not going to do it as romantically as I'd intended to."

He stopped on the roadside, grasping Edith's slender shoulder. "Will you marry me, Edith? When you agreed that we were courting, I assumed—"

"Oh, *yes!* Yes, Asa, I will!" she cried out as she grabbed him in a hug.

Asa savored the warmth of her embrace, the immediate joy she'd shared with him. This road-side moment would live in his memory forever, scented by lilacs and lit by the morning sunshine. He would have to think of a fitting engagement gift—ways to show her he truly loved her, and to compensate for his oversight.

"Truth be told, I sewed my wedding dress yesterday," Edith admitted as she smiled up at him. "And Loretta and Rosalyn have agreed to be my *newehockers.* So you're not the only one who's been making assumptions."

Asa chuckled with relief. "Just another way we seem to be on the same page, aware of what the other one's hoping for and dreaming about," he murmured. "I—I love you so much, Edith."

"And I can't think straight for being so in love with you, Asa," she replied.

The rest of the morning went by in a haze of happiness. Asa gave Aaron Brenneman a large deposit on the shop building, and his examination with Andy Leitner went well, and then Asa handed Luke a down payment for the house and the land that would soon be Detweiler property. He and Edith chatted briefly with Nora and picked up the checks for the clocks, rugs, and baskets she'd sold. Then Asa, Edith, and the twins—the four of them—were on their way.

The four of us. The sweetness of their togetherness made Asa an ecstatically happy man. He was aware of discussing the erection of the exterior shop walls on Monday, and talking about the final details of his property arrangement with the Hooleys, but he was mostly focused on Edith's happy smile, her lilting voice, and the way her love for Leroy and Louisa shone every time she spoke to them or touched them.

On their way back to the Riehl place, Asa waved his arm high above his head when he saw Will driving the mule team with the planter behind it. Will waved back, looking exultant even from across the field.

"What a glorious sight those Percheron mules make," Asa remarked, shading his face to get a better view. "They're so tall. And they step in time with one another, even while making the turn at the end of a row."

"Will's happy to be working with them, and to be farming for the Hooleys," Edith remarked with a nod. "He's a different man from the fellow who argued with you about fathering the twins awhile back."

A different man. As Asa gazed at Edith's dear face, he loved the way her dark brown bun was so neatly tucked up under her white *kapp* as its strings fluttered in the breeze. He knew all about the way a man's life could change the moment one important person believed in him.

CHAPTER FIFTEEN

During the following week, Edith considered the rainy days a blessing. She and her sisters couldn't work in the garden, so they spent most of their time painting at the house where she and Asa would make their home. With the windows open, a cool breeze kept the paint fumes to a minimum. The babies entertained themselves with little stuffed animals and the mobile Edith had attached to the playpen.

"The kitchen looks so much better now," Rosalyn said as she poured the paint from her roller pan back into the can. "I've never understood some of the odd colors English folks use in their rooms."

Loretta laughed. "*Jah*, sorry to say it, but the walls in here reminded me of something from the twins' diapers. A couple coats of butter yellow are a big improvement."

"And the fresh white on the cabinets makes the whole room look bigger, too," Edith said with a satisfied sigh. "Asa said Adam Wagler—the guy with the big remodeling wagon—would take down that far wall, so we might as well move on upstairs to the bedrooms."

"At the rate we're going, we'll be finished in a couple more days." Loretta glanced up at a battery clock they'd hung on the wall. "I'll head back to the house so Dat won't think we've forgotten about his dinner."

Edith slipped her arms around her sisters' shoulders, chuckling at their paint-splattered old dresses and kerchiefs. "*Denki* so much for your help," she murmured. "Doing all these rooms by myself would've overwhelmed me."

"Many hands make light work," Rosalyn quipped.

"It's fun to work where you and Asa will soon be living," Loretta put in. "And with the rooms being empty, it's a lot easier than painting at home would be—even though we'll have to tackle that chore one of these days."

"I don't see how Dat stands working downstairs, as dingy as those walls have gotten. But I shudder to think about moving his clocks and workbenches around to freshen up his shop." Rosalyn slipped into a plastic rain poncho and then playfully lifted Leroy from the playpen. "Let's get home, little man. You'll be fussing for your bottle pretty soon."

"I'll be right behind you with Louisa," Loretta said. "Won't take us long to stir up some pancakes and eggs. We've got leftover ham, too."

Edith nodded as she gathered their painting equipment. "I'll wash these trim brushes and be right there. We've got a package of new roller covers for this afternoon, when we change to pale blue, so we're all set."

The house got very quiet after her sisters left with the twins. Edith enjoyed having this time at the kitchen sink, getting the feel of the room where she'd be spending so much of her time someday soon. Living in this house with Asa would be an adjustment, after having Rosalyn and Loretta for her constant companions—especially during the day, when Asa worked in his shop. But she would have the twins to occupy—

"Aha! Here you are, the queen of this kitchen!"

Edith jumped at the sound of an unexpected voice. "Asa! I wasn't expecting to see you so soon after you spent the weekend here."

Asa grinned mischievously. He shook the rain from his straw hat and draped his slicker over the screen door as he closed it. "Thought I'd surprise you while I was out delivering a set of furniture," he replied. "We've got a buyer for our shop in Clifford. It's just a matter of signing off on the paperwork once the money comes through, so we're finishing our current orders before we have to move everything out."

"Oh, that's wonderful-*gut* news!" Edith returned his steady gaze, adoring the way he made her feel so pretty. When she realized she'd left the water running, she continued to rub the white paint from her brush. "I'd hug you, but I've got paint all over my hands."

"You've been busy. The kitchen looks fabulous." Asa slipped up behind her, wrapping his arms around her shoulders as he bussed her temple. "I can't wait until we're living here, you and I. The day will be here before we know it—"

"It's only four more days until Bishop Tom announces our intent to marry," Edith interrupted with a happy sigh. "My life feels so much fuller, so much more blessed, now that you're in it, Asa."

"I know all about that, pretty girl," he murmured.

When Edith turned her head Asa kissed her, as she'd hoped he would. Her cheeks went hot as she hurried to finish rinsing the paintbrushes. "How about if you join us for dinner? It'll only be pancakes and eggs, because Loretta and Rosalyn have been helping me, but—"

"Can't stay this time," Asa murmured apologetically. "But I'll return as soon as I can. This weekend, most likely."

Edith nodded. "You've got a lot to do. And truth be told, Dat's cranky today, so maybe it's best you'll not be surprising him."

Asa plucked his slicker from the door. "He'll have to get used to me sooner or later. But I'm glad we'll have our own place, instead of living at your house the way a lot of newlyweds would," he remarked. "Drew's fixing up an apartment above the shop, so our home'll be real cozy with just you and me, Edith. See you this weekend."

She returned his smile, her whole body aglow. "I'll be waiting."

Asa blew her a kiss and slipped out the door. A few moments later, Edith watched his two black horses pull an enclosed delivery van down the lane toward the road. It tickled her that he'd gone out of his way to see her again, if only for a few moments. How had he driven in without her being aware of it?

You were lost in your pretty thoughts. Focused on the future . . . But maybe he came the back way, on a path between the fields.

Through the window above the sink, Edith saw the van stop at the new metal building beside the road, where the Brennemans were working inside on this rainy day. The three brothers and Asa had spent most of Monday erecting the building, with the help of several local men, so now the putty-colored structure with its pumpkin metal roof stood as the most recent testament to Willow Ridge's growth. By the time Bishop Tom announced Asa and Edith's plans to marry on Sunday, the shop's interior would probably be finished enough that Asa and his brother could move their equipment and furniture into the new Detweiler Furniture Works.

This is happening so quickly and efficiently—and it's happening to me! Edith mused as she rinsed paint from the last brush. When she saw the van take off down the road, she blew Asa a kiss. She washed her hands and headed home to help with the noon meal, feeling so happy she didn't mind the rain or the puddles that soaked her old tennis shoes.

"Hello, Will!" she called out as she approached the house. "Too wet to do any planting today, *jah*?"

"Sure is," he replied as he rose from the porch swing. He was holding Louisa, feeding her a bottle. "Your sisters assigned me to the twins while they fix dinner. I believe the kids've put on another pound or two since I last saw them."

"They slurp down their goat milk, that's for sure," Edith said with a nod. She crossed the porch to lift Leroy from the playpen, and picked up the bottle that rested on the swing. "They've been *gut* supervisors while we were painting today."

"I saw Asa stop by the house, as well. I waved when he came out of his new shop, but I guess he didn't see me." Will held Edith's gaze as he swayed gently from side to side with the baby. "Seemed like he was in a hurry. I'm surprised he didn't come over to see the twins."

Edith considered this—and laughed at Leroy when he grabbed hold of the bottle to begin drinking. "Could be Asa had a certain time he was expected to deliver his furniture, and he knew he'd run late if he played with the babies. He was excited because they've sold their shop in Clifford."

"Wow, *that* happened faster than he'd figured on. Things are moving along."

"This Sunday Bishop Tom's publishing our plans to marry, too," she said. "So, see there? Lots of *gut* things have come from that confrontation you had with him on the roadside."

Will's eyes widened. "Please tell me you're planning on a long courtship, Edith," he pleaded. "Take it from me, marriage requires a lot of patience and adjusting even when it's just the two of you, let alone adding twins to the picture. I—I've wondered lately if I leaped before I looked when I hitched up with Molly, you know?"

Edith blinked. Was Will another naysayer, suggesting that she and Asa were rushing their relationship? "We haven't set the date," she hedged, hoping to avoid a troublesome conversation.

"Don't get me wrong. I loved Molly dearly," Will murmured. "But a couple more months of courting her would've revealed a *big* secret that would've changed everything. Just saying."

Edith didn't reply. She focused on Leroy's little fingers gripping his bottle . . . on his wispy hair, which was getting darker now, and on his deep blue eyes. The baby gazed up at her with so much love and trust; Edith's heart swelled at the thought of being his *mamm.*

For a fleeting moment, Leroy's forehead puckered, and his tiny eyebrows tilted down toward his nose. Edith held her breath. *Asa looks exactly that way when he's puzzled—or bothered by something.*

When the wee boy resumed sucking on his bottle, however, Edith's doubts disappeared. She'd been thinking about Asa so often lately that she'd momentarily superimposed his features over Leroy's. As often as her sisters tended the babies, neither of them had ever mentioned a resemblance to Asa, so she wouldn't go looking for one, either.

"Shall we help your aunts with the pancakes?" Edith murmured. "I'm thinking it's time for you and your sister to try some of the applesauce we'll be serving, too."

Leroy's laughter made Edith laugh, as well. His plump, happy face looked nothing like Asa's.

There you have it. Don't let your imagination run away with you.

As the courting buggy rounded the last curve and headed toward Willow Ridge on Saturday afternoon, Asa couldn't stop smiling. After a day of painting the new shop's interior, with help from the Riehl girls and Will, he and his brother could begin moving their furniture from Clifford. He'd just ordered a sturdy wooden sign from a fellow in Morning Star, and his hopes were flying high. Detweiler Furniture Works would reopen sooner than he'd ever thought possible.

"I'm glad we rode over to order the shop's

roadside sign from that fellow Luke told me about," he said to Edith. "Now that I've seen Morning Star, New Haven, and Higher Ground, I'm even more certain we'll have several places to sell our refurbished furniture. I was glad to see that poster about the upcoming flea market, too."

"*Jah*, this was my first visit to Morning Star," Edith remarked. "I liked the consignment shop there—in case I find time to make more baskets than Nora wants to carry."

Asa slowed the horse, hoping to enjoy this ride for as long as possible. "Seeing the refinished kitchen table and chairs there made me wonder about your preferences in furniture," he began softly. "We have a lot of rooms to fill, Edith. It would be more economical for me to refinish the bigger pieces myself, but . . . maybe you'd rather have a new kitchen or bedroom set. I really like what the Brennemans make—"

"*Jah*, I've been eyeballing their pretty pieces at Nora's," she cut in, "but their prices nearly stop my heart."

"You get what you pay for, sweetie." On a hunch, Asa steered the horse up the next hill. "They dovetail the joints and drawers, and they take extra pains selecting just the right wood for each set they make. Their finishing work is top-notch, too."

He smiled at Edith, determined to keep her brown eyes sparkling forever, just the way they were now. "In the long run, you save money by buying *gut* furniture one time, instead of having to replace it after a few years," he went on. "Let's stop at Simple Gifts before Nora closes for the day, and we'll browse in the Brennemans' shop sometime soon. I want you to pick out a roomful of furniture—without looking at the price tags—and that'll be your wedding present."

Edith's stunned expression startled him.

"Did I say something wrong?" Asa murmured as he urged the horse up Nora's lane.

She let out a nervous laugh. "Oh, no, I—well, I've never gotten to pick out furniture," she admitted in a rush. "We've had everything in our house since before I can remember."

"Perfect. I want this to be the most special gift you've ever received, Edith."

As she grabbed his hands and squeezed them, Asa thanked God for giving him such a fine idea. He worked on furniture nearly every day, so Edith's sudden joy over getting to select the pieces for their new home was a gift in itself. After he hitched the horse to the railing and helped her down from the buggy, Asa took her hand to enter Simple Gifts.

Just outside the door, Edith hesitated. "If I see something here I like, wouldn't it be better to ask Seth if he could make us something like it?" she asked in a tiny voice. "Nora tacks a considerable percentage onto the items she carries."

Asa was so in love with her, he couldn't speak for a moment. "I admire your frugality, Edith," he murmured. "But it might be a while before Seth and his brothers could get a roomful of furniture made for us—and after the way they set aside their other work to build my shop so quickly, I couldn't expect them to do that for me again. If you see what you want, say the word, and it's yours."

"Oh, Asa," she murmured. "You're so *gut* to me."

Asa's body thrummed as they entered the store. A few other customers strolled the aisles toward the back and upstairs, but no one else was looking at the furniture display. Asa couldn't miss the enchantment on Edith's face as she slowly walked the length of a beautiful oak table that was extended far enough to have ten matching chairs around it. A small printed card said there were two more leaves that went with the table, and four more chairs.

"*Gut* afternoon, Asa and Edith!" Nora called from the upstairs loft. "If you have questions, just holler. I'll be down in a bit."

Asa waved at her, grateful that Edith could shop uninterrupted. The expression on her dear face made him glad he'd spoken for her before some other man had caught her fancy. Edith was so easy to please—and so eager to please *him*. He could search the Plain world forever and not find another woman who made him feel so happy. So complete.

When Edith wandered over to a maple sleigh bed with a mirrored dresser and chest of drawers, Asa continued watching her. If this was the set she wanted, he might ask Seth to fashion them a matching bed in a larger size. Maybe the crowded shop was affecting his perception, but he suspected his feet would bump the tall, curved footboard.

Edith looked up at him. "This seems *short,* ain't so? It's a beautiful piece, but an open-ended bed might work better for you, Asa."

When her cheeks turned a modest pink, Asa chuckled. "You've been reading my thoughts again. When I was at the Brennemans' shop, I saw lots of other beds in progress, so—"

"I want *you* to find our bedroom set," she said earnestly. "It would be really special to know you'd refinished the wood and chosen the pieces especially for our room."

"I'll be happy to do that," he replied. "Next time we're at the house, we'll choose which room will be ours, and I'll get its dimensions."

"Oh, it's the one in the back corner, overlooking the pastureland." Edith grinned at him. "I painted that room myself—a clear blue that's a few shades lighter than your eyes."

Asa was too awestruck to think. She could have asked him for every piece of furniture in the store, and he would've bought it, just to keep the dazzling smile on her face.

"May I have this oak table and chairs, along with the hutch?" Edith asked after a few more moments of contemplation. "To my way of thinking, the kitchen table's the soul of a home. It's where folks gather each and every day to be nourished and to share their lives. It's where individual people become a *family*."

Asa felt such a welling up of emotion, he wasn't aware of Nora's coming over to join them.

"What a wonderful sentiment," the storekeeper murmured. "If you want this table set—or anything else in my store—for your new home, I'll deduct my consignment fees. As your wedding gift."

"But on a table and fourteen chairs—and the hutch," Asa protested, "you'd be cutting yourself out of hundreds of dollars, Nora. I wouldn't feel right if you did that for us."

"I wouldn't feel right if I didn't." Nora glanced toward the customers at the cash register. "I can have Seth deliver it whenever you're ready— no charge for that, either. I'm happy you'll be making your home with us in Willow Ridge, Asa."

Half an hour later, Asa left Simple Gifts feeling jubilant. The furniture Edith had chosen had cost more than he'd figured on paying for her wedding gift, but what more worthy person could he spend his money on? Edith was grinning, clasping her hands like a delighted little girl as she sat beside him in the buggy. It was a moment he knew he'd always recall—and in his excitement, he couldn't hold back.

"What if we set our wedding date for a week from this Thursday?" he blurted. "It's not as though my family will be coming from far away—"

"Nor mine. The ones who don't live in Roseville aren't able to travel anymore," Edith said in a tight, excited voice. Then she frowned. "But if that's the fourteenth of May, I'm pretty sure it's Ascension Day. I'm not sure how they celebrate here in Willow Ridge, but ordinarily folks are holding big family reunion picnics, playing games together, and—"

"So the day after that will be *perfect*," he insisted. "We can invite our family and friends to be here for Ascension Day and to stay for our wedding—we don't have to marry on a Thursday, after all," Asa pointed out. "And why not ask the Witmers to do our wedding meal at the Grill N Skillet? You and your sisters wouldn't have to worry about all that cooking, or serving the meal in your house."

"Oh, my. Hosting a dinner at our place would take more redding up and cooking than we could possibly do on such a short notice," Edith mused aloud. A giggle escaped her. "I like it! Let's do it! We've already got the house, and your shop, and my wedding dress, and—"

"And we'll be able to adopt the twins sooner that way, as well," Asa said as he stroked her cheek. "Will believes that, at this point, their father will never step forward. He's told me he wants us to raise Louisa and Leroy, with his blessings. He'll sign the papers once we start the adoption process."

"And then they'll be ours. We'll be a family," Edith murmured prayerfully. "That's the best reason of all for marrying sooner rather than later, don't you think? It sets their future. Folks will stop speculating about Molly—and Will can put the past behind him."

As the magnitude of this decision struck him, Asa's heart filled to overflowing. "I love you so much, Edith," he murmured. "You always put others first, and you put your whole heart into everything you do. You're such a blessing."

Edith sighed contentedly. "It's settled, then. I promised to watch the kids while you found their father, and now I've promised to be your wife," she said. "Simple vows, but they've set us on a path together forever. Nobody can change that."

"I'm yours, you're mine, and the twins will be ours," Asa murmured with a decisive nod. "I believe God's been blessing us every step along the way."

CHAPTER SIXTEEN

The next morning at church, Edith could hardly sit still. All during Preacher Ben's sermon about Jesus's ascending to heaven forty days after His resurrection, she peered between the heads of the older women seated in front of her, hoping for a glimpse of Asa. Did he feel as fidgety as she did? He'd asked Bishop Tom to announce their wedding date along with their official intent to marry, but otherwise they hadn't told a soul. Not even Loretta and Rosalyn, seated on either side of her, knew the secret that had kept Edith awake most of the night. She'd been too excited to sleep as she made mental lists of the many things they needed to do before the fifteenth of May.

After a hymn and a prayer, her father stood to read the passage Bishop Tom would preach on during the second, longer sermon. Dat looked appropriately solemn as he held the big Bible, facing the congregation gathered in Ben and Miriam Hooley's home. "Hear the word of God as found in Ecclesiastes, the third chapter," he began in his sonorous voice. *"To every thing there is a season, and a time to every purpose under the heaven. A time to be born, and a time to die; a time to plant, and a time to pluck up that which is planted."*

Edith listened to the familiar verses, smiling at the twins as they dozed in their baskets between her and her sisters. *A time to marry and become a family,* she added as her father kept reading.

"A time to rend, and a time to sew; a time to keep silence, and a time to speak," Dat continued. *"A time to love, and a time to hate; a time of war, and a time of peace."*

As he closed the Bible, her father paused to find her in the crowd. The expression on his face said it all: during his upstairs meeting with the church leaders, while the congregation was singing the first hymn, Bishop Tom had revealed the news of their wedding date. Dat was *not* pleased, but he sat down without comment.

When Bishop Tom stood up to preach, Edith's heart pounded so loudly she could hardly hear him. "As I've thought about the age-old list of times in our lives, just read for us by Deacon Cornelius," he began, "I'd like to add another one or two. Seems to me we need a time for patience—a time to allow God's plans to unfold the way He intends. And we often need a time for correctin' mistakes we've made on account of doin' things our own way instead of His way."

Edith felt the blood drain from her head. *Is the bishop going to spend the next hour expounding upon the way Asa and I decided to marry so soon after we met? Is he predicting we'll someday regret our decision—and spend the rest of our lives dealing with a monumental mistake?*

As Tom continued to speak, Edith noticed that many *kapps* in front of her bobbed in agreement as the sermon touched upon the perils of rushing ahead with projects that please us, oblivious to the consequences for our families. Everyone seemed to think Bishop Tom was speaking directly to him or her, for his thought-provoking message was inspiring pensive expressions on the men's faces, as well. Edith had come to realize that the bishop of Willow Ridge had a real talent for applying the truths of the Bible and the principles of their faith to their everyday lives. This morning, he was in fine form.

"I'll conclude by remindin' us that Jesus loves us even when we disregard His will for our lives," Bishop Tom said as he gazed out over the faces in the crowded room. "It's our job to seek His counsel, and to tell our neighbors when we believe they've strayed from the path—and it's our Christian obligation to forgive them when their words and actions hurt us. Patience and humility will lead us to the peace God intends for us."

After a prayer and the final hymn, the bishop pronounced his benediction. Then, as always, came the time for making announcements that concerned individual members and the church district. Edith held her breath. She wrapped her

264

arms around the twins' baskets, gazing into their precious faces as she awaited what Tom would say next. Her pulse was still pounding, but she felt strong now—confident that she and Asa had made the right decisions for the right reasons.

"It's my pleasure to publish the intention of Asa Detweiler from Clifford to marry our own Edith Riehl," the bishop announced. "You're all invited to their wedding on Friday, May fifteenth—a sort of extension of our Ascension Day festivities."

A moment of stunned silence filled the house. Then her sisters gasped, grabbing her arms.

"Edith! We'll hardly have time to breathe, much less clean," Rosalyn whispered.

Loretta gazed intently at her. "I knew you two were serious, but why so soon? Why—"

"Edith and I invite you all to join us for our wedding feast at the Grill N Skillet, as well," Asa said above the crowd's chatter. "And because our house is not yet furnished, it seems the perfect place for our wedding service. We hope you'll bless us—and our new home—with your presence a week from this Friday."

Edith's heart stilled. Asa stood confidently, smiling at the crowd and then focusing on her. Although he hadn't discussed holding the wedding at the new house, it seemed the perfect solution to the problems her sisters were protesting about.

"See there?" she whispered to Rosalyn. "The rooms are empty and freshly painted, so we'll have no cleaning to do at home—and no cooking, or dishes and table linens to wash the next day. Our dresses are made, so once we call our friends and family in Roseville, we're ready for the wedding, ain't so?"

Her sisters gaped at her. Edith suspected they had questions and doubts, but they gripped the twins' baskets so they could head toward Miriam's kitchen to help set out the common meal. Edith moved between the pew benches with them. The large front room quickly filled with the men's chatter as they began to set up tables. The kitchen became a beehive of activity, as well—abuzz with the women's comments.

"My word, this wedding's coming on like a stampede!" Lydia Zook exclaimed.

"Do you want a bunch of us to make pies, dearie?" Naomi Brenneman asked as she grasped Edith's hand.

"Oh, that would be wonderful-*gut*," Edith replied gratefully.

"And how about a wedding cake?" Miriam Hooley held little Bethlehem against her hip, gazing intently at Edith. "I've made a *gut* many of those—"

"And Miriam's cakes are much tastier and prettier than any I could make." Savilla Witmer joined in with a bright smile. "I could hardly keep it to myself when Josiah whispered to me before the service that you and Asa wanted us to cook for you. Congratulations, Edith!"

Millie Hooley slung her arm around Edith's shoulders. "Seems Ira and I started a whole new tradition, holding our wedding dinner at the café!" she said with a laugh. "Some of the older folks shook their heads about us doing things so differently from how they'd always done them, but I didn't hear one complaint about putting all the plates, glasses, and silverware in the café's dishwasher."

"*Jah*, there's that," Nazareth Hostetler agreed as she gripped Edith's hand. "I wish you and Asa all the best as you make a home for the twins."

The congratulations continued during the meal preparation and while everyone ate. Edith noticed the pensive expression on Will's face as he sat beside Asa at a table filled with men. She couldn't miss her father's somber mood, either, as the fellows around him carried on animated conversations. She'd had no illusions about how her father would react to today's announcement, so she refused to cower as he approached her when folks stood up to clear the tables.

Dat grasped her shoulder, leaning close as he spoke. "Your mother's rolling in her grave," he muttered. "Folks here are speculating about why you and Asa have to marry so quickly, too.

But you've made your bed, and you'll lie in it. I hope you're happy, Edith."

As he walked toward the door, Edith clenched her jaw to keep from crying. Just this once, couldn't Dat share her excitement? Even Bishop Tom and Preacher Ben had expressed their congratulations, saying they were pleased that Asa had asked them to perform the wedding ceremony.

Loretta, standing beside her, sighed. "I'm sorry Dat was so gruff with you," she murmured. "Seems he's not happy about anything these days."

"We think Asa's a fine man," Rosalyn chimed in. "Even if your wedding's blowing in faster than we'd imagined, we're excited for you, Edith—and tickled to be your side-sitters, too."

Edith grasped their hands gratefully. "Asa says his brother Drew and Will are going to stand up with him. "It'll be a wonderful day, no matter what Dat thinks. And everything's fallen into place for our marrying so we can adopt the twins. That's what matters, really."

Edith gazed into the sweet faces of the two little babies who were wiggling in their baskets, eager to play. If she remained focused on Louisa and Leroy's future—their welfare— surely God would bless her and Asa as they became man and wife.

Thursday evening, Asa gazed around the large front room of the house, which was filled with pew benches for the wedding, and let out a satisfied sigh. Everything was ready for the wedding tomorrow.

Because Ascension Day was a holiday, the Witmers had closed the café Wednesday evening to prepare for the wedding meal. They had set up more tables in the Grill N Skillet and cooked up a feast of grilled meats and side dishes, along with the traditional creamed celery and chicken and stuffing "roast" served at most Amish weddings. The neighbor ladies had baked an incredible number of pies, and Miriam Hooley's wedding cake stood proudly on the wedding party's *eck* table, lightly covered with cheesecloth to keep it fresh.

When Asa and Edith had gone in to give the Witmers their final approval this morning, Edith had looked thrilled about the white tablecloths and nicely arranged tables in the café. During the day she'd met his parents and a few other relatives who'd come to the Ascension Day picnic Bishop Tom and Nazareth had hosted, and they'd gotten along fine . . . even if his folks had remarked at how *quickly* the relationship had bloomed. Although they'd been too polite to ask, Asa had assured them that this was by no means a shotgun wedding.

Will's *mamm*, Marian Gingerich, had come to Willow Ridge with his two older brothers, Homer and Harvey, and they seemed pleased that Will was farming here and getting a fresh start. Molly's parents, Orva and Ruth Ropp, had shown up, as well—which had startled Will, because he hadn't invited them. Bishop Vernon Gingerich had graciously asked the Ropps to sit with him and Jerusalem at the picnic. They had exclaimed over how plump and perky the twins were, so Asa sensed a spirit of goodwill had been maintained despite the situation's initial awkwardness. Once again Asa had witnessed Willow Ridge's gen-erosity at work, because all of these out-of-town guests were staying with the Hostetlers, Preacher Ben, the Brennemans, or Luke and Nora.

"So where are *you,* Drew?" Asa murmured as he glanced out the front window of the quiet house. Dusk was falling, and the picnic crowd across the road was breaking up. He had assumed his brother would escort their parents to town, but Drew still hadn't made an appearance.

Climbing the stairs, Asa reminded himself that his brother had never been one to follow other people's schedules—or to mix and mingle in a crowd of strangers. Drew would introduce himself to Willow Ridge on his own terms, and he was looking forward to being a side-sitter, so Asa stopped wondering about him.

He gazed at the antique bedroom set he'd moved into the large back bedroom Edith had chosen to be theirs. He'd bought the set at an estate sale a while back because the curved lines of the tall headboard, and the way it came around both sides of the bed to form small night tables, had intrigued him. The auctioneer had raved over the Art Nouveau style—not that Asa had cared what era the furniture dated back to.

As he studied the bed, the low dresser with its round mirror, and the matching armoire, he knew every hour he'd poured into refinishing the set this past week had been worth his effort. Rosalyn had made up the bed with a set of sheets she'd embroidered. A quilt from Edith's hope chest topped the bed, and two of Loretta's colorful rugs graced the floor on either side of it. As his wedding gift, Drew had replaced the caned seat of a bentwood rocker that fit nicely into the room. Asa could imagine Edith's contented smile as she rocked Leroy and Louisa. . . .

He planned to provide furniture for the twins soon, so Edith could return all the items the neighbors had loaned her. And then there was an empty front room to furnish, and a couple of spare bedrooms—

To everything there is a season, Asa reminded himself as he went back downstairs. Adam Wagler had removed the wall between the kitchen and the dining room, creating a space that now showcased the oak hutch and allowed the table to be extended to its full size. Asa ran his finger along the flawless tabletop, smiling. He'd centered the table in the kitchen with six chairs around it, but he dreamed of the family dinners that would fill this clean, airy room with laughter and happy voices.

Edith was so right: the kitchen table was the soul of a home, where individual members became a family. And tomorrow morning at the wedding, that dream would come true.

Whistling a tune, Asa left the house and strolled toward the shop. He'd slept in the apartment above it the previous evening and had decided to spend his final night as a bachelor there, as well. Velvety darkness was settling over the countryside. The folks at Bishop Tom's picnic had gone home, and the long tables in his yard had been put away. A peaceful hush surrounded Asa as he continued down the long lane. As he approached the other end of the shop building, he noticed the glow of a lamp in one of the windows in the apartment.

He closed the entrance door behind him and started up the stairs. "That you, Drew?" he called out.

His brother let out a short laugh. "Who'd you think it was? Your sweet little Edith?"

Asa entered the sparsely furnished apartment, frowning. Drew sat on their old sofa with his feet on the coffee table. He lifted a can of beer to his lips—which probably explained his questionable remark about Edith. "I was hoping you'd show up for the picnic, maybe visit with the parents today," Asa said as he lowered himself onto the other end of the couch. "They were asking about you, as were the other guests."

Drew shrugged. "Never been much of a party animal, you know. Ready for the big day?"

"*Jah*, I am."

"Still time to back out," Drew teased. He gestured toward the corner, where an apartment-sized gas stove, a sink, and a fridge served as a kitchen. "Grab a beer, brother. We'll toast your last night as a free man, and your long, happy life of wedded bliss."

It was common for single guys to joke this way, and not unheard of for them to keep beer around, yet Asa wasn't amused. "I'll pass. Something tells me you've had my share and yours both."

Drew's dark brows arched. "You're sounding pinched, Asa. Is the little lady already laying down the law, leading you around by the nose?"

Asa leaned closer to his brother, gazing into his eyes. "I've heard enough smart remarks about Edith, got it? If you're lucky, you'll find a woman half as caring and considerate as she is."

Drew opened his mouth, but then clapped it shut. They sat in silence for a long while as the shadows deepened around the single lit lamp. Drew drained his beer can. As he crumpled it, he stood up to look out the front window. "Sorry about the mood," he said with a sigh. "It's just now hitting me that we've made this big move, and that you're getting married—and that we'll not be doing everything together anymore."

Asa considered this. "I asked you to come along when I was talking to Luke about this farm, and when I was planning the shop building," he pointed out. "Once you got past how quickly things were falling together—and realized how much better our business would do here—I thought you were okay with all of this."

"*Jah, jah*, it's just a lot of change," Drew said with a dismissive wave. "I'm fine with it. Just feeling a little uprooted. I'll get over it."

"You can still have a room at the house," Asa insisted. "It was never my intention to leave you out, or—"

"Nope, I came of my own free will, and I prefer this apartment. You've found a really nice girl, while my romantic efforts can be summed up as *the one who got away*." Drew shrugged. "It is what it is. I'm going to make a peanut butter and jelly sandwich and call it a day. Want one?"

Asa wanted to quiz his brother about the romance that apparently hadn't worked out, but he thought better of it. Although they were very close, Drew had never been one to confide about the girls he'd gone out with—to the point that Asa had stopped asking. "I was so busy chatting with folks at the picnic, I didn't eat much today," he remarked. "PB and J sounds like a great bedtime snack."

Drew laughed and grabbed the bread bag from the small kitchen table. "It might be our breakfast, as well. It seems neither of us thought to stock the fridge."

Rather than saying how busy he'd been refinishing the bedroom set, moving most of their belongings to Willow Ridge, and checking on wedding preparations, Asa didn't respond. He stood up to stretch, and then slipped into the small bathroom. As he did his business and washed his hands, Asa wondered if there was more to Drew's thorny mood than he was admitting—but Asa didn't want to pry, thinking it would only prolong his brother's bad attitude. When he came out, Drew was setting their sandwiches on the coffee table—and then he poured two big glasses of milk.

"*Denki*. You'll make somebody a fine wife someday," Asa teased as he took his seat on the couch.

Drew let out a short laugh and shoved his sandwich into his mouth. The soft store-bought bread and salty-sweet filling didn't take long to eat. After Drew had gulped half his milk, he eyed

Asa. "Seconds? If I say so myself, that tasted mighty fine."

"It hit the spot," Asa agreed. "Sure, I'll take another one." He rose to gaze out the front window, savoring the sight of the lamplight in the homes across the road—hoping the comfort food would help both Drew and him sleep better. Tomorrow was the biggest day of his life, and he wanted everything to go perfectly.

By the time he'd polished off his second sandwich, Asa realized how tired he was from the day's activities. "Well, tomorrow's an early day," he murmured. "You want the bed or the couch?"

"Take the bed. You'll sleep better." Drew smiled at him. "Sweet dreams, brother."

Was it his imagination, or was he getting muzzy-headed? Asa felt so exhausted and heavy, he slipped between the sheets in his clothes. When his head hit the pillow he was already asleep.

CHAPTER SEVENTEEN

E dith felt so fidgety she had to consciously stop shifting as she sat on the front pew bench Friday morning. It was her wedding day! It felt wonderful to be holding church in the house where she would soon live with Asa, with every pew filled. Family members and friends listened to Preacher Ben expound on the scripture her *dat* had read—the thirteenth chapter of Corinthians, which told of the unconditional Christian love that would make for a blessed marriage. Loretta and Rosalyn sat with her, and the twins' baskets were positioned between them. Asa faced her from the men's side, smiling confidently across the small space the preachers occupied. Will was there, too. Both men looked so handsome and solemn in their crisp black trousers and vests, wearing new white shirts.

But where was Asa's brother?

Bishop Tom had delayed the church service that preceded the wedding, holding a whispered conference with Asa—who finally insisted they begin, in hopes that Drew would be able to perform the wedding ceremony. "I thought he was coming to the picnic yesterday, but I haven't seen hide nor hair of him—and neither has anyone I called in Clifford," Asa had murmured. "We'd best get started."

Although Asa had told her his brother wasn't as outgoing as he was, or as keen on making the move to a new town, Edith thought it odd that Drew hadn't come to Willow Ridge to see the new furniture shop or to meet Luke and his other new neighbors. He'd been delivering furniture or seeing to the sale of their building in Clifford— necessary activities, yes, but folks who'd been eager to meet him had become puzzled as time had passed by and he'd made no appearance. Dat, of course, had pointed to Drew's absence as just one more reason Edith shouldn't marry into the Detweiler family—at least until she knew what she was getting into and with whom she'd be dealing.

Asa's smile, however, brought Edith out of her troublesome thoughts. His raven hair was swept back from his face, brushing his white collar as he gazed raptly at her with his indigo eyes. Even as the congregation stood to sing the final hymn, Asa watched her intently over the top of the hymnal he shared with Will.

Bishop Tom paused again after the song ended, looking around the crowd as if expecting Drew to come forward for the wedding ceremony. "This really is too bad," he murmured as he approached the men's side. "I hope nothing's happened to your brother, Asa."

Asa stood up, his forehead furrowed with concern. "He'd better have a *gut* reason for missing my wedding," he said under his breath. "I'll give him the what-for if he's just—well, never mind that. We can't keep the bride waiting on her big day."

When Asa gazed at her in invitation, Edith rose from the pew bench to stand beside him, in front of the bishop. She felt shimmery inside, glowing with the excitement of this anticipated moment— the solemn highlight of her life, second only to her baptism into the church. She'd been too excited to sleep last night, yet she didn't feel a bit tired. Edith focused on Bishop Tom's kindly, weathered face as he began the age-old Amish wedding ceremony. Through the years, the words and ritual had remained unchanged, binding couples with the same irrevocable vows their parents and grandparents before them had taken.

A movement to her right made Edith blink. Why was Will hurrying down the side aisle toward the door?

Asa frowned, and then focused forward again. Bishop Tom followed Will's exit with a concerned glance.

"Said he was feeling funny," Asa whispered urgently. "Something he ate at the picnic yesterday. Just keep going."

A worm of apprehension squirmed in Edith's stomach. Not only was it unheard of for a *newehocker* to slip away during the wedding service, but *nobody* told the bishop how to conduct a ceremony. Glancing up, Edith noticed how Asa's jaw was working. A trickle of sweat an down his cheek. After years of attending weddings, she knew that after the bishop preached a brief sermon on the duties of a steadfast husband and a devoted wife, he would lead them in their formal vows.

Is Asa getting cold feet? In all the hours she'd spent with him, he'd seemed so confident and sure he wanted to marry her and be a *dat* to Leroy and Louisa. It occurred to Edith that Bishop Tom was speaking of important matters—issues she needed to know about to be an Amish wife dedicated to the faith—so she gave her full attention to the clergyman's words again.

"We come now to the exchange of your vows," the bishop said in a solemn voice. "The words ya repeat after me will bind ya as man and wife before God forever. This is the moment where all doubts must cease. Any hesitation must be set aside as ya promise to be faithful to one another, believin' that only death will separate you—even as *nothing* shall separate us from the love of God in Christ Jesus, whom we honor and serve above all else."

Bishop Tom gazed at each of them as though peering directly into their hearts. "Understanding the finality, the solemnity, of these vows, are ya ready to proceed?"

"*Jah*, let's do it," Asa murmured. He clasped and unclasped his hands as though wondering what to do with them.

"And you, Edith?" asked the bishop.

Edith glanced over at Louisa and Leroy, who watched her from their baskets. She nodded.

Bishop Tom began to read the vows of holy matrimony, line by line, which Edith repeated in the strongest voice she could manage. She'd imagined feeling exuberant and sure of herself at this moment, yet the importance of what she was promising suddenly struck her so hard her knees shook. Maybe all brides felt this nervous. Maybe the same sensation had rendered Asa fearful, too, for as he began to repeat his vows, his voice sounded strained and higher-pitched than she'd ever—

The door flew open so hard it hit the wall. "Edith, stop! You're marrying the wrong man!" someone cried out.

Everyone gasped and turned toward the door. Wide-eyed and stunned, Edith watched Will enter the main room with his arm around a taller man who appeared dazed and disheveled, wearing clothes he must have slept in. As she took in the fellow's midnight hair, broad shoulders, and height, her hand flew to her mouth. He gazed at her as though he knew who she was, but was too disoriented to speak coherently.

Edith then stared at the man standing beside her,

observing identical hair and features to those of the poor fellow who was with Will. "What's going on here?" she demanded in a shaky voice.

The man beside her swallowed so hard his throat clicked. He wouldn't look at her, wouldn't answer her. Edith suddenly felt ill.

Preacher Ben rose from the bench, gazing first at the groom and then at the fellow Will was leading down the aisle. "My stars, they're identical twins," he said as murmurs filled the big room.

"*Jah*, they are," Will replied, shaking his head in disgust. "The longer I sat by the groom during the service, the more I noticed little things about his voice and attitude that didn't match up with the Asa Detweiler I've come to know. *This* is Asa," he announced, gesturing toward the man he'd guided to the first row of pews. "That fellow's his brother, Drew. And Drew has a whole lot of explaining to do about why I found Asa dead asleep in the shop apartment."

Outbursts of shock and dismay filled the room. As Will's words sank in, Edith hugged herself hard, grateful when Loretta and Rosalyn came to stand on either side of her. Her sisters gently urged her to sit down on the front pew bench.

Dat stood up and raked his hand through his hair, glaring at both Detweilers. "This is even worse than I predicted," he blurted. "Not only have you humiliated my daughter and my family, you've made a travesty of the marriage ceremony.

What do you have to say for yourself?" he demanded, jabbing Drew's chest with his finger. "You're not leaving this room until we hear—"

"What on God's *gut* earth is wrong with Asa?" a short woman called out as she came up the aisle from the women's side. It was Fern Detweiler, Asa's mother, and from the opposite end of the room came tall, barrel-chested Ernest Detweiler. Edith had only met these folks yesterday at the picnic, but she could tell they were as upset as she was.

Drew turned, as though to bolt from the house, but his father brusquely grabbed his arm. "While we're all in church, it's a *gut* opportunity to confess, Andrew," Ernest stated in a no-nonsense voice. "From what I can tell, you intended to marry Edith and pass yourself off as Asa. How long did you think you'd get away with that?"

"This is the most despicable thing I've ever witnessed!" Will put in. "When I followed my hunch and looked in the shop apartment, I found Asa sleeping so hard I almost couldn't wake him. What'd you do to him?" he demanded. "Had I returned just a few minutes later, you and Edith would've been man and wife—a knot that couldn't have been untied, even though it was absolutely *wrong*."

As she heard what these men were saying, Edith's thoughts whirled so fast she felt dizzy. She couldn't believe anyone would attempt such a brazen trick—much less do it to his identical twin brother. When it occurred to her that she'd almost married a man she'd never even met, she got lightheaded and queasy.

"Take deep breaths," Loretta urged. "You're white as a sheet, Edith."

"Put your head between your knees so you don't pass out," Rosalyn suggested, pressing down on Edith's shoulders.

Inhaling desperately, Edith remained upright on the pew to watch Will help Asa sit down on the pew bench across from her. Asa appeared totally confused, as though he couldn't quite grasp what was going on but he sensed it was gravely serious. He rubbed his face, gazing from her to his brother.

Oh, Asa, what's happened to you? Why on earth would your brother—your twin—do this to you?

"Andrew, we're going to sit down and wait for your explanation of all this," Ernest Detweiler insisted. "You owe every one of us in this room a confession and an apology."

Edith heard a quiet sob as Asa's mother sat down beside him, lightly smacking his face to keep him focused. Bishop Tom, Preacher Ben, and Dat stood a few feet in front of her, conferring in hushed whispers about the correct procedure for a wedding situation no one had ever encountered. The babies began to kick and squirm as Loretta and Rosalyn tried to soothe them and keep watch over Edith at the same time.

Then Nora appeared, kneeling in front of her. "Edith, do you want to leave?" she whispered. "If this were happening to me, I'd be running down the road screaming like a crazy woman."

Edith focused gratefully on Nora's freckled face. "*Jah*, get me out of here," she rasped. "I—I can't face these people—"

"That settles it." Nora stood up, turning toward Bishop Tom. "You men decide what you need to do, but it seems to me the two people who most need to hear an explanation are in no shape to listen to it right now. I'm taking Edith home."

"Asa, we're going with them," said Fern Detweiler as she stood up. "Are you able to walk with me, or do we need—"

"I'll help you, Mrs. Detweiler. I'm a registered nurse," Andy Leitner explained as he came up beside Asa to help him stand. "This is the last place Asa needs to be right now, and I need to look him over."

"I'll go with you," Luke Hooley said as he came down the aisle. "I can support him from the other side."

"I'm staying here so I won't miss a word of this," Will said. "Catch you later, Asa."

"I'll watch the twins, Edith," Rosalyn insisted. "Go on home, sweetie. I'm so sorry."

Relieved that Asa and the babies were in

competent hands, Edith rose to go. With Nora in front and Loretta behind her, she made her way down the narrow aisle between the pew benches. She kept her head down, unable to bear the sight of so many women watching her, clucking over this unthinkable situation. Once outside on the porch, she released the sob that had risen from the depths of her soul, thankful that her sister and her friend embraced her to keep her from keeling over.

"No, *no!*" Edith cried out. "I can't believe—"

"Neither can we, honey," Nora murmured as she led them away from the doorway. "Let it all out."

"—that Asa's twin brother would pull such a nasty—"

"Despicable," Loretta put in, wiping her own tears. "Will had it right."

"—and that I didn't realize it wasn't Asa standing beside me," Edith blurted. "I feel so—so *stupid* and cheated and betrayed—"

"*Jah*, there's the right word for it. Betrayed," Fern Detweiler muttered as she came out onto the porch. "Never in my life would I have seen *this* coming. And my own flesh and blood to blame for it, no less."

Edith sniffled loudly, straining to regain some control over her emotions. Luke and Andy were guiding Asa toward the porch swing, and once he was seated, the nurse began looking into his eyes. When Andy took hold of Asa's wrist to check his pulse, Asa peered over at her. He looked so befuddled, so helpless. . . .

"Asa, how many fingers do you see?" Andy asked.

Asa blinked, trying to focus. "Two."

"*Gut*. And who are these people sitting with you?" the nurse continued.

Asa glanced to his left and then to his right. "It's . . . Luke and—and my *mamm*," he replied. "I don't understand what's . . . happening."

"We'll figure it out, Asa. You're doing fine—take some deep breaths, okay?" Andy said reassuringly. "Luke, if you'll sit with these folks, I'm going inside to quiz Drew. We need to know immediately if Asa's recent concussion is causing his confusion—or what his brother gave him to put him out."

Edith's mouth dropped open. If Drew had given something to Asa so he'd sleep through the wedding . . . What if that substance had affected Asa's brain permanently, so soon after his concussion? What if the man she'd intended to marry wouldn't recover? Asa was still gazing desperately at her, as though trying to figure out who she was. *And if that's the case, how can I watch Asa struggle against this—this demon inside him, for who knows how long? What does this mean for Louisa and Leroy? How will I make it from one day to the next without Asa to love me as his wife?*

Suddenly overcome by unthinkable possibilities, Edith turned. "Take me home," she pleaded as she gripped Loretta's and Nora's hands. "I can't handle any more of this."

Luke shook his head, watching his wife and Loretta escort Edith down the lane toward the Riehl place. Troublesome ideas twisted around in his mind as he considered what this incredible turn of events meant for the young man who'd just built a new shop with the twin brother who'd tried to steal his wife. Luke wasn't sure he could ever trust Drew Detweiler. What if Asa remained so impaired that he could no longer work?

What's the connection between this ruined wedding and the way Asa's brother never showed up to look at the house or the new shop? Has Drew been planning this all along? How did he figure to get away with it?

A loud sniffle made Luke glance at the pudgy middle-aged woman who sat beside Asa, mopping her face with a handkerchief. "I'm really sorry this has happened, Mrs. Detweiler," he said gently. "We've all been glad that Asa's come to Willow Ridge with his furniture business, and that he and Edith have fallen for each other."

"Please call me Fern. After meeting everybody at the Ascension Day picnic, I feel right at home here," she replied before blowing her nose loudly. "Ernest and I were so tickled that Asa had found a nice girl—even though it blew up so sudden-like, and he's moved farther from home. But who could've foreseen *this* ordeal?" Fern shook her head dolefully. "Drew has always lived in his brother's shadow, but I never guessed he'd stoop so low as to . . . I suspect there's more to this story than we want to hear."

Drew has always lived in his brother's shadow. Luke considered that statement in light of how he and Ira had always been close. As the older brother, he'd done his share of teasing and starting trouble that he'd left Ira to get himself out of, but he would *never* have horned in on Ira's bride. He'd always understood identical twins to be like two halves of a whole—emotionally closer from the moment of conception than other siblings—so he couldn't imagine what had driven Drew to pretend he was Asa on the most important day of his brother's life.

Was Drew truly heartless? Or was he incredibly desperate and shortsighted?

They all looked up as Andy Leitner came back out to the porch. His expression remained somber, but he seemed relieved by what he'd learned. "Asa, do you ever take sleeping tablets when you have trouble falling asleep?"

Asa blinked and shook his head. "Sleep's never a problem for me."

"That's what I was hoping you'd say," Leitner remarked. "Drew's refusing to give a full confession in front of a roomful of people he doesn't know, but when I told him your life depended on it, he admitted he'd crushed some over-the-counter sleeping tablets and put them in a peanut butter sandwich. Does that ring any bells?"

Asa made a choking sound. "He—we ate PB and J sandwiches before bed last night. Two of them," he murmured. "So it's pills that are making me so groggy? Even now?"

Andy nodded. "Your system's not used to the sleep-inducing ingredient they contain. You would've eventually slept off the pills' effect, but Will woke you before they'd run their course."

"Sleeping pills?" Fern looked away, her expression horrified. "What if Drew had given him too many? What if—"

"Asa's going to be fine, so let's not dwell on that," the nurse insisted as he squeezed her hand. He looked at Asa again. "If you think a nap would make you feel better, I'm not concerned about any repercussions now. Luke could walk you down to the apartment—"

"My bed's upstairs, here at the house," Asa insisted with a frown. "I'll not be sleeping in Drew's apartment anymore—not that I'm inclined to nap after all *this* stuff has come to light."

"You sound like you're coming out of your fog," Luke put in. "How about if I get you a glass of water?"

"*Gut* idea. That'll clear his head faster and keep the sleep medication moving out of his system." Andy sighed. "I'm sorry this has happened, Asa."

"So . . . you're telling me that my brother drugged me with the intention of—of marrying my Edith?"

Luke headed for the door, relieved that Asa's head was clearing and that no permanent damage had been done. Inside the house, folks were holding intense conversations about the morning's events. As Luke walked down the narrow aisle between the pew benches toward the kitchen, Cornelius Riehl called for silence.

"In light of how the Witmers have closed their café today for our wedding festivities—and how they've prepared food for more than three hundred of us," he announced in his booming voice, "I invite you all to be our guests for dinner. Josiah says they can be ready in twenty minutes."

As Luke reached the kitchen, the chatter grew louder. He found a glass and then took a pitcher of cold water from the fridge. The beautiful table and chairs in the center of the kitchen made him wince. Asa had chosen such a fine gift for his bride—and Edith had painted the rooms in this home, fully intending to share it with her new husband. What would happen now? Would one or both of them change their minds about marrying, after they got to the bottom of Drew's deception?

"Hey—why not have the wedding after we eat?" one of the young men in the front room called out. "It's not like Asa or Edith is to blame for what's happened today. They still want to get married."

Luke stood absolutely still. When the chatter in the front room quieted, his older brother spoke.

"Ya saw how devastated Edith was, and how dazed Asa appeared," Ben said ruefully. "I believe some important matters have to be cleared up before those two stand up together. They deserve a happy wedding day without clouds of deceit and distress hangin' over their heads."

"I'm all for that," Bishop Tom chimed in. "Both families have some sortin' to do. Let's take a moment to hold the Riehls and the Detweilers in prayer, and to thank God for the food we're about to eat. Even when it seems our lives have taken a turn for the absolute worst, we're to believe that God will provide everything we need."

Luke bowed his head, gripping the glass of cool water. *We humans mess things up pretty bad sometimes, Lord. Hold Edith and Asa—their families—in Your hand as they try to make sense of what happened today. Forgive us our debts as we forgive our debtors.*

CHAPTER EIGHTEEN

E dith sat in the old rocking chair in the front room, staring at nothing as she aimlessly pushed up and rocked down, pushed up and rocked down—anything to avoid thinking about what had happened during her wedding. She was grateful that Nora and Loretta didn't feel the need to chat or to console her. What could anyone possibly say to make her feel better? Or to make sense of the way Asa's brother had behaved? The clocks in the room ticked off the minutes and then, one after another, chimed ten times.

Only ten in the morning. How am I going to get through the rest of this horrible day?

Footsteps on the porch made the three of them look toward the door. Rosalyn entered with Leroy in his basket, followed by Will, who carried little Louisa against his shoulder.

"Time for these kids to have their bottles. They're getting fussy," Rosalyn said with a quick squeeze to Edith's shoulder. "Dat invited the wedding guests to eat the food the Witmers have prepared, so it won't go to waste. How about if I fetch us some carryout?"

Images of the white tablecloths in the Grill N Skillet's dining room and the dozens of pies covering the kitchen counter flashed through

Edith's mind. "I couldn't eat a bite, but you folks go ahead," she murmured. She grimaced and hugged herself to keep from crying again. "Don't let them cut our wedding cake! This is all so wrong!"

"Exactly what I was thinking," Rosalyn reassured her. "I'll ask Miriam to freeze it for you. If you think of anything else, let me know, Edith."

"I'll warm the twins' bottles." Loretta rose, taking Louisa from Will.

When her sisters had gone to the kitchen, Will took a seat on the end of the sofa nearest Edith. He rested his elbows on his knees, looking as though he knew things he didn't want to reveal.

"So what else happened after we left?" Nora asked. "Is Asa going to be all right?"

"*Jah*, he's with his *mamm* and Andy and Luke. They, uh, found out that his brother crushed sleeping pills and mixed them into a peanut butter sandwich last night," Will replied with a disgusted shake of his head. "But Drew's refusing to say anything else."

"Nobody's going to stand for that!" Nora snapped. "If Drew's too much of a coward to tell his story, Bishop Tom and Ben—and Luke—will keep after him until he answers their questions and comes clean to Asa and Edith. Then they might just run him out of town!"

"Sleeping pills?" Edith demanded. She gripped the arms of the rocking chair, trying to process this information. "What did Drew think would happen once Asa woke up? Did he really believe I'd stay married to an imposter?"

Edith sprang from the rocking chair and went to the window, unable to fathom that any man would concoct such a vile—flimsy—scheme. Across the road, a stream of people came out of the home where she'd planned to live with Asa for the rest of her life. As the guests turned toward the Grill N Skillet, on their way to eat the special meal the Witmers had cooked, several of them gazed toward the house as though to catch a glimpse of her—

That poor bride who was too stupid to realize she was standing beside the wrong man . . . That silly goose who didn't listen to the warnings about how this romance was galloping way too fast . . .

Edith moved away from the window. She couldn't watch them acting as though they'd attended a normal ceremony and were on their way to celebrate her and Asa's union with a wonderful meal.

"Thank goodness you followed your hunch, Will," Nora said. "If you hadn't found Asa when you did, we'd be in even more of a pickle once the truth came out."

Edith felt Will gazing at her as she paced, but she couldn't look at him.

"It was his attitude this morning, an edge to his remarks that didn't sit right with me." Will let out a long sigh. "I've only known Asa about a month, but even when he was arguing with me about not being the twins' father, he didn't sound so demanding. So impatient."

"Which explains why Edith didn't pick up on those differences," Nora said gently. "Like most brides, she didn't see the groom until they both showed up for the service this morning. She hadn't spoken to him or heard him talking until she was standing beside him in front of Bishop Tom. And you sure can't tell them apart by looking at them."

Edith blinked. "It was only when he told Bishop Tom to keep going—when you got up and left in such a hurry, Will—that things seemed strange," she murmured. "I thought Asa was just nervous, like I was—"

"You had no way of knowing." Nora came over to stand in front of Edith, gazing into her eyes as she grasped her shoulders. "I want you to stop feeling stupid, all right? Who on earth would ever figure on a twin's taking his brother's place at a wedding? Especially when you didn't even know there *was* a twin."

Edith let out the breath she didn't realize she'd been holding. "*Denki*, Nora. You tried to tell me to—well, you're a true friend, taking my side instead of saying 'I told you so.'"

Nora smiled. "I've taken my turn at playing the fool, honey."

"*Jah*, me too," Will chimed in ruefully. "I'm glad we've figured out who bamboozled you, Edith, because I still don't know who got Molly pregnant before she married me."

Edith's pulse thudded as an appalling idea struck her. "What if it was Drew?" she blurted. "What if he pretended to be Asa when he was with Molly, just like he did with me?"

Will and Nora gaped at her as they considered this. Loretta and Rosalyn stepped out of the kitchen to follow the conversation, each of them holding a baby and a bottle of milk.

"That seems like a wild stretch of your upset imagination, Edith," Rosalyn said, shaking her head.

"It sounds outlandish," Loretta agreed. "But then, who knew Asa's brother was his identical twin? None of us had met him—"

"Which smacks of a *plan!*" Will said, pounding his palm with his fist. "Drew never came to Willow Ridge because everyone would've seen that he looked exactly like Asa. I think he'd been planning to displace the groom for quite a while."

"But why?" Edith demanded. "Why would he want to marry me when he'd never met me?"

Nora glanced out the window, toward the house across the road. "Looks like most of the guests have left for the café," she said. "I can't think the Detweilers would allow their wayward son to join the dinner party, so it seems like a *gut* time to go over and ask Drew some questions. Are you up for this, Edith?"

The thought of confronting Drew made Edith's head pound, but it wasn't as though she was the only person he'd duped. Asa had been betrayed on a much deeper level than she had—and maybe Drew should be answering to Will, as well. Edith stood taller, inhaling deeply to fortify herself. "*Jah*, it might be best if Drew has to face everyone he's tricked at the same time," she replied resolutely.

Will stood up and headed for the front door. "I'm not leaving until I get answers. He owes every one of us the truth."

Asa looked sadly at the beautiful new table he'd bought for Edith. With help from Luke and Ben, he'd put in all the leaves and fetched the rest of the chairs. The kitchen was filled with family members and friends, but this wasn't the type of gathering he'd envisioned when Edith had chosen her wedding gift.

Edith, he thought with a loud sigh. *Lord God, please hold her close, because after what happened today she might not want* me *to hold her ever again.*

Asa's mother and Ruth Ropp—Molly's *mamm*—were filling glasses with water, handing them around as folks took seats at the table. It seemed like paltry hospitality, considering the other wedding guests were enjoying the special meal the Witmers had prepared at the Grill N Skillet—not that Asa could've swallowed a bite of food. His stomach churned, and his temples throbbed. Most of the grogginess from the sleeping pills had worn off . . . but would he ever get over the ache in his heart?

My brother Drew—my closest friend since before we were born—drugged me so he could marry the woman I love.

It clawed at his heart, this doubt and betrayal. Asa wondered if his brother had been planning to steal his bride for a long time—which would explain Drew's excuses for not visiting Willow Ridge. But too many pieces of the puzzle remained hidden for Asa to have a complete picture of his brother's treachery. It was the Old Order way to forgive and forget, but it would take a long, long time to rebuild the trust his twin had shattered.

The folks around the table stopped chattering and looked toward the doorway.

"Edith," Bishop Tom said as he stood to welcome her. "Here, take my seat—"

"No, she can sit here," Vernon Gingerich offered as he, too, rose from the table.

"Let's scoot around to make room for Nora and Will," Luke suggested. He didn't seem surprised to see that the two of them had come over.

Will waved off his offer. "Couldn't sit still if

my life depended on it," he said. He glanced warily at Drew, who leaned against the counter by the sink. "I'll stand behind my *mamm*."

Asa was vaguely aware of other remarks being made and of the scraping of chairs against the floor, but his gaze remained on Edith. She was so lovely in her royal-blue wedding dress and crisp white apron—clothing she'd sewn to wear on the biggest day of their lives. Her pink-rimmed eyes and pale complexion attested to the shock she'd endured. As she looked at the folks around the table, however, she seemed stronger. Determined to deal with whatever Drew chose to say to everyone.

Asa swallowed hard and opened his arms. He had no idea what he'd do if Edith had decided she no longer wanted to be with him. Her sorrowful smile as she hurried into his embrace was a balm to his battered soul.

"Asa—Asa, I'm so sorry," she murmured.

He clung to her slender body. "No need for *you* to apologize, sweetie," he whispered.

Edith eased away, aware of their audience. "Are you all right?" she asked.

"I'll make it now that you're here with me," Asa replied. He glanced toward the table, where Preacher Ben was gesturing toward two empty chairs. "Let's sit down. I—I'm not sure I'm ready for what Drew might say, but I hope he'll be truthful."

"*Jah*, we have a lot of questions," Nora remarked quietly as she sat down next to Luke. "And you two deserve more than just honest answers."

Asa pulled out a chair for Edith and then sat beside her. When she took hold of his hand, twining her small fingers between his, he felt her strength seeping into him. He could better endure this ordeal because Edith had set aside her disappointment and heartache to be with him.

Bishop Vernon Gingerich, who sat beside Will's mother, Marian, spoke up in a voice that hushed the chatter. "Let's come before the Lord in prayer," he said earnestly. "God our Father, we're grateful for Your presence as we gather to talk with Drew and to discern Your truth in this difficult situation. Open our hearts and minds. Forgive us our debts as we forgive our debtors. Amen."

Asa opened his eyes. His mother and father were gazing at Drew as though he had disappointed and shamed them beyond words. Cornelius Riehl, his brow furrowed, appeared ready to launch into a lecture Asa didn't want to sit through—and Edith shouldn't have to endure, either—so Asa spoke first.

"What were you *thinking*, Drew?" he asked tersely. "For the love of God, man, why did you try to marry my bride? You hadn't even met Edith before today!"

Drew cleared his throat nervously. He'd remained standing against the sink, not meeting anyone's eyes. "*Jah*, I had," he murmured. "I stopped through town with a wagonload of furniture a while back, and . . . and I also slipped in a couple of weeks ago when she was painting this room."

Edith's face turned a sickly shade of pale. "I was so surprised and glad to see you, because I thought you were—and you *kissed* me," she cried out. Her hand fluttered to her mouth as though she wanted to vomit.

"You believed I was Asa, and I—I didn't correct your perception." Drew licked his lips, glancing nervously at Asa. "I've been to Willow Ridge a few other times, as well. Did you think I'd agree to transplant the furniture business—my life—without knowing something about the town we'd be moving to?"

"When were you here?" Asa demanded. "Why didn't you come along with me when I asked you to, instead of—of sneaking around behind my back?"

Drew's responses made Asa stiffen with anger and resentment. His twin wasn't as outgoing as he was, but Asa had *never* figured Drew would deceive him. He clasped Edith's hand, awaiting Drew's answer . . . already sensing it would make his actions more incriminating.

"I was here the day you bought this place—or rather, the day Hooley had already snapped it up and told you we'd be buying the house and buildings from him," Drew replied testily. "Amazing what you can hear from behind the windbreak of evergreens along the road."

Luke scowled and sat up taller in his chair. "Why didn't you participate in that transaction? This was your new home—your new place of business," he pointed out sharply. "I'm guessing some of the money going toward the purchase was yours, as well."

Drew shrugged—not that it dislodged the chip on his shoulder. "Asa was the one who was in such a lather to relocate," he muttered. "Asa's always been the take-charge guy, you see. I'm just along for the ride."

Although Asa regretted that his brother was airing his grievances in front of so many people, he also noticed that the expressions on their faces mirrored his own disbelief. He had repeatedly suggested that Drew come along to Willow Ridge with him, but his brother had always had other more important priorities—or he'd pretended to, anyway. "So you're saying that instead of being in Clifford, supervising the painting of our building that weekend, you were skulking around, spying on me."

Drew's lips twitched. "Those painters did a *gut* job. You said so yourself," he countered. "And meanwhile, you and Miss Edith were out running the roads in a courting buggy—"

Edith sucked in her breath. "That was *you* behind the bushes! I *thought* I saw something moving when we came out of the pizza place," she said in a hoarse whisper.

"And where else have you been hiding, spying on folks?" Cornelius demanded as he rose from his chair. "What I'm hearing makes me very leery of your moving to our town, Detweiler. If you'd do this to your own brother—"

"Let's let Asa and Edith finish with him," Bishop Tom suggested as he took hold of Cornelius's forearm. "The rest of us can ask our questions later."

"*Jah*, we've got questions, all right," Will muttered as he kneaded his mother's shoulders. "I've never heard the likes of such carryings-on— of one brother so outrageously deceiving the other concerning their business and a marriage."

Asa noticed how grim his father's expression was, and how Mamm looked ready to burst into tears. It was a sad day, indeed, when parents witnessed such a confession from a son they'd raised to know right from wrong . . . a son who didn't sound particularly sorry for what he'd done.

"Since you asked, Mr. Riehl," Drew continued in a tight voice, "I also witnessed the scene between my brother and Will Gingerich—the day Edith marched down the road and told them to lower their voices because they were upsetting the babies in the buggy. Once again, the windbreak served my purpose. I heard every word—"

"Why did you follow me here that day?" Asa interrupted. "Why would you—"

"The real question," Will insisted, "is why the phone message I'd left concerned *you,* Drew. When my wife Molly confessed her love for Asa as she lay dying, was she really talking about you? Had you pretended to be Asa when you got involved with her, so Molly believed—"

"Watch what you're sayin', son," Preacher Ben warned as he gazed at Will. "You're makin' a mighty big leap—"

"Not when you consider that Drew's been masquerading as Asa to fool Edith," Will countered. "When Asa and I had a long talk about who fathered the twins, I could tell he was sincerely puzzled about Molly's crying out his name. The only thing we had to go on was a business card from Detweiler Furniture Works, with both men's names on it—"

"So you're saying Drew got our daughter in the family way? *He*'s the father of those little twins?" Ruth Ropp asked shrilly. Her work-roughened hands quivered as she fiddled with the ties of her *kapp.* "When I suspected Molly was . . . Well, I quizzed her about being with a man, and she denied it. Wouldn't tell me who she'd been dating, either."

Everyone around the table got wide-eyed and quiet.

When Drew tried to clear his throat, he made a choking sound. "Molly and I were . . . I wanted to—I loved her so much, but before I could propose marriage, she broke up with me," he admitted as his face contorted with agitation. "I had no idea there was a baby—er, babies. Honestly."

Molly must be the one who got away, Asa thought as he stared at his twin. He was sorry his brother had lost a woman he'd loved, but that didn't excuse his behavior. "If you loved her so much, why'd you tell Molly you were me?" Asa asked incredulously. "What were you going to say when she found out you'd lied to her about who you were?"

"Not a *gut* way to treat a woman you loved— or to treat your brother, either," Edith muttered. "This is beyond comprehension."

Will's jaw was working in his slender face. He leaned over his mother's shoulder to level his gaze with Ruth Ropp's from across the table. He'd never been fond of Molly's mother because she seemed so negative about every-thing. "So you *knew?*" he whispered harshly. "You suspected Molly was pregnant when you and Orva encouraged me to court her—and you tossed in the rental farm to sweeten the deal?"

Orva Ropp shifted uncomfortably. "What're parents to do in that situation?" he implored Will. "Figured it was better to match Molly up with a nice young fellow to start a family than to send her off to have the baby and give it up."

"You misled my boy from the beginning?" Marian Gingerich challenged as she reached up to grip Will's hand.

In the silence that followed, Asa's stomach felt as if it were twisting into knots. "Every bit of this trouble circles back to you, Drew," he muttered. "And you did all these dishonorable deeds in my name."

"Oh, what a tangled web we weave when first we practice to deceive," Cornelius quipped dramatically. "Seems apparent to me that—"

Asa smacked the table with his palm, silencing Edith's *dat* and making everyone else jump. "Why?" he demanded loudly. "Why did you pass off your—your scheming and lying on me, Drew?"

Drew's cough rattled like a hot wind blowing through a drought-stricken cornfield. "I followed you to Willow Ridge that first time because I— I heard Molly's name in Gingerich's phone message. I—I wanted to find out if it was the Molly I'd dated, and I couldn't believe she'd died," he said in a strained whisper. "Then—when I got here and saw there were babies involved—I realized they might be mine. I thought if I could get Edith to marry me, I could raise my children with a woman who obviously loved them. I saw it as a way to take responsibility for—"

"You thought it was *responsible* to pretend you were me? And to deceive Edith?" Asa blurted out. "I don't believe that for a minute, Drew."

"You've crossed the line, son," their *dat* muttered with a shake of his head. "This whole situation's turning my stomach."

Asa released Edith's hand and stood up so fast his chair fell backward and hit the floor. He strode to the opposite side of the kitchen for fear he'd grab Drew around the neck and choke him. The Old Order preached that peace was to prevail in family relations even when one member had done hurtful things to another, but Asa found this situation too disturbing to tolerate.

"Why?" he cried out. "I won't stop asking you that until I hear something that'll pass as an answer. Everyone here has a right to know."

Drew stood against the sink, holding his head in his hand. His Adam's apple bobbed as he swallowed. His shoulders shook as he struggled to gain control of his emotions, but Asa didn't feel a bit sorry for him.

"You really don't see it, do you?" Drew finally murmured. "You never have."

Asa remained ramrod straight, glaring at his twin from across the kitchen. He'd always realized that Drew wasn't as outgoing or as confident as he was, but he hadn't suspected his brother was so desperate—so despicable—that he'd use their identical appearance to his advantage with two different women. "You're right, I don't see it. Spell it out for me."

Drew raised his eyes toward heaven as though beseeching God to lift him away from this painful moment of reckoning. He glanced at the two bishops and Preacher Ben, perhaps hoping for words of wisdom that would get him off the prongs of this pitchfork situation.

"All my life I've wanted to be you, Asa." Drew gazed at a spot on the wall, speaking in a faraway voice. "You were always quicker to catch on at school. The guys all wanted to be on your team for baseball and the girls—well, the girls whispered among themselves about how cute and smart you were, and how they hoped to go out with you someday," he continued bitterly. "I could never hold a candle to you, Asa. I might've looked exactly like you, but the folks we grew up around knew the difference."

Drew paused, clenching his fists at his sides as he stared at the floor. "It was the same at home with Mamm and Dat. They always loved you best—"

"That is *not* true," their mother protested as tears streamed down her face.

"We treated you both the same," Dat insisted. "You boys had different personalities from the day you were born, but when one got a pony the other did. When one got lectured about something, the other one had to listen—"

"But it was always me getting the lecture," Drew protested plaintively. "In your eyes, Asa could do no wrong, and I could never measure up."

"Envy." Bishop Vernon solemnly raised his hand to stop the discussion. "The book of Job tells us that wrath kills the foolish man, and envy slays the silly one. You two brothers are mouthpieces of wrath and envy right now."

"And likewise, Ephesians warns us not to be provoking one another or envying one another," Bishop Tom chimed in. "There comes a point when questions and answers are more about provocation than the sincere desire to clarify what's been goin' on. You've passed that point, fellas."

Asa opened his mouth to protest, but Tom's direct gaze stopped him. Asa let out a long breath. "After all Drew has put Edith through, she deserves the truth from—"

"I've heard all the truth I can handle for one day." Edith folded her hands on the table, gazing at Asa. "Let it be, Asa. No *gut* can come from the two of you going on and on about this. We've all witnessed enough."

The people around the table nodded, appearing weary from the onslaught of information they'd endured. Asa's mother dabbed at her eyes with a handkerchief, while his *dat* gazed at Drew as though he couldn't believe a son of his had committed such heinous sins.

"Let's depart in peace after a word of silent prayer," Bishop Tom said as he bowed his head. "We each have concerns best held up to God alone."

In the hush of the next few moments, Asa felt anything but prayerful. He lowered his head, but instead of closing his eyes he watched Edith. Her shoulders slumped, and her forehead nearly touched the table as she prayed.

What must Edith think of Drew? Does she still want to marry me, or will she want nothing to do with me now?

As the bishops scooted back their chairs, the others around the table opened their eyes. Cornelius stood up with a deep sigh, glancing from Asa to Drew before he addressed their guests. "I hope you folks will head on over to the Grill N Skillet," he said. "They've cooked up plenty of food, and you might as well enjoy a *gut* meal before you get on the road."

"Fine idea," Luke murmured, grasping Nora's hand. As the two of them left the kitchen, Luke squeezed Asa's shoulder. "Sorry about all this stuff you've uncovered."

"Now that the wound's been opened, we hope it'll have a chance to heal," Nora said quietly. "Let us know what we can do for you."

Asa nodded, appreciating their concern. Preacher Ben got up to follow his brother and sister-in-law. "It's in God's hands now," he murmured. "It'll work out the way it's supposed to."

Asa wanted to believe that. It was difficult, however, to fully accept Drew's testimony—his twin had deceived him and Edith so many times, how could anyone know if some of the answers he'd just given were fabricated, as well? His parents' pale faces attested to their sorrowful hearts as they approached him.

"Guess we'll start back home," his *dat* said wearily. "Not sure I've got the stomach for food that was intended as a celebration of your marriage, Asa."

"*Jah*, it'll take a while to get beyond what we learned today," Mamm said. She looked over her shoulder, to where Drew still stood at the sink, alone. "I hope you boys can make peace between yourselves. You've got some forgiving to do—and so does Edith, bless her heart. In a different way, Drew must forgive you, as well, if only because he believes you're so much better than he is."

Asa turned to follow his folks outside, until a shrill voice made him turn around.

"All things considered, I cannot leave Molly's innocent little children here in Willow Ridge," Ruth Ropp declared shrilly. "They belong with family—not anywhere near the man who ruined my daughter's chances for a solid marriage."

Asa's heart pounded as he saw Edith's stricken

expression. "From what we've heard, it was Molly who kept her pregnancy a secret—from you, and from Will and Drew," he pointed out urgently. "Those wee babies are in a *gut* home with Edith. She loves them—"

"I brought Leroy and Louisa to Willow Ridge because I trusted the Riehls to care for them when I couldn't—while you were caring for your *mamm* after her heart attack," Will insisted. "Anyone can see how they've blossomed since they came here. Asa and Edith plan to adopt them, with my blessings. With all due respect, Ruth, I think you should—"

"You don't have a leg to stand on, Will. They're not your children—and anyway, you should've brought them to our house when Molly died." Ruth stood up, her expression resolute as she focused on Edith. "Where are they? We'll collect their clothes and—"

"Ruth, maybe you and I should discuss this," Orva murmured as he rose beside her. "We've got our hands full with your—"

"Nonsense. Our grandchildren need the stability of a Christian home, and I'll not have these—these Detweilers raising them!" Molly's mother said with a scornful glance toward Drew. "Who knows what other insidious situations that man's gotten himself into? He might have fathered them, but anyone can see he's not fit to be a *dat*."

"Please reconsider," Edith implored the Ropps

as she went around the table to stand before them. "We've gotten all manner of help from the bishop and his wife—from the women around town. I vowed I'd take care of Louisa and Leroy, and no matter what Drew has done, I'll stand by my word."

Asa's heart went out to the lovely young woman who should have been his wife by now. He went to stand beside Edith, praying for persuasive words. "We've got their new room ready upstairs, and we're ready to be a family—to raise them as our own children," he insisted. "Drew's revelations today don't change that."

One of Mrs. Ropp's eyebrows bent like a snapped twig as she glared at Asa. "Drew's revelations change everything," she muttered. "You still have to deal with him, because he's your brother and your business partner, but I do not. Let's fetch the twins now so Orva and I can have them home by dark."

Asa's heart lurched. He looked at Tom, hoping for his testimony to Edith's mothering skills. "Bishop, you surely know how the babies have grown since they've been here—partly because of your wife's goat milk," he added. "Edith's devoted herself to their care, and—"

Bishop Tom raised his hand for silence as he joined their uncomfortable little circle. His sigh sounded apologetic yet resolute. "It's always been my belief that kids should be raised by their own kin, if possible," he said. "I'm not denyin' Edith's love or motherin' skills, understand. But because of the circumstances—because you and your family have a lot to work out amongst yourselves, Asa—I think it's best if these grandparents take the babies home."

When Edith's mouth fell open, a sad gasp escaped her. She looked away, appearing torn between arguing with the bishop and running off to cry.

"*Denki*, Bishop," Ruth said triumphantly. "It's a relief to know there's one responsible, trustworthy man here in Willow Ridge." She looked at Edith then, her sharp features softening slightly. "I'll understand if you don't want to be present when we take the babies. If you'll just show us which house—"

"Come with me," Cornelius put in. "If the bishop says you're to have the twins, then that's the way it'll be."

Asa detected a note of reluctance in the deacon's tone, and he couldn't miss the way Cornelius avoided looking at Edith as he escorted the Ropps toward the door. Had the deacon come to love Louisa and Leroy? Or did he think the twins would be better off with his daughter than with the surly, middle-aged Ropps? Bishop Tom gripped Edith's hand, and Vernon patted her shoulder, and then the two church leaders followed the others through the front room.

"I can't believe that just happened," Will said with a sorrowful shake of his head. "That's not what I intended, Edith. I'm really sorry. I—I don't even know why they came to the wedding, or how they'd have known about it."

Edith squeezed her eyes shut against her pain. "Could be they got wind of it after Dat called Reuben to tell him about the wedding—and about us having babies in the house," she murmured in a quivering voice. "Dat's *mamm* was a Ropp, so some of his cousins could've mentioned it, too." Her head dropped forward, and she began to cry.

Will sighed. "Let's get you a bite to eat, Mamm," he murmured. "Asa, Edith . . . I owe you both more favors than I can count. I'll do what I can."

Asa nodded, but he didn't feel encouraged by Will's support. As he wrapped his arms around Edith, sorrow welled up inside him until he couldn't see straight. Unshed tears made his throat ache as the sound of Edith's sobs tore at him.

After a few minutes, she eased out of his embrace. "I've got to go over there," she said as she mopped her face with her sleeve. "The twins will be confused by—and I can't let those wee ones go without saying *gut*-bye."

As Edith hurried out of the kitchen, Asa knew he'd never find a more loving, steadfast, devoted woman . . . but did she still want him? Did she feel wary about her future as his wife because Drew would live above the shop and work with him every day?

He started for the door, but then turned toward his twin. "See what a mess you've made?" he said bitterly. "You're my brother, and I'm supposed to forgive you, but you've made that very, very difficult, Drew. Stay out of my sight for a while. Got it?"

His brother's indigo eyes held pain and yearning and regret, but Asa walked away. He had his own pain to deal with.

CHAPTER NINETEEN

E dith entered the house, bracing herself . . . preparing herself to say good-bye to the two babies she'd come to love so completely. As she'd anticipated, Loretta and Rosalyn were each holding a twin, appearing confused and overwhelmed as they listened to Dat. When Louisa and Leroy spotted Edith, they laughed and held out their little arms to her, ignoring the other folks in the room.

"I know you weren't expecting this," Dat was saying to her sisters, "but the Ropps are the twins' grandparents. They've asked to take the babies home, and Bishop Tom has agreed that it's best if they do."

When her sisters stared at Edith, hoping for an explanation—or a correction—she had to swallow a lump in her throat before she could speak. "It's like he says," she murmured. "You won't believe what happened over at the house—"

"I'm so glad the children weren't there," Ruth cut in. She was trying to coax Leroy from Rosalyn's arms, but he was turning away from her. "Drew Detweiler is exactly the sort of man we should protect these innocents from. Come to Mammi now," she murmured in a lower voice.

Leroy swiveled his head to avoid looking at

Ruth. Louisa sucked on her fingers, gazing doubtfully at Orva before burying her face against Loretta's neck.

"This, um, might take some doing," Rosalyn murmured. She focused on Ruth as she swayed from side to side to keep Leroy from fussing. "Do you have clothes and bottles and—"

"No, but if you'll pack us a duffel, we'll be fine," Ruth replied crisply. "They'll get used to us in time."

"They take goat milk in their bottles," Loretta insisted. "If you don't have goats nearby, maybe you'd better leave them with us, at—at least until they're on solid foods."

"That must be why they're bigger than I remember. A lot more energetic," Orva remarked. He seemed hesitant to touch Louisa for fear she'd start crying. "You can't miss the way they look just like their father, though."

It was easy to see that the Ropps weren't comfortable with the twins. Had they not spent time with Leroy and Louisa after they were born? Had they been so caught up in caring for their dying daughter that they'd had no energy left for the babies?

Or do they resent the fact that Drew Detweiler's blood runs in the twins' veins? Will they blame every little quirk and misstep on him as time goes by?

Unable to bear another moment of this distressing scene, Edith strode toward the stairway. "I'll pack them a bag," she said, forcing her voice to remain strong.

As soon as she reached her room, however, Edith sobbed. How was she supposed to part with Louisa and Leroy? Blindly grabbing a duffel from the top shelf of her closet, Edith tried to gather her thoughts. She feared that if she didn't pack necessities like diapers, onesies, and shampoo—and bottles—it might be a while before the Ropps could acquire some of those items. She hesitated to send the toys and clothing local ladies had loaned her, because those items should be returned to their owners . . . shouldn't they?

My friends here will understand, Edith consoled herself as she stacked little shirts and dresses in the duffel. *Better to send along what they need and replace the outfits and toys we borrowed, rather than wonder if Leroy and Louisa have what they're familiar with . . . what makes them happy. And that will take more than a duffel.*

As she descended the stairs with the bag, the twins' frightened crying tore at her heart. Edith passed quickly through the front room, dropping the duffel near the door. She focused on her packing so she wouldn't splinter into a million pieces. She found a box and filled it with bottles, bibs, and little dishes, and then stuffed cloth toys around the glassware so it wouldn't break in transit. Half a pail of goat milk sat in the mudroom refrigerator. Edith quickly poured it into bottles, packed them in a cooler, and placed ice cubes around them. She prayed the Ropps wouldn't put the twins on formula because it was more convenient.

With a heavy sigh, she carried the cooler and the box to the door. Dat was sitting on the edge of the rocking chair, ready for the Ropps to leave. Orva and Ruth each held a crying grandchild, frustrated because they couldn't seem to quiet them.

"Bring the buggy, Orva," Ruth ordered tersely. "Let's go."

Orva, relieved to have an assignment, thrust Louisa at Edith and headed out the door.

"Ma-ma-ma!" the little girl exclaimed tearfully as she embraced Edith's neck. From a few feet away, Leroy was stretching his arms toward Edith, trying to escape his grandmother.

Why don't you just rip out my heart and take it with you? Edith thought as she fought another round of tears. She stepped outside and sat down on the porch swing, savoring these last few moments in one of the twins' favorite places. Ruth came out, too, and deposited Leroy in her lap. As Mrs. Ropp toted the duffel down the porch steps, followed by Dat carrying the box of bottles, Loretta and Rosalyn came out with the twins' baskets.

"This is so hard," Loretta lamented.

"It's just plain wrong," Rosalyn murmured, blinking rapidly. "The Ropps may be the kids' grandparents, but it's easy to see—what brought this on, Edith?"

Edith sighed, cradling the twins' sweet bodies against hers. "Long story. We'll save it for later when we can't sleep," she whispered as Ruth came back to the house.

Too soon Orva drove the buggy up the lane. With all the love she could muster, Edith hugged and kissed the twins and quickly tucked them into their baskets. "God go with you, wee ones," she murmured hoarsely. "I'll always love you."

The babies began to fuss as soon as Ruth grabbed the handles of their baskets. Edith went into the house, thinking to make it easier for the Ropps to tuck the twins into the buggy. When Loretta and Rosalyn joined her, the three of them huddled close, holding each other in the kitchen as they cried.

"Only a month they were here, and yet they were such a part of our lives," Loretta said between sobs.

"I can't believe they'll be better off with the Ropps," Rosalyn blurted. "What was Bishop Tom thinking? What if they don't have any goats nearby?"

Edith shook her head mournfully. "It's mostly because of the way Drew lied to us and pretended to be Asa—"

"No! Who would pull such a stunt?" Rosalyn demanded.

"What do you mean?" Loretta asked with a frown. "Why would that matter to Mrs. Ropp?"

Edith sighed. She didn't have the energy to recount the entire story, but her sisters might as well know the punch line. "Drew is the twins' father. He, um, was dating Molly Ropp before she broke up with him and married Will—"

"And Will had no idea she was pregnant?" Loretta asked.

"That's just wrong!" Rosalyn declared.

Edith nodded, wishing she could rewrite this entire story. "Drew claims he didn't know about the babies, either, until the day he followed Asa here to find out if the Molly in Will's phone message was the young woman he'd dated. It's a twisted tale, and I don't want to get into the rest of it right now."

The bang of the screen door made them stand tall and wipe their eyes. Edith heard Dat pause in the doorway, but he didn't speak for a moment. "Drew told a story so outrageous I don't think he could be making it up," he said tersely. "How about if I fetch us some go-boxes of the meal they're serving at the café? While I'm there I'll ask Josiah about how to handle the leftovers we don't have room for in our deep freeze."

"It would save us from cooking," Rosalyn murmured.

"Maybe later I'll feel like eating something," Loretta said glumly. "What a shame we're not at the party."

Jah, *today's all about shame,* Edith thought as their father left. *Shame on Drew for the lies he's told. Shame on Asa for not insisting that Drew come to Willow Ridge sooner. Shame on me for being blinded by my love . . . and for needing those babies so much . . .*

Around one o'clock, Asa ambled across the road toward the Riehl place because he was too wound up to stay in his big house alone, and he didn't want to be in the shop building where Drew was. Wedding guests were still at the Grill N Skillet, but the café was the last place he wanted to go because people would ask questions—or they'd look at him with pity in their eyes because his wedding had gone awry and they were eating the food intended for the celebration. He supposed he should offer to pay for the wedding feast Cornelius had provided them, but he wasn't sure he was in a civil enough mood to discuss that topic yet.

Asa lowered himself onto the Riehls' porch swing. Through the screen door he heard voices drifting from the kitchen. Aromas of grilled meat, hot bread, and other delectable food tantalized him, but he listened for a bit . . . distinguished the voices of Loretta and Rosalyn, but heard no sign that Cornelius sat at the table with them. He was glad Edith's father wasn't belaboring all the things that had gone wrong this morning with Drew, because that sort of talk would only make Edith feel worse than she already did.

His stomach rumbled painfully. He'd had nothing to eat since the peanut butter and jelly sandwiches Drew had made the night before, so he decided to see if the Riehl girls would allow him to share their meal. Asa stood up and went to the door.

"Knock, knock," he called into the house.

After a moment, Loretta peered out from the kitchen. "Asa? Is that you?"

"*Jah*," he replied, sad because she was asking which brother he was. "Not to worry—Drew's in his apartment."

"Come in! Dat brought us some of the wedding dinner, and—" Loretta glanced over her shoulder. "Well, Edith could use some company. She took it hard when the babies left."

Asa stepped inside. He paused in the kitchen doorway to survey the carry-out boxes of food that cluttered the center of the table, but when Edith met his gaze, her pink-rimmed eyes and desolate expression cut a big hole in his heart. "I—I'm so sorry," he murmured as he approached her chair. "I had no idea any of this stuff about Drew was going on before today."

"I know." Her tremulous sigh filled the quiet

kitchen as she rose to get him a plate. "Sit down, Asa. Have some dinner."

"*Denki.* I'm really hungry." Asa took the seat beside Edith's, but sensed she wasn't in the mood to chat. "Wow. Looks like the Witmers outdid themselves. Grilled chicken, Savilla's mac and cheese, pulled pork, potato salad—"

"It's all fabulous, too," Rosalyn remarked as she chose a chicken thigh from the carton. "Dat brought this for us and went back to talk to Josiah about freezing the leftovers. I think he's too agitated to eat."

"I can understand why. My brother took us all for quite a ride this morning," Asa said quietly. "It's going to take me a while to forgive all the lies he's told—and to believe anything he says going forward. That's a sad state of affairs, when you consider that Drew and I have always done everything together."

Loretta nodded. "I—I've never heard of anyone's wedding getting interrupted the way yours did. But thank God Will sensed things weren't quite right, or we'd have had an even bigger mess to sort through when we discovered Edith had married Drew."

"I can't understand why he thought he wouldn't get caught," Rosalyn murmured. "The moment you showed up, everyone would've known he'd . . . betrayed you. Sorry to say it that way."

"It is what it is. And while I'm not sure I believe

all the answers he gave while we were quizzing him," Asa said as he began to fill his plate, "I was stunned by his talk of always wanting to be me because everyone—especially our parents—supposedly loved me best."

"Oh, my." Rosalyn pressed her lips into a line as she considered this. "There's no future in his thinking that way. He'll always be Drew, and you'll always be you, Asa."

Loretta buttered a slice of bread. "Almost makes you wonder if his feelings led him to do other things over the years, out of envy," she murmured. "I mean, if he tried to marry Edith, and he told Molly he was you . . . who's to know?"

"I've thought of that, *jah*," Asa said. "Right now I'm still too flummoxed to explore that possibility."

They ate in silence for a while. Asa suspected the girls were all grieving the absence of Leroy and Louisa. The two wooden high chairs in the far corner of the kitchen taunted him. Nothing he could say would compensate for the emptiness Edith was feeling. She looked so sad, so fragile that she might shatter if he wrapped his arm around her or talked about the twins.

Asa polished off a second plateful of the wonderful food and pushed back from the table. "I really appreciate your sharing your dinner with me. It'll hold me for the rest of the day." He glanced at Edith, who'd been moving her food around on her plate rather than eating it. "Whenever you want to talk, or—well, I'll be glad to see you," he murmured. "Take your time. You've had a tough day."

Her brown eyes appeared so lusterless, Asa would've moved heaven and earth to make her smile. "One of these days I'll have to move on," she murmured. "I know where to find you."

He excused himself, bidding the Riehl sisters good-bye. Asa stepped out onto the porch, and as he glanced down the road, he recalled the heated conversation he'd had with Will Gingerich last month—when, unbeknownst to them, Drew had been hiding behind the windbreak of spruce trees. Even if it wasn't the most productive use of his time, Asa knew he'd be running the events of the past five weeks through his mind again and again, rethinking them in light of the way his twin had been eavesdropping . . . sneaking around.

Asa scowled as his gaze followed the gravel road until it disappeared around the curve. One mystery remained unsolved, and he figured he might as well ask Drew about it rather than pick at the mental scab for days on end. He crossed the street, waving at a couple of buggies that had pulled out of the café's parking lot—hurrying along rather than talking to the drivers. He entered the new metal shop building and took the stairs up to the apartment.

Without knocking, he stepped inside. Drew sat

at the tiny table with a beer can in front of him, his head resting in his hands. "Yeah? Whaddaya want?" he murmured.

Asa crossed his arms. "Was it you driving the buggy that was going hell-bent for leather, after Gingerich left the twins with Edith? Midnight and I both got hurt, you know."

Drew didn't move. "*Jah*. I had to get home so you wouldn't know I'd been listening in on you."

"So you left me on the side of the road, out cold?" Asa demanded. Once again he felt his temper rising, and he couldn't stop it. "Your *secret* was more important than how badly I might have been hurt? That stinks, Drew."

"It does. I'm sorry."

Appalled by his twin's lack of compassion, Asa spun on his heel and left. He slammed the apartment door, filling the furniture shop with the clatter of his boots on the wooden steps. The fresh walls of the showroom were a big improvement over what they'd had in Clifford, but Asa was in no mood to appreciate his new workplace. He just wanted to be away from his brother, even if it meant spending the night totally alone in the house in which he'd planned to begin his new life with Edith.

Such a sweet dream their marriage had been, but now he wondered if it would ever come true.

CHAPTER TWENTY

Monday morning Nora sat at her small desk recording her weekend's sales on her computer spreadsheets. It was drizzling outside, and she was so immersed in her bookkeeping she didn't hear the bell above her shop door jingle. When she sensed someone's presence, however, she glanced around the shelves containing the pottery display.

Edith was standing near a dining-room set the Brenneman brothers had brought in after Asa had purchased the previous table and chairs for her wedding present. Nora nipped her lip. The poor young woman appeared lost and listless, as though she'd forgotten why she'd come into the shop. No one could possibly understand the depth of Edith's disappointment—not only because her wedding had been canceled, but because the twins had been taken away, as well—so Nora quickly considered what she could do to make Edith feel better.

"Hey there, Edith, it's *gut* to see you," Nora began in an upbeat voice. "I'll have you know I've sold every one of those baskets you brought in—so I hope you've got more goodies for me in that big tote you're carrying?"

Edith blinked. "Oh—*jah*, Loretta's finished

another rug," she replied in a voice Nora could barely hear. "I got a big shipment of basket-making supplies a while back, but I couldn't focus this weekend. My hands and my head seemed miles apart."

"You've had a lot on your mind," Nora said as she went to stand beside Edith. "How can I help you? Would you like to bring your supplies here to work for a while? Maybe a change of scenery would make you feel better," she suggested as she removed the woven oval rug from Edith's bag. "Oh—this blue, yellow, and cream color combination looks very nice! Fresh and soothing."

Edith's smile didn't reach her eyes. "Loretta misses the twins so much, she spent all day Saturday finishing this rug and starting another. We . . . we all think we should return what's left of the baby things the local ladies loaned us," she continued with a sigh. "So I've come to ask if you could swing by in your van to fetch them. I—I also want to pay the gals who loaned us the clothes and toys Mrs. Ropp took."

Nora considered her answer. She could understand why the Riehl girls didn't want reminders of Louisa and Leroy around the house, yet she hoped that by some stroke of luck or God's grace, the babies would come back to Willow Ridge. "What if I store that stuff for you—in case the twins return?" she asked gently.

Edith glanced away, pain shadowing her face.

"Oh, Ruth Ropp—the twins' grandmother—was pretty clear about the wee ones being raised by family, and about how she didn't want them anywhere near Drew Detweiler."

Nora slung her arm around Edith's shoulders to guide her toward the office. The rain was coming down heavily enough that it drummed against the roof of Simple Gifts and made the store appear shadowy and more subdued. "How about some tea? And I have some really cute cookies Lena Witmer decorated, too."

Edith shrugged. She entered the office and sat in the padded chair Nora gestured toward. A few moments later the electric teakettle was steaming, and Nora had brought in two mugs and plates from the store's pottery display as well as some of the wrapped sugar cookies she kept in a basket near the cash register. She dropped peach teabags into the mugs and poured steaming water over them, hoping the fruity fragrance would lift Edith's spirits. As Nora unwrapped two large, cheerful butterfly cookies, however, she sensed her guest wasn't going to be enticed by the refreshments . . . so perhaps some straightforward talk was what Edith needed.

"How are you and Asa getting along?" Nora asked as she sat down beside her guest. "Now that Drew's storm has blown over, are you setting another wedding date?"

Edith glanced glumly into her tea as she stirred

it. "He ate dinner with us Friday afternoon, but I haven't seen him since. He, um, left it up to me to reopen the conversation."

Nora didn't like what she was hearing. Last week Edith had been so in love with Asa, so eager to marry him, that nothing was going to stand in her way. "So Drew's in the apartment above the shop, and Asa's in that big house by himself?" she asked gently. "Any reason you haven't been over to talk to him?"

With a shrug, Edith sipped her tea. She broke off a wing of her butterfly cookie, but left it on the plate. "I don't know what to say."

Nora thought hard as she bit into her cookie. Was Edith still despondent about the twins' being taken away? Or was there a lot more to the situation between the Detweiler brothers than Nora had heard? "Have your feelings for Asa changed now that you've met his brother? Even though your relationship with him came on fast and furious, I thought the two of you would make a *gut*, steady couple—and strong parents for the twins."

"But with the babies gone . . . I just don't know," Edith murmured. "It seemed God—and Will—were answering my prayers by providing the children I couldn't have. As I think about that big house with just Asa and me rattling around in it like two peas in a shoebox, I'm not sure my days would have meaning. And it wouldn't be fair to

Asa if I married him, because he loves children as much as I do."

"You might be surprised at how much joy and love you and Asa could discover if you have time together, just the two of you. Luke and I certainly have," Nora insisted with a smile. "And then you can find other babies to—"

"But I love Louisa and Leroy!" Edith blurted. "I'm so worried that the Ropps won't get them the goat milk they need, and that those poor little babies will never feel truly loved. It was easy to see that Ruth and Orva weren't comfortable with them," she went on in a rush. "They took the twins out of a sense of duty, because they didn't approve of the man who fathered them.

"And the whole scenario got even more twisted because the twins' *mamm* thought Asa was the father."

Nora was glad Edith had gotten these difficult issues off her chest, because she would find no healing, no peace, if she dwelled on the unfortunate details that had been revealed after her canceled wedding. The mug Nora was holding—and the cookie she bit into—gave her another conversational path to follow. "Children can make all the difference in a marriage—for better or for worse," Nora began, tapping Edith's plate with her fingertip. "For instance, the lady who makes this beautiful pottery? Amanda lost her first husband, and was raising her three girls when another attractive fellow came along—and Wyman had five kids. When they married, it seemed like a match that met everyone's needs, until Amanda snapped. Ran away from home."

Edith's doleful brown eyes widened. "Amanda left her girls—the whole raft of kids? I can't think Wyman stood for that!"

Nora smiled. She loved picking up pottery at Amanda Brubaker's place because their home was always busy and bubbling over with the children's activities—but Nora also knew she'd go crazy trying to mother eight children. "Wyman had expected Amanda to slip into his first wife's place, in his previous home, so his life could go on as it had before," she explained. "But that didn't work for Amanda."

"I should think not. Raising eight kids is a lot different from caring for three of your own girls—and in a different house, no less," Edith replied with a shake of her head. "That would take a huge adjustment, no matter how much you loved your husband."

"*Jah*, it would. Wyman eventually realized that he had to make some adjustments, too, so now the Brubakers are one big, happy family," Nora remarked. She unwrapped a cookie shaped like a tropical fish, decorated in bright pink and yellow frosting. "And Lena, who makes these cookies in her home kitchen, came to Willow Ridge with Josiah Witmer last winter when she was carrying his child, but not married to him. She wanted to be a mother and a wife more than anything, but Josiah couldn't commit to such responsibilities."

"Lena was in a tough spot, between an Amish rock and an Old Order hard place," Edith quipped. She drained the tea from her mug and picked up the wing of her butterfly cookie. "And yet, from what I've seen of Lena and Josiah, they're devoted to each other and to baby Isaiah."

"They are," Nora agreed. She was pleased to see Edith perking up now that they were discussing other couples' difficulties. "They have a nice home just outside of town, and they took over the restaurant business from Miriam Hooley—after the place burned down and was rebuilt—and now their marriage and their café are both a huge success. Their families are very happy about the way things have worked out for them, too.

"But Lena's parents originally believed that Josiah was bad news all around, and they wanted him out of their daughter's life," Nora continued, dunking her fish cookie into her tea. "Lena had to do some tough talking—had to let Josiah know exactly where she stood and what she wouldn't stand for. Amanda did, too. They'd be miserable today if they hadn't spoken up and told their men what they needed. What they couldn't live without."

Edith bit into her cookie, closing her eyes. "Lena bakes a mighty fine cookie," she murmured.

"So, you're telling me I need to speak my mind to Asa?"

"It's the only way he'll know what you need, Edith. Men sometimes let on as though we're to be seen and not heard—although Luke knows better than to expect that of me!" she replied with a laugh. "Most husbands truly want to make their wives happy. They just need to know how. They can't read our minds . . . and they're *guys,* after all. They never catch on to the emotional stuff as fast as we do."

Edith's smile brightened her face. "*Jah,* you've got that part right," she replied. "My sisters and I have given up on believing Dat will ever understand why we feel the way we do—about the twins, for instance. He took off for Kansas City again this morning, to buy clock parts. He seems to need a day away after he gets riled up."

How many clock parts could Cornelius possibly need? Nora wondered as she finished her cookie. *Wouldn't ordering them through the mail and getting them delivered be cheaper than hiring a driver?* She kept these questions to herself, however, because Edith seemed to be coming out of her shell.

"Asa impresses me as a fellow who shares a lot of your hopes and dreams, Edith," Nora said. "By the time we left the house last Friday, after hearing Drew's answers, I could tell Asa was worried about the impression his brother was

337

making on you. If you love him, he needs to know you don't blame him for what Drew did—and that you don't believe he'll allow Drew to interfere with your relationship anymore."

Nora observed the subtle changes in Edith's expression. She was really listening, thinking about what she might say to Asa—and that was a step in the right direction.

"I'll keep you and Asa—and Drew—in my prayers, Edith," Nora said softly. "It seems like such a little thing sometimes, praying for people. But I believe God listens."

Edith's lips curved. "Sometimes having somebody listen makes all the difference," she murmured. "*Denki* so much for being my friend, Nora, and for helping me through a rough spot."

Nora nodded. "Happy to help. Do you still want me to come fetch the baby things? If it would be less painful not to have them around—"

"I think we'll gather everything into the spare bedroom, at least for a while," Edith replied in a pensive voice. "If we sisters pray for the twins, believing that God will find the best home for them to grow up in, maybe someday soon they'll come back to Willow Ridge. If I think happy thoughts of Leroy and Louisa when I look at the playpen and the toys, that'll be a lot better than crying—no matter how God answers us. I'm really tired of crying."

Nora squeezed Edith's hand. "I bet if you share

that idea with Asa, he'll pray for Leroy and Louisa, too. It's obvious he loves them and wants what's best for them. So does Will."

"*Jah*, they do. That's a fine idea." As sunlight shone through the small office window, Edith smiled at it. "Look what you've done, Nora! You've chased away the rain and my gloomy thoughts, like this beam of heavenly sunshine."

A short while later, as Edith left for home, Nora returned to her bookkeeping with a smile on her face and a sense of satisfaction. She couldn't take credit for the heavenly sunshine, but if she'd spread some cheer while lifting Edith's spirits, she'd done a good day's work.

Asa sucked in air and bit back a curse word when he nicked his thumb with his carving knife. He immediately pressed the wound together between his other thumb and forefinger, but before he could resume his work on the headboard he was restoring, he had to stop the bleeding. Getting a bandage to stay on his thumb would be a challenge.

"Cut myself," he muttered to Drew as he headed for the door.

His brother looked up from his sewing machine, nodded, and went back to stitching the pleats for the skirt of a couch he was reupholstering.

Asa sighed as he hurried toward the house. Once upon a time, Drew would've at least expressed some concern or helped him find Band-Aids, but their communication had been as scarce as hen's teeth since his twin's revelations last week. It was Tuesday, four days since he'd learned of his brother's duplicity. The silence in the shop was deafening. The evenings alone in the house while Drew remained in his apartment stretched into forever, as well.

"Asa! Wait for me!"

Thinking he was hearing imaginary voices, Asa turned to see Edith hurrying up the lane toward him, carrying a picnic basket. His heart did a cartwheel. For a few seconds he forgot about his wound and the blood that was seeping out of it. He drank in the sight of Edith's lovely smile, daring to dream that she was coming back to him, forever.

"Edith, it's so *gut* to see you," he murmured when she'd caught up to him. "I'm going to the house for a bandage—"

"Oh, my! That's a nasty cut." She set down her basket and grabbed a napkin from inside it. When she'd wrapped the napkin tightly around the wound, she looked up at him. "We'd best get you into the house and clean up the cut before the paper sticks to it."

Asa gazed at her small, sturdy hands as they clasped his and felt better immediately. After a moment her words sank in, so he began to walk toward the house, keeping his strides short enough that she wouldn't have to jog—and she wouldn't have to let go of him. *Lord, please, please don't allow her to let go of me ever again,* he prayed as they approached the house. "You—you left your basket—"

"It'll be all right. I thought you—and Drew—might share some lunch with me," she replied as they stepped up onto the porch. She grabbed the doorknob and then stopped, gazing up at him. "Asa, these past few days have been impossibly quiet without you and the babies," she confessed. "I can't not talk to you anymore. We have to figure out how we feel and what comes next—but first, we'll fix your thumb."

Asa nodded, willing to go along with whatever she said if it meant an end to the torture of wondering how Edith felt about him . . . and about getting married.

"Stick your hand under cool running water," she instructed as they entered the kitchen. "Where do you keep your first-aid stuff? Bandages and antiseptic."

"Upstairs bathroom," Asa murmured. "But I'll warn you. We bachelors don't keep much of that stuff around."

The sound of Edith's quick footsteps on the stairs soothed him. He stuck his thumb under the water, gingerly peeling away the paper napkin as he washed away the blood that had seeped all over his hand. Before he'd had time to assess the seriousness of his wound, Edith was beside him, setting down the box of Band-Aids, a roll of wound tape, and the ointment she'd found.

"Doesn't look like we'll have to amputate," she teased as she again took hold of his hand. "Might not hurt to have Andy look at this, though, in case it's deep enough for stitches—"

"It's not *that* bad," Asa protested as he reached for a towel. "Just an ordinary, everyday cut like guys in my profession get all the time. But thank you for caring," he added gently.

Edith flashed him a smile. "You men are all alike. It's a wonder more of you don't die from neglecting basic first aid and hygiene. Here—I'll wrap it tight with this until the bleeding stops. I don't see anything else to use."

Asa couldn't believe it when she leaned closer to his hand and wrapped one of her long *kapp* strings tightly around his thumb. "But you'll have a bloodstain on your—"

"Just an ordinary, everyday fix for a problem we girls deal with all the time," she quipped. "But thank you for caring."

You have no idea how much I care—how much I've missed your smiles and upbeat chatter. Asa didn't say this out loud because he was savoring Edith's earnest nursing . . . the warmth of her slender body as she stood close to him, holding his hand between hers.

"We have to forgive Drew," she said softly. It

was a no-nonsense statement that brooked no argument, yet she wasn't bossing him. "And we must pray for Leroy and Louisa, that they'll find the home God intends for them, even . . . even if it won't be here, with us."

Asa sighed and slipped his arm around her. It had cost Edith a great deal to say that, because she loved the twins even more than he did. She had also gotten right to the point of his recent feelings, because until he forgave his brother there would be no moving forward—in his business dealings or in the home life he wanted to share with this wonderful young woman. The silence between him and Drew felt as over-whelming as that proverbial invisible elephant folks talked about, occupying all the space and every moment they shared. There wouldn't be enough room for Edith in his life—in this house—if that silent, enormous elephant continued to dwell here.

"*Jah*, you're right," he finally admitted. "But I don't know what to say."

Edith turned her face so she could look up at him as she kept her *kapp* string wrapped around his finger. "I know exactly how that feels. I figured you fellows are probably sick of cooking for yourselves, so lunch might be a *gut* way to get us all talking."

Asa's body relaxed as a light, airy happiness seeped into places where he'd been feeling so tense and grouchy. "You're a genius, Edith," he whispered. "And you're a blessing, too. Even if Drew doesn't take the bait and start talking to us, *I* have plenty to say to you alone, girlie."

Her cheeks flushed a pretty shade of pink. She gently unwrapped her *kapp* string and studied the cut on his thumb. "If we put a big Band-Aid up and over your thumb, and then wrap some tape around and around it, I think it'll stay on while you work. But you'll need to change the bandage every day and keep it clean."

"Maybe you could be my nurse, Edith. It would mean I'd get to see you every day," Asa murmured. "After the lonely weekend I've had, your company will be just what the doctor ordered."

Edith let out a short laugh. "Anything to avoid visiting Andy at the clinic, *jah*?"

Asa laughed. Although she hadn't known him for long, she knew him pretty well. When his thumb had been covered with a Band-Aid containing antiseptic ointment and then neatly wrapped with the tape, the two of them headed outside. He grabbed the handle of the picnic basket and motioned for Edith to precede him into the shop. "Somebody took pity and brought us lunch," he called out.

But the chair at Drew's sewing machine was empty.

Asa went to the foot of the apartment stairs.

"Drew, Edith's here with a picnic," he called up toward the open door. "We'd like you to join us."

Silence. Then his brother said, "Nah, you two go ahead. I don't want to intrude."

"Phooey on that!" Edith blurted as she joined Asa at the stairway. "We three are going to make our peace—over fried chicken and fresh rhubarb pie. If you really want to get on my bad side, stay right where you are. We'll eat your pie."

Asa cleared a space on one of his worktables, wiping it with an old towel. Bless her, Edith had brought a jug of lemonade, warm chicken that filled the shop with its savory aroma, homemade rolls, slaw—and an entire pie. "What a feast," he murmured as she placed three plates on the table and opened the packets of food. "You're a saint, Edith. An angel come down to save me from myself."

With a glance toward the stairs, Edith shrugged and sat down in one of the chairs he'd set around the table. "Let's pray and eat. He'll come downstairs, or he won't."

Asa took hold of her hand and bowed his head. Denki *Lord for blessing me with Edith's company and her can-do attitude today. Heal what's hurting inside Drew. Open our hearts to the forgiveness You would have us extend to each other.*

For a moment he gazed at Edith's bowed head, her serene expression, as she prayed. Footsteps on the stairs made them both glance toward Drew, who looked at the table as though wondering if they were setting some sort of trap. He stood behind the empty chair for a moment, inhaling deeply. "Wow, you weren't kidding. Sure beats PB and J sandwiches."

"*Jah*, those things can lay you low," Asa blurted before he'd thought about it.

A rueful smile flickered on his brother's face as he sat down. "Not one of my better ideas, feeding you those sleeping pills, Asa," he said in a voice they could barely hear.

Edith passed Drew the plate of chicken. "We all do things we regret. But the real damage is done when we let those inner wounds fester, because they eventually poison us—not that I'm here to preach a sermon," she added quickly. "I just thought you fellows might enjoy a meal somebody else cooked."

Drew took a dinner roll, sniffing its yeasty aroma as though he'd never experienced such a treat. "You're being incredibly generous, Edith, considering the way I—I tricked you during the past several weeks and messed up your wedding. I'm sorry. I'm really sorry."

Edith's eyes shone like cups of tea brewed to triple strength. "I accept your apology, Drew. And I forgive you."

Asa marveled at her composure, her serenity. She made forgiveness look so easy, considering the way his twin brother had ripped her dreams to shreds on Friday. Even so, Asa preferred to wait out whatever his brother might say to him rather than echoing Edith's simple goodwill. Drew had double-crossed him in several ways, after all.

His twin seemed content to bask in Edith's kindness, devouring three pieces of chicken along with large helpings of the side dishes she'd brought. Drew appeared to be starving for more than food, however. His face seemed tight, and he was avoiding Asa's gaze as they ate.

Edith finished her meal and looked at Asa and his brother. "I need your help with something before we have our pie," she said softly. "Nora has suggested that we pray for Louisa and Leroy, asking that they find the family who will best be able to love and care for them. Three prayers are stronger than one, I'm thinking."

Drew looked at her closely. "Why don't you just ask God to bring them back here to you? You *know* that's what you really want."

"Who am I to tell God what to do?" she countered calmly. "He knows what I want, just as He knows what's best for those wee ones. Shall we?"

Edith extended her hands across the table toward Asa and his brother, gazing steadily at them. Asa took Edith's hand in his, and so did Drew, but when it came to clasping hands with another man, both brothers hesitated. Amish guys weren't into being touchy-feely—but Edith's silent, relentless plea finally got to him.

Asa stuck out his hand. He realized then that Edith had a strategy for bringing him and Drew together, if only during the time it took to pray for the babies. And if Drew wouldn't complete their circle, he stood out as the one who couldn't get beyond old behaviors to embrace new ones.

Once again Asa marveled at Edith's fortitude. Her courage. She'd come here today with no guarantee that her food or her request for prayer would be appreciated, yet she'd taken that risk to initiate the forgiveness process. She'd realized that sheer stubbornness might keep him and his brother from having more than short, surface conversations, and she was trying to break through the invisible barrier they'd erected.

Several seconds ticked by. Asa didn't move his hand. Edith didn't stop gazing sweetly at Drew, as though willing him to comply with her wishes. The rhubarb pie sat in the center of the table, the ultimate enticement.

Finally, sighing loudly, Drew took Asa's hand and bowed his head. Edith smiled, bowing hers, as well. Asa sat for a moment, taking in this scene and the power of this simple moment. When he gripped Drew's fingers, his brother returned the pressure—and suddenly, Asa was filled with a hopeful yearning. The separation they'd known these past four days had taken more of a toll than he'd realized. Yes, his twin had played some unthinkable tricks on them, but Drew had also admitted to a lifetime of feeling unworthy—less than acceptable, even to their parents.

As Asa bowed his head, he couldn't imagine the pain his brother, his closest kin and friend, had suffered for so long. Asa had never known rejection, yet Drew had felt inferior—lacking—every day of his life. *I can't change the past, Lord—can't change the way Drew feels—but maybe I could be more aware now, and try to understand him better. He and I need each other more than we're willing to admit.*

Asa paused in his prayer, savoring the feel of Edith's and Drew's hands . . . the bond the three of them shared during this quiet moment. That's how it would be when he married Edith, too—Drew would always be in the picture. And Asa wanted him there, needed him there, despite the way Drew had tried to marry his intended bride.

Big mistakes call for big forgiveness, even if he doesn't apologize any further.

Releasing the breath he'd been holding, Asa vowed to fully love his brother again—for he and Drew were truly each other's keepers. Edith was wise enough to realize that, and to bring them to this moment of reckoning and reconciliation.

Hold Leroy and Louisa in Your hand, God, and bless them with the family, the upbringing, You deem best. Guide Edith and me toward the way You would have us live, with those kids or without them. Amen.

When Asa opened his eyes, Edith was beaming at him. They waited a few more moments, until Drew raised his head. Their hands were still joined in a circle, and it remained intact for a few more moments.

"*Denki* so much for putting in a *gut* word for the wee ones," Edith murmured as she eased her hands from theirs. "I feel a lot better now that we've prayed as a family. I hope we'll do that many times as the years go by, because I believe there's great power when two or three gather together in Jesus's name. I also believe in the power of pie."

Asa blinked. Drew's eyes widened. Edith reached for a knife and cut into the golden-brown dessert, maintaining a perfectly straight face.

Laughter bubbled up from deep inside Asa, and as the sound of his mirth rang in the rafters, Drew laughed along with him.

Edith giggled, grinning at both of them. "That's what I like to see—folks laughing together. Sharing dessert and joy. We all need more joy, ain't so?"

Asa sighed gratefully as she placed a large wedge of pie in front of him. "You're the wisest woman I know, Edith. *Denki* for coming to our rescue today."

Drew nodded, accepting his generous slice of pie. "I agree on all counts. You're a *gut* woman, Edith, and I hope my wrongdoing won't keep you from marrying Asa," he murmured. "I can see now that I almost messed up a match made in heaven, and—and I hope you both can forgive me."

Edith's smile softened. "Consider it done, Drew."

"*Jah*, I want to wipe the slate clean and start fresh, brother," Asa said as he extended his hand across the table. "It's just no *gut* when we're not getting along."

When Drew gripped his hand and shook it, Asa sensed a shift in the atmosphere, a lifting of the heavy burden he'd borne since last week. "I feel so relieved," Drew murmured. "I knew what I'd been doing was desperately wrong, and now I can start over. I made so many stupid mistakes and assumptions, Asa—and you're the last person on this earth I should have betrayed. I'll be in your debt forever, because you've given me another chance."

Asa nodded, his throat tightening with emotion. Confession didn't come easy. His twin appeared truly remorseful—and perhaps ready to discuss other matters that weighed heavily on him.

"I can also admit that you'll be a much better *dat* for those kids than I'd ever be, Asa," he continued in a stronger voice. "I—I sure hope I haven't messed that up. The Ropps are doing what they think is right, but . . . they're such unhappy people. Molly couldn't wait to be married to get away from them. Guess I'll never know why she left me to take up with Will."

"May God rest her soul," Edith whispered. "She must've had some regrets, if it was your name she thought she was crying out before she died."

Asa nodded. This lunchtime conversation had given him a lot to think about—but first he enjoyed every mouthful of his rhubarb pie, and agreed to a second piece when Edith offered it. Drew took seconds, as well. It felt so good to be sitting at the table together again, sharing a meal with Edith and his brother.

"I owe apologies to Will and the Ropps, as well. I had no idea Molly was pregnant, but when I saw how much those babies resemble me, there's no wiggling out of it. I caused Molly's condition by being careless," Drew murmured pensively. "And I owe a huge apology to your *dat*, Edith, because he paid for your wedding meal at the café and the party was ruined."

"It would be a gesture of *gut*will on your part to speak with them," Edith agreed. "Don't be surprised if you stir up their resentment, however. I've heard preachers tell Dat he holds a grudge longer than he should."

Drew shrugged. "If I hadn't told so many twisted tales, nobody would need to forgive me. Again, Edith, I'm grateful you've been so quick to accept my apology."

"You've come to Willow Ridge for a new life—a fresh start," Edith pointed out. "It's not easy, leaving all your friends behind, so I hope folks here will give you the chance to settle in and become a respected member of our church district. You and Asa have a lot to offer our little town."

A little later, as Asa escorted Edith down the lane, he took her hand. "You're nothing short of a miracle worker, Edith. Would've taken Drew and me a long time to come to speaking terms again if you hadn't brought us together."

Edith shrugged modestly. "I had to give it a try."

Asa stopped in the shade just before they got to the gravel road. "There's something I really want to know, though. You don't have to answer now."

Her brown eyes gazed steadily into his. Wise woman that she was, she waited him out.

"Will you still marry me, Edith? I—I want that more than anything, even if the twins don't make it back to Willow Ridge," he said softly. "If I have you by my side, I know we can make a life together. I believe God will bless us, according to His will."

For the longest moment she stood motionless, as though his words had turned her into a statue. Then her face lit up like the springtime sun, and she wrapped her arms around his waist. "*Jah*, I will, Asa," she replied. "I believe God has truly blessed us today, and He won't stop. I love you even more now than I did last week."

Asa's heart swelled as he embraced her. He couldn't ask for any better than Edith had just given him—her love, and her life.

CHAPTER TWENTY-ONE

"You invited *how* many people here?" Dat demanded crossly. "Sunday is our day of rest. It's the only day I don't work on clocks."

Edith glanced at her sisters as they all sat at breakfast. It had been apparent ever since Dat had come to the table that he wasn't in the best of moods, but she refused to change her plans—and the resolute expressions on Loretta's and Rosalyn's faces told her they were looking forward to having guests as much as she was. Rosalyn passed him the platter of lemon cheesecake rolls she'd baked yesterday, while Loretta rose to fetch the coffee pot.

"There's no church, so it's a visiting Sunday, Dat," Edith reminded him gently. "And with Asa, Drew, and Will not having family nearby, I invited them to join us for dinner—along with Nora and Luke, and Bishop Tom and Nazareth."

"Why do I want to deal with the Detweilers—and Gingerich and the bishop—on my day off? Un-invite them."

Edith recalled times when her father's withering glare would've made her do his bidding simply to keep the peace. Yesterday, however, she and her sisters had decided to stand firm and face up to him together—so she was determined that

Dat's grumpiness wouldn't ruin her plans for a nice meal with their closest friends.

"You know that wouldn't be polite," Loretta murmured as she topped off his coffee.

"Polite? Why must I always be polite?" Dat countered.

Rosalyn caught his gaze and held it. "Because, for one thing, Drew wants a chance to apologize," she said firmly. "When someone who's wronged us asks for the opportunity to make amends, it's our place to listen."

"Puh," Dat said as he rolled his eyes. "Detweiler can't face me like a man? Has to have a crowd of supporters?"

"Dat, really," Loretta murmured as she returned to her seat. "Maybe you should go back upstairs to bed, and then get out of it on the right side this time."

Their father scowled in righteous indignation. "And maybe you three should remember to honor your father—and your mother," he added sternly. "Have you forgotten what day this is?"

Edith sighed. She and her sisters had anticipated this topic . . . the way Dat called up his mourning to get things to go his way. "Of course we remembered Mamm's birthday," she murmured. "We baked a cake for today's dessert—"

"And you know how Mamm loved to entertain folks," Rosalyn chimed in. "It's only fitting that we celebrate instead of sitting around—"

"Well, you go right ahead and *celebrate,*" he said as he rose from his chair. "Act as if her death means nothing to you. Count me out."

As he crossed the kitchen floor toward the stairs, Edith sighed. Loretta ran a finger beneath her eyes while Rosalyn blinked rapidly.

Their father slammed the basement door behind him.

"That didn't go so well," Loretta murmured.

"Why does he throw his grief in our faces as though it's wrong to move beyond Mamm's passing? As though we don't miss her too?" Rosalyn asked in a tight voice. "One of these days Bishop Tom's going to insist that Dat find another wife—"

"Especially because we'll all most likely marry someday soon," Edith put in. "I certainly won't miss these unpleasant discussions after I move across the road with Asa."

"I refuse to remain under this roof with him— even if I don't marry," Loretta muttered. "That's an unkind attitude, but I've *had* it with his manipulation. His refusal to move on."

"*Jah,* we've got plenty of incentive to find husbands," Rosalyn said. "When Dat's left all by his lonesome, maybe he'll realize he shouldn't have driven us away."

They sat in silence for a few moments. Loretta picked at the rest of her breakfast and then pushed back her plate. Rosalyn held her mug glumly between her hands, gazing at her coffee as though she hoped to find a cure for Dat's grief there.

Edith stood up to scrape the dishes. "If he stays in the basement all day, so be it," she said in a low voice. "We'll just tell the others he's pouting—"

"Bishop Tom'll have none of that," Loretta said with a smile. "He'll be going downstairs to have a little talk with Deacon Cornelius about his un-Sunday attitude."

"I wouldn't put it past Nora to go down, too, saying she wants to see where Dat works on his clocks." Rosalyn chuckled as she rose to help clear the table. "Dat might think he'll have the day to himself, but we know better."

"I figured Dat would likely be in a low mood on Mamm's birthday," Edith said as she carried their stacked plates to the sink. "But I was so pleased that Drew asked how best to apologize to him, I planned a gathering anyway. We have to give Drew a chance. If he doesn't believe folks in Willow Ridge accept him, he'll never settle in."

"And if he moves away, Asa—and their furniture business—will never be the same." Loretta began running hot water into the sink. "Nora's told me that she and Luke think it's a positive sign that three young men have recently moved to town. It means Willow Ridge won't dry up and blow away like other settlements where the young people leave for places that hold more promising jobs and affordable farm land."

The three of them quickly washed the dishes, discussing how to organize the noon meal and minimize work on a Sunday. As they spoke together, Edith's spirits lifted. She hadn't told her sisters about the other topic of conversation she'd raise when everyone got here, and having a secret made her smile as she wiped their plates with her towel. . . .

Rosalyn elbowed her. "Penny for your thoughts, Edith."

"*Jah*, somebody's mind surely isn't on drying the dishes," Loretta teased as she nodded toward the open cabinet. "You put those last two plates away without drying them, silly."

Edith giggled, quickly retrieving the wet plates. "Asa volunteered to bring a ham, but I—I was just wondering what Nora might come with, seeing's how she doesn't cook much."

"*Jah*, sure you were," Rosalyn said with a chuckle. "Your little grin had Asa's name all over it."

Shrugging, Edith allowed herself to smile again. "Is that a bad thing? After our chat with Dat, I'm grateful to have something to be happy about."

"And I suppose we should also be glad that we'll have two other unattached fellows to ourselves today," Loretta remarked. "I heard Katie Zook and Nellie Knepp talking about Will and Drew the other day when I was in the market."

"Savilla Witmer's closer to those fellows' age," Rosalyn pointed out. "And then there's Rebecca—"

"Oh, she's too deep into her computer business to join the Amish church," Edith said. "Next time I'm in Simple Gifts, I'm asking Nora to show me the new Web site Rebecca designed for Detweiler Furniture Works. Asa says it's finished now, and he's tickled with it."

The morning passed quickly as the three of them put the leaves in the table and set it with a fresh tablecloth and Mamm's better dishes. They had made a big bowl of potato salad yesterday, along with a cake and slaw, so once the kitchen was ready for guests, they headed for the porch to read the latest issue of *The Budget*. When a piece of paper fluttered out of the door frame where it had been wedged, Edith picked it up.

"It's a note from Will, saying he got called away on some family business," she said as she skimmed the note. "He won't be joining us for dinner, but he plans to stop by later in the afternoon. And then he drew a big smiley face."

Loretta settled on the porch swing. "At least it doesn't sound like anyone's ill."

"Maybe he and his *mamm* and brothers are getting together—and that would be a *gut* thing," Rosalyn said. She sat down beside Loretta and handed her a section of the newspaper. "As I recall, they had a falling out when Will's older brothers took over the family farm."

Edith smiled as she settled into the wicker chair near the swing. "I'm sure we'll hear about it, or he wouldn't have added that smiley face. Now we have something else to look forward to!"

The morning sun and a breeze made the next hour pleasant as the three of them relaxed together. Reading *The Budget* was a great way to catch up on the news from Roseville, as well as the Plain settlements where their far-flung cousins lived and their friends had moved to. They were trading sections of the paper when a familiar voice called to them.

"There's a picture we don't often see! All of the Riehl sisters sitting down at the same time," Nora teased as she and Luke walked up the lane. "Hope you're ready to try my very first deviled eggs. And I figured I couldn't ruin a cottage cheese and pineapple salad."

"Actually, the eggs were a team effort," Luke put in. "It's a *gut* thing we boiled plenty of them, because they kept disappearing as we spooned the filling into them."

"Hullo, you Hooleys and Riehls—and you Detweilers!" Nazareth called out from the road. "Everybody must be getting hungry at the same time."

"I like the looks of that roaster you're carryin', Asa—or maybe it's Drew," Bishop Tom added as he waved to everyone. "I take it for a sign we've got some serious meat headed for the table."

As Edith rose to greet their guests, it felt good to have company coming onto the porch carrying pans and platters—and a roaster that gave off the delicious aroma of well-seasoned ham. "Looks like a feast!" she said as she held the door for everyone.

Loretta and Rosalyn got the potato salad and slaw from the fridge, while Nora and Nazareth arranged their deviled eggs, salad, and a big pan of apple slab pie on the kitchen counter. "I baked banana bread yesterday with some whole wheat flour from your mill, Luke," Nazareth said as she took the covering off her other plate. "Made little sandwiches out of it, with apricot jam and goat cheese for the filling."

"The ham's warm and ready for a platter," Asa said as he set the enamel roaster on the stove. "Hope everybody likes it with barbeque sauce."

"That's why it smells so *gut*," Bishop Tom said as he clapped his hands on the brothers' backs. He glanced around the kitchen and then into the front room. "Cornelius must be upstairs makin' himself presentable, *jah*?"

Edith and her sisters glanced at one another as they placed serving utensils on the plates of food. "He was cranky at breakfast, so he excused himself to the basement," Rosalyn explained. "Today would've been Mamm's birthday, you see."

"Those sorts of anniversaries can affect ya in ways ya don't anticipate," Tom replied as he headed for the basement door. "I sure hope he's not workin' on a clock or—"

The door opened, and Dat stepped up into the kitchen. "*Gut* morning to you, Bishop. Happy to see you Detweilers and Hooleys, too," he added. His smile looked tight, but he appeared ready to tolerate guests for their noon meal. "I've heard English fellows call their getaway places *man caves*—and with three daughters in the house, I need to slip into my cave every now and again."

Luke and the Detweilers chuckled and went over to greet Dat while the bishop shook his hand. Edith was relieved that her father had come upstairs before Tom had gone down to check on him. She suspected Dat secretly did some clock repairs or cleaned his shop on the Sundays when they didn't attend church—and she and her sisters knew better than to catch him at it. When she lifted the lid of the roaster, however, all distracting thoughts of her father drifted away with the spicy-sweet steam that rose from the ham.

"Oh, this smells really yummy," Edith said as she placed some of the thinly sliced meat on a platter.

"We figured a spiral-sliced ham would be easy to fix—and something everyone would enjoy," Asa said. He held the sides of the roaster for her so it wouldn't move as she picked up more slices with her fork. "It was Drew's idea to separate the slices and add the sauce before we warmed it."

"Wow, this reminds me of something the Witmers would serve at the Grill N Skillet," Nora said. "We've got quite a nice meal to enjoy."

"*Jah*, better than Tom and I would've been eating at home," Nazareth said with a laugh.

While Edith placed the platter of ham with the other food on the counter, her sisters set pitchers of tea, water, and lemonade on the table. "Shall we pray before we fill our plates?" she suggested.

It felt special to have their closest friends gathered in the kitchen, and Edith couldn't help smiling as she bowed her head. *Be with Will and his family today,* she prayed, *and we ask Your presence with Drew as he seeks reconciliation. Bless Dat with an open heart—and a happier attitude—as we entertain our friends on Mamm's birthday. Thank You for surrounding us with Your love.*

Happy chatter filled the kitchen as everyone spooned up their food at the counter and sat down at the table. Edith sensed that having ten people here for dinner made the meal much more pleasant than it would've been with just the four of them—even if Dat wouldn't admit it. He sat at the head of the table with Bishop Tom and Luke on either side of him, and they were asking Asa and Drew about how their furniture business was doing. Edith relished having all the women together so they could hold their own conversation, although it was a special treat to be seated next to Asa. Every now and then he smiled at her as though waiting for the right time to share their special news.

"I—I really appreciate you Riehls inviting us for dinner today," Drew said in a voice that prompted the other conversations to stop. "And while we're all together, I'd like to say again that I'm sincerely sorry for the trouble I've caused— the wedding I ruined and the way I betrayed everyone's trust. I hope you can find it in your hearts to forgive me—especially you, Cornelius. You had a lot invested in Edith's wedding day, and I made it all go wrong."

Stillness settled over the kitchen. Dat sat up straighter as he set down his utensils. "I can't recall ever feeling more humiliated than at the moment Will Gingerich brought your brother into our wedding gathering," he said in a low, stern voice. "It hurt me a great deal to see the pain on Edith's face—and the expressions of disbelief and shock our guests wore—when we realized what you'd done, Detweiler. But it's the bride and groom who need your apologies."

"He's already talked to us, Dat," Edith said. "Asa and I have sorted things out with Drew and forgiven him."

"Drew and Asa have met with me, too," Luke

said as he smiled at the two brothers. "Far as I'm concerned, we're squared away with their purchase of the acreage from the farm across the road. They're paid in full, money-wise and for explanations, as well."

"Drew's come over for a couple of sessions with me, as well," Bishop Tom chimed in. "Asa's gonna join us next time so the two of them can understand each other's feelings better—concernin' that anger and envy we talked about after the wedding was canceled."

Dat cleared his throat loudly. "So you came to me last?" he challenged Drew. "Were you too afraid to show your face around here—"

"Matter of fact, I've been finishing some upholstery work so I could repay you for the wedding dinner at the Grill N Skillet," Drew interrupted as he reached into his shirt pocket. "This is the amount Josiah Witmer said he charged you, but if it's not enough, let me know what I owe. Again, I'm sorry I ruined your family's big day and your special dinner."

Dat closed his mouth over the retort he'd been ready to deliver. He glanced at the amount on the check and folded it into his shirt pocket. "I have to admit I wasn't expecting such a gesture, but I appreciate it," he murmured. "You've at least made restitution for what that day cost me financially, although I suspect it'll be a while before I can forgive and forget—"

"You can forgive Drew in the time it takes to say three words," Bishop Tom insisted. He held Dat's gaze for several seconds to drive home his point. "From what I've seen, he's been sincere in his apology, so the rest is up to you, Cornelius. We'll let you deal with that in your own way, in your own time, however. Your forgiveness should flow as freely as Drew's apology and his money."

Edith could see Dat wasn't very happy about receiving a personal sermon from the bishop, in front of all the folks around the table, but she was grateful to Tom for putting this matter in perspective. Asa squeezed her hand under the table.

"With that in mind, I'll tell you all that Drew has also offered to pay for dinner at the café on the new wedding day Edith and I have chosen," Asa said as he smiled at everyone around the table. "We've decided on Friday, the twelfth of June, and we hope you'll all honor us with your presence."

"Oh, Edith! That's fabulous news!" Loretta squealed. She threw her arms around Edith's shoulders while Rosalyn rose from her place across the table to embrace Edith from behind her chair.

"I'm so happy for both of you," Nazareth said as she beamed at Edith and Asa.

"I—I'm guessing the absence of Leroy and Louisa doesn't affect Asa's feelings as much as you thought it might?" Nora asked as she held Edith's gaze from across the table.

Edith reached over to clasp Nora's hands. "I can't thank you enough for talking me through my feelings," she murmured. "I didn't have to ask. Asa told me himself that we'd still be a family if God didn't bring Leroy and Louisa back into our lives."

"And we saw no reason to wait a long time before we set another date," Asa put in. "I loved Edith the moment I met her, when she stood up for the two babies Will and I were quarreling about. I loved her even more after she talked with Drew over a picnic she brought over to us. And I especially loved the way she was able to pull herself together after he spoiled our original wedding day. She's a strong woman, Edith is."

"*Jah*, you've got that right, son," Bishop Tom murmured. "She could've handled her disappointment a lot differently. Edith's a special young woman—an example to us all about movin' past our regrets and resentment."

As Edith's cheeks got hot, she glanced at Dat in time to catch him shaking his head at the bishop's comment. He held his tongue, however. Despite her father's reaction, Edith accepted the congratulations from everyone else in the kitchen and enjoyed the affection in Asa's eyes as he smiled at her. Her sisters cleared everyone's dinner plates while she and Nora cut the chocolate cake and Nazareth's apple slab pie—which filled a large rectangular cookie sheet and looked as big as three regular pies.

"How about if we put these on the table and everyone can help themselves?" Edith suggested. "I'll get a couple of metal spatulas—"

"You can set that pie right down here by me," Luke teased as she walked past him. "Apple's my favorite, and it looks like Naz used a lot of cinnamon."

"It's the drizzle of white icing I'm eyeballing," Drew said when Nora set the pan at the men's end of the table. "I predict there won't be much of this pie left by the time we leave."

When everyone had a dessert plate and a mug for coffee, Edith and the other women sat down again. She wasn't surprised that each of the fellows took a large square of the pie, while the women chose the chocolate cake. Noting Asa's euphoric expression as he chewed his mouthful of pie, she nudged him with her elbow.

"What's your favorite kind of pie, Asa?" she asked as she cut into her cake.

Asa swallowed, grinning at her. "Whatever kind you put in front of me, Edith."

Everyone at the table laughed. "You've got it right, guy, and you're not even married yet," Luke teased. "Whatever the wife fixes, your best response is '*denki*, dear, this is the most wonderful-*gut* stuff I've ever put in my mouth.'"

Across the table, Nora let out a short laugh. "*Jah*, that works—even when she's only warmed up a can of soup. Luke, poor man, often finds himself at the stove anyway, just so there's food on the table."

Luke wiggled his eyebrows. "I didn't marry you for the way you cook in the kitchen, Nora-girl," he shot back at her.

As their banter continued, Edith hoped that she and Asa would share a deep love like the one Nora and Luke showed so openly. Amish folks didn't display their affection in public, yet she found it endearing when couples defied some of the old traditions in positive ways. Could there ever be such a thing as too much love between a husband and a wife? If such love was a gift from God, surely it wasn't wrong for married folks to show their feelings when they were with their family and friends.

Everyone took more pie and cake, lingering over dessert and coffee as they visited, so it was nearly two o'clock before the men went out to the backyard to sit in lawn chairs. Their voices and laughter drifted in through the windows as Edith, her sisters, Nora, and Nazareth made quick work of washing the dishes and putting away the food.

"Well, Edith, I guess we'll be washing and pressing our new dresses to wear at your wedding—again," Rosalyn added with a chuckle. "Not many gals can say that."

"Nor do they want to go through what Edith and Asa did on their original wedding day," Nazareth pointed out. "It's commendable of Drew that he's repaid your *dat* for the first meal at the café, and is also treating us all to another banquet in a few weeks."

"*Jah*, I was wondering what Dat might say about having to pay twice," Loretta remarked in a low voice. "If he'd made a fuss, though, Rosalyn and I would've done it for you, Edith."

Gratitude welled up inside Edith as she pulled the drain stopper. "You two are the best sisters and friends I could ever have—"

"Hullo in there! Anybody want to let me in?" a familiar voice called from the front door. "I've got a surprise—well, *two* surprises!"

"That's Will," Loretta murmured as she tossed down her towel and headed to the front room. A few moments later, her delighted laughter prompted everyone in the kitchen to turn toward the door. "Edith! Edith, come and see who's home!"

Edith's heart hammered as she quickly dried her hands. *Can it be? Have my prayers been answered?* she thought as she hurried into the front room. The sight of two earnest little faces, two pairs of extended arms and kicking legs, stopped her heart. Edith couldn't speak for the sheer joy that flooded her soul when Louisa and Leroy began babbling at her.

"Twins!" she cried as she rushed toward them.

"Louisa and Leroy! Oh, but we've missed you in this quiet house."

Scooping one baby and then the other from the baskets Will was holding, Edith hugged them to her shoulders. It was heaven to feel their little arms clasping her neck, to hear their laughter and gurgling chatter as they wiggled excitedly against her.

"What's happened? I've been trying to convince myself that it's God's will for the Ropps to raise them," Edith whispered as she gazed at Will. "So why are they back? These two are the reason you went to see your family today, *jah*?"

Will smiled fondly at her. "Molly's *dat* called me last night and said they couldn't handle two babies while they were looking after Ruth's *mamm*. She's the one who had the heart attack when Molly died, remember?"

Edith nodded, amazed at this turn of events. "I hope this doesn't mean Mrs. Ropp's mother has taken a turn for the worse."

Will shook his head, chuckling. "No, but the babies' crying upsets her to the point that her doctor's concerned about her blood pressure and other issues—not to mention that she becomes more demanding," he explained. "Orva had tried to talk with Ruth about this before they left here with the twins, remember. So now he's put his foot down."

Nazareth, who'd come from the kitchen with

Rosalyn and Nora, cooed at the wee ones and stroked their wispy hair. "Were these angels fussy because they had to drink formula again? I'm going home to get a bucket of this morning's milk from my fridge so these kids can have a meal that agrees with them."

"*Denki* so much," Edith called after the bishop's wife. She gazed into Louisa and Leroy's faces, unable to get enough of their smiles—yet aware that during the week and a half they'd been away, they'd lost some weight. "And *denki* to you, too, Will, for going to fetch them. See there?" she said to Nora and her sisters. "It's a *gut* thing we didn't return the high chairs and playpen and such things to their owners."

"I have a box and a duffel of their stuff in the buggy. I'll go get it." Will's smile widened as he watched Loretta and Rosalyn take the babies from Edith's arms. "I was so relieved to be bringing them back into this home—knowing they'll get all the love they'll ever need with Edith and Asa raising them," he added. Then he raised an eyebrow. "Or at least I *hope* you and Asa plan to be together."

"The wedding's June twelfth," Loretta said excitedly. "Better get your church clothes ready and make plans to celebrate with us—for sure and for certain this time."

"Best news I've heard all day. Congratulations, Edith."

"You missed Asa's making the announcement— and you missed some mighty fine food, too," Rosalyn put in.

"We'll be getting the high chairs out, and washing the bottles for Naz's goat milk," Loretta said, "so you might as well join us in the kitchen, Will. Feeding you is the least we can do!"

Will shrugged modestly. "Happy to help the twins. They're my final connection to Molly, after all."

As Edith watched Will head out the front door, she couldn't stop smiling. "Hasn't *this* been a fine day?" she murmured as she watched her sisters fussing over the babies. "Let's take Louisa and Leroy out back for a moment so the men can see them. It feels so *gut* to have them home again."

CHAPTER TWENTY-TWO

O n Friday the twelfth of June, Edith smiled at Asa, who sat facing her from the men's side of the room with Will and Drew beside him. It felt a little odd, as though she was having a recurring dream, to see the handsome fellows on the pew bench a second time—but with all three of them present. As her father stood up to read the morning's scripture passage, she told herself to focus on the message instead of on the man she loved.

"From the fifty-first Psalm come these familiar words, a petition to remain in God's *gut* graces," Dat said in a resounding voice. *"Create in me a clean heart, O God; and renew a right spirit within me. Cast me not away from Thy presence; and take not Thy holy spirit from me,"* he read. *"Restore unto me the joy of Thy salvation; and uphold me with Thy free spirit."*

Today's about joy, Lord, but we remain eternally grateful that You've not cast us away because of the mistakes we've made, Edith prayed. *We're especially thankful that Drew has made his amends and that You've created clean hearts for him, his brother, Will, and me.*

After a prayer and a hymn, Preacher Henry

Zook rose to preach the first sermon. He spoke in a low voice, and while his message was sincere, Edith found her attention wandering. She reminded herself to be patient, because they had an entire church service to sit through before the wedding began.

Beside her, Loretta leaned closer to whisper, "Are you nervous?"

Edith realized that she felt altogether confident, believing she would come away as Asa's wife this time. "No, I'm fine," she murmured.

"Then stop squirming."

Edith sat taller. She'd been so intently focused on Asa, she hadn't realized she'd been wiggling on the pew bench.

To settle herself, she ran her fingers over Leroy and Louisa's velvety cheeks, pleased that they were such calm, quiet babies now that they'd resumed their goat-milk diet. Soon they would be her and Asa's son and daughter, because Will had contacted an adoption agency to begin the process of giving them the Detweiler name—and all the love their hearts could hold for these special babies. Drew was pleased that he'd be living close by to watch his children grow up, as well.

After more prayers and another hymn, Preacher Ben rose to address the congregation with the second, longer sermon. "Seems the perfect morning to recall the passage from Revelation that's often used at funerals, but which speaks to the young folks in the first rows this morning," he began as he looked at the three men and then at Edith and her sisters. *"And God shall wipe away all tears from their eyes, and there shall be no more death, neither sorrow, nor crying, neither shall there be any more pain: for the former things are passed away,"* Ben recited in a ringing voice. *"And he that sat upon the throne said, 'Behold, I make all things new.'* That's what we celebrate today, folks—God's made this situation new for Edith, and for the Detweiler brothers, and for Will and the little twins. Praise be to our Jesus."

Edith smiled gratefully at Preacher Ben as he continued his sermon. *Behold I make all things new.* It reminded her of the way Asa took old, broken furniture and created a useful piece with fresh stain and the skill of his carpenter's hands. The passage also reminded her that Drew had walked away from the lies he'd told, and Will had found a fresh start farming for Luke Hooley. The Lord had opened a different door for Leroy and Louisa, as well, and Edith felt blessed to be raising them as her own children.

"It's almost time for the wedding," Rosalyn murmured as everyone stood up to sing the final hymn of the church service. "I'm so happy for you, Edith. Asa's a blessing to our family."

Edith smiled—even though Dat was eyeing the

three of them sternly, as he had when they'd been young, talkative girls in church. Nothing was going to spoil her absolute joy today as she stood beside Asa and promised to love and honor him for the rest of her life—an exchange of simple vows that would forever bind them together. Because she'd almost unwittingly married his twin, however, Edith cherished these moments of anticipation . . . the knowledge that this time the vows she repeated would be honest and meaningful. Today no one would interrupt the ceremony with the jarring news that she was standing beside the wrong man.

Denki, *God, for delivering us from our sins and loving us in spite of them,* she prayed as the last words of the hymn died away. Denki *for the way our family has come together again in forgiveness—and is now growing. Your will be done.*

As folks sat down on the wooden benches, Bishop Tom gestured for Edith and Asa to join him in the small open spot in the center of the room. More than two hundred people had gathered to celebrate this day with them, and Edith could feel the love and support that filled the home she and Asa would soon share. From the preachers' bench, Bishop Vernon Gingerich smiled at her with twinkling blue eyes. Such a blessing he'd been to Will and his family, helping them patch up the holes that resentment had caused in their relationships, and easing Will's grief after Molly's passing.

"We're gonna do this again," Bishop Tom said, smiling at the men and then at the women. "But this time we'll get it right!"

Gentle laughter filled the room and lifted Edith's spirits. Asa gazed down at her. He looked so handsome in his black vest and pants with his shiny raven hair brushing the collar of his white shirt. She knew she would remember this special moment forever. Once again Bishop Tom began the ancient Old Order wedding ceremony, and Edith repeated the words with joy and confidence.

As Asa said his vows, his face radiated the deep love and commitment Edith hadn't felt when she'd stood beside Drew a month ago. She'd attributed the little differences in the groom's mannerisms to his nervousness—the same jitters she'd been feeling that morning—but today Asa's voice filled the big front room with his strength and purpose.

When at last Bishop Tom pronounced them man and wife, Edith drew a deep breath. Asa turned and took her hands in his, gazing at her with indigo eyes that shone with devotion. "I love you so much, Edith," he murmured.

"I love you, too, Asa. Forever and ever."

As their guests rose from the pew benches, Dat stood up to address the crowd. "You're all invited to the Grill N Skillet to celebrate with us," he announced. "We're grateful to Drew Detweiler for providing our meal today. God has greatly blessed us with His abundance and love, which we in turn share with our families and friends. We're glad you all came today."

Edith and her sisters gathered around the small table where Bishop Tom was laying the marriage certificate. "Dat's in fine form today," Loretta remarked as Edith and Asa signed their names.

"Dare we hope he's moving forward now, a happier man?" Rosalyn asked as she wrote her name beneath Edith's.

"That would be a *gut* thing for all you girls," Will said as he waited for Loretta to sign and hand him the pen. "Especially now that Edith's taking her sunny disposition across the road."

Drew was nodding as he signed the certificate and returned the pen to Bishop Tom. "We should make it our mission to see that Cornelius carries today's happiness forward with him. He's suffered long enough."

"That's a commendable attitude, kids," the bishop remarked as he, too, penned his name on the proper line. "I'm glad you'll all be close at hand to help him—and each other—with that project. But for now, let's go up the road and celebrate with a fine dinner! It's a happy day in Willow Ridge."

Edith couldn't have agreed more as she and Asa accepted congratulations from the folks who gathered around them. Ernest and Fern Detweiler beamed at her, welcoming her to the family, and then Marian Gingerich gripped her hands, as well. "I feel we've turned the page and started a new chapter in the family story," she said with tears in her eyes. "I'm so relieved that Leroy and Louisa will be your children now—and so grateful for the way you've led Will to a fresh opportunity."

Edith's body thrummed as she accepted similar congratulations from Bishop Vernon and Jerusalem Gingerich and Preacher Ben and Miriam Hooley. Nazareth and Jerusalem agreed to mind the babies during the meal so Edith and Asa would be free to visit with their guests.

It was a special moment when Dat came up to her, gazed at her wistfully, and then embraced her. "Wish your *mamm* could've been here to share this day," he murmured, but he quickly put a smile on his face and extended his hand. "Asa, it's *gut* to have another man in this family— another rooster to keep after these busy hens!"

Everyone around them laughed. As the guests made their way to the door, Edith was grateful that so many of their friends and family members had come a second time to share this special day with her and Asa. The lane and the road filled with people talking and laughing, all the way to the Grill N Skillet. Edith walked among them, her hand enveloped by Asa's larger, stronger one.

She felt loved and cherished. She felt blessed and beautiful.

Behind her, Edith heard the rapid patter of footsteps. Nora caught up to her, her freckled face pink with excitement. "The next event," she said eagerly, "is to be a baby shower at my place, Edith. As we baked pies and set the tables for today, all the ladies agreed it was time the twins had their own clothes and toys."

Edith stopped walking and threw her arms around Nora. "*Denki* so much for all the ways you've helped me. Knowing you is like having a *mamm* and a big sister and a best friend all rolled into one!"

Nora eased away, blinking rapidly. "That's one of the nicest things anyone's ever said to me," she murmured. "You're welcome, Edith. I'm glad you're finally Mrs. Detweiler—and so happy that you'll be raising Louisa and Leroy here in Willow Ridge."

When they arrived at the café, Edith, her sisters, Will, and the Detweiler brothers filled their plates with the grilled meats and delicious side dishes that awaited them on the buffet table. They took their places at the raised table in the corner, where they could look out over the crowd as everyone ate. Aromas of grilled meats, creamed celery, and the traditional "roast" made of chicken and stuffing filled the air. The kitchen serving counter was covered with slices of pie on plates—an inspiring sight—but it was the regal white wedding cake with its pale blue borders that made Edith sigh with gratitude.

"What a beautiful cake Miriam's made us," she murmured. "It survived the first wedding day, held its shape in the freezer, and now it's standing tall and sturdy and sweet . . . like a prize for enduring all the setbacks we encountered along the way."

"Tall like me, sturdy like the twins," Asa said as he gripped her hand, "and sweet like you, Edith. But *you're* the prize, and I'm the big winner. I don't know where I'd be if you hadn't stuck by me these past weeks."

Edith gazed into her husband's indigo eyes, loving the way she saw herself reflected in them. "We don't have to worry about that anymore," she murmured. "We're together now in Willow Ridge—a little slice of heaven right here on earth."